For the Love of Catherine

For the Love of Catherine

Carole Llewellyn

ROBERT HALE · LONDON

© Carole Llewellyn
First published in Great Britain 2012

ISBN 978-0-7090-9572-9

Robert Hale Limited
Clerkenwell House
Clerkenwell Green
London EC1R 0HT

www.halebooks.com

2 4 6 8 10 9 7 5 3

Printed in the UK by the MPG Books Group,
Bodmin and King's Lynn

To Barrie with love.

ACKNOWLEDGEMENTS

I wish to thank the following people for their help and assistance in my research: Mary Gahan, Customer Service Assistant, National Railway Museum and Andrew Croxton/Search.Engine@nrm.uk

Louise Macfarlane, Imperial War Museum – www.iwmcollections.org & IWM@reference-service.info

Sources

BBC History Online
BBC News UK/Titanic
Titanic – A voyage of discovery/survivor.htm.
Timeline of events 1914–1918/World War One
Historic-UK.com
Salvation Army/workhouses/bibliography online

Chapter One

On 10 April 1912 the Titanic, *the pride of the White Star Line, set sail on her maiden voyage from Southampton to New York. On board 2,223 passengers and crew.*

AT 11.40 ON the night of Sunday 14 April 1912, Mair Parsons woke with heart thumping. A loud noise had vibrated through the ship. She left her cabin – the one she shared with her 2-year-old daughter, Catherine, and her future mother-in-law, Ethel Jenkins, who were both still sound asleep – and made the long trek from steerage, third-class accommodation, to the upper decks of the *Titanic*.

She returned quickly in a state of panic.

'Wake up, Ethel! Ethel! Wake up!' Mair cried, frantically shaking the woman by the shoulders.

'What is it? Whatever's wrong?' a bleary-eyed Ethel asked.

'Come on. Get up. Quick, we need to get ourselves up onto the Boat Deck. Something has happened. I think it's serious.'

'Happened?' Ethel squinted at the old wind-up alarm clock, the one she'd insisted on bringing from home. 'Good Lord, girl. It's barely midnight. Why are you dressed in your day clothes?'

'I – I've been to the upper decks and, I tell you, everyone's rushing about up there. It's frantic. I heard someone shout that the ship has collided with an iceberg. The ship's engines have stopped. I saw the crew preparing the lifeboats! Oh Ethel … we're all going to die!'

'Mair, please calm down. You're frightening me.' Ethel had never seen Mair so agitated.

'Calm down? Didn't you hear what I said?'

'Yes, I heard you. But I really can't believe we're in any danger. Only the other day the *Daily Express* quoted Captain Smith of the

Titanic as saying, "even God himself couldn't sink this ship," and I believe him.'

'No, Ethel, you really have to trust me on this. Now hurry. Please get dressed while I see to Catherine. We shall need plenty of warm clothes. It's very cold up on the Boat Deck. I still can't believe that you slept through that awful noise!' Mair admonished.

'With our cabin situated in third-class down in the bowels of the ship, it's taken me all of the last few days to find my bearings and get used to inhaling the salty sea air by day and engine fumes by night. I tell you, I was that done in, I'd have slept through anything.'

'Well, thank God, I didn't,' Mair said tensely. 'The noise frightened me that much, I just had to go and investigate. Now will you get a move on? Or I swear I'll take Catherine and go without you!'

Ethel's eyes went to young Catherine who was sound asleep, her light-brown hair gleaming with health and soft curls surrounding her lovely face, a beautiful child, and one whom Ethel loved very much. A love made deeper, at least for Ethel, knowing as she did the circumstances leading to her birth – although she often doubted the same could be said of Mair. Sometimes the way Mair looked at her daughter – as if Catherine's mere existence reminded her of her attacker – gave Ethel goosebumps.

Ethel nodded. 'I'll do as you say, but I'm sure there'll be no need for us to actually leave the ship.'

Minutes later Mair, with Catherine in her arms and walking at a fast pace, led the way up to the Boat Deck and into the chill April night.

'I thought that the allotted space for third-class passengers was the Poop Deck,' Ethel offered, out of breath.

'That's as maybe, but it's not where the lifeboats are!' Mair told her.

The speed at which Mair had alerted them and the way she cleverly circumnavigated her way past the Poop and the Well Deck, meant they made it onto the Boat Deck at around 12.30. Captain Smith, the ship's captain, had only just given the order to load the lifeboats – women and children first – and, although the deck was beginning to fill up with first-class passengers, Mair, Ethel and Catherine were among the first in line for lifeboat number 10 situated port-side. Crew members were busy handing out life jackets and instructing everyone to put them on.

Mair held a sleeping Catherine close to her. It was freezing cold on deck, and she folded her own coat around the child for added warmth. Ethel frantically struggled with her life jacket, eventually having to be helped by a young crew member.

'Would you like me to assist you with yours, Miss?' the young man asked, holding out a life jacket to Mair.

She didn't answer, her eyes transfixed, staring into the blackness and out to sea.

'No. My daughter-in-law's fine at the moment,' Ethel interjected. 'If you like, I can take charge of hers. I'll make sure she puts it on later.'

Over the years Ethel had grown to love Mair and was proud to call her daughter-in-law. The fact that she and Ethel's son, Frank, were not yet married made no difference at all although, if the truth be known, with all that Mair had been through during her short life, Ethel secretly feared for the girl's mental health.

As the crewman handed Ethel the extra life jacket, he managed a forced smile. 'I'm sure it's just a precaution,' he said.

Mair's whole body stiffened with fear. The lifeboats looked so small. The drop to the sea below so vast … what if the lifeboat toppled and they all fell out? She couldn't swim … she didn't want to die! Oh why wasn't Frank there to protect her? Why had she been so eager to leave Wales and make this trip? The situation she found herself in filled her with fearful anxiety – so different from the excitement she'd felt the morning the letter arrived from her stepsister, Rhiannon Hughes, a celebrated music-hall star presently on tour in America.

'Oh Ethel, you'll never believe it,' Mair had squealed with excitement when she read the letter over breakfast at John Jenkins' comfortable house in Ponty. It was a small mining village in South Wales, where she, Frank and Catherine lived with Frank's mum, stepfather and two younger sisters.

'What is it?' Ethel asked.

'Rhiannon's due to appear at the Colonial Theatre in New York, and she wants me to go out with Frank and spend a month with her and Gus at the Plaza Hotel on Fifth Avenue!'

'Well I never. New York, you say?'

'Yes, Ethel. Apparently she's already contacted the shipping company and booked our passage. She says I'm to think of it as a belated present, for my seventeenth birthday in January. All *we* need to do is send the company our personal details to confirm the persons travelling.'

'There's exciting. When is it booked for, then?' John Jenkins asked.

'Oh, not until early April, so there's plenty of time to get passports organized.'

'She expects you to stay for a month, you say?' Ethel pulled a face.

'Yes, that's right. Why the face? You don't mind us going, do you?'

'No, of course I don't. It's just that I can't see Frank being able to up and leave his regiment for that length of time, can you?'

'I hadn't considered that. And I don't suppose Rhiannon did either,' Mair confessed. 'It would be awful if we had to turn down this wonderful chance to travel to America. I'm sure if Frank explained the circumstances to his commanding officer....'

'You should have learnt by now how seriously Frank takes his duties as a soldier and to his regiment,' Ethel reminded her.

'Look, with Frank due home on leave from Maendy Barracks this Friday, why don't we wait and see what he has to say on the matter, eh?' John Jenkins suggested, by way of placating the two women.

Frank and Mair had been together as a couple for more than two years. Although they'd known each other far longer than that, nearly ten years to be exact....

Mair clearly remembered the day she and her mother, Nellie Parsons, having been given the position of housekeeper to Dai Hughes and his daughter, moved into his tied colliery house. From the first day they moved in Mair had been overwhelmed by the way everyone, especially Frank Lewis and his family who lived next door, had welcomed her.

A year later, when Dai Hughes actually upped and married her mother, she couldn't have been happier to have Rhiannon as her step-sister and Frank, a brother-like figure, whom she could always depend on....

Unfortunately, her mother's flighty ways led to Nellie running away with her fancy man, ending her marriage to Dai and deserting her own daughter. Thankfully, Mair still had Dai, Rhiannon ... and Frank, to love and care for her. And in later years when Mair found herself with child and feeling at her lowest, Frank proposed to her, making her the happiest girl in the world.

Mair and Frank desperately wanted to marry but, as Mair was underage, by law she required parental permission. With her father dead and her mother God knows where, it looked as if they would have to wait until she reached the age of twenty-one. Despite this, when Catherine was born Frank Lewis, fully aware that he was not the child's father, begged Mair, telling her how proud he would be to be named as such on Catherine's birth certificate, 'A name that will be rightly yours too, when we are allowed to marry,' he'd reasoned.

An offer Mair had eagerly accepted.

When Friday eventually came and Frank arrived home on weekend leave from his army barracks in Cardiff, Mair could hardly wait for him to get through the front door, before giving him the news of Rhiannon's invitation. The last thing she expected was for him to be so dismissive.

'I'm sorry, Mair, love, but my mam's right. I'll never get the time off,' Frank said.

Mair's disappointment showed on her face. 'You don't know that for sure. At least, not until you ask,' she argued.

'Oh yes, I do. I can just imagine my CO's reaction if I actually had the cheek to ask for a month's leave. He'd have me up on a charge and that's for sure. No. I'm afraid, as much as I'd love to come with you and Catherine, it's completely out of the question.'

'Oh Frank, it won't be the same without you. And if you don't come, it'll mean we'll have to travel all that way on our own.'

'I'd much rather you didn't. I'd be worried sick about you,' Frank said.

'You mean you'd rather I didn't go? But—'

'No, don't be so silly. Of course you should go to see Rhiannon. I'm only saying that I'd feel a lot happier if you had someone with you.' He pondered for a while. 'You say Rhiannon has already booked tickets for two adults and a child, is that right?'

'Yes. That's right.'

'So why not take my mother with you instead?'

'Me! Travel to America!' Ethel cried out. 'Whatever will you think of next?'

'Oh, Frank. That's a great idea. Ethel, it really is the perfect solution. And just think how pleased Rhiannon and Gus would be to see you.' Mair urged.

Ethel turned to her husband, 'What do you think, John?'

'I say go. It'll be a trip of a lifetime. I can't think of a single reason for you to turn it down, can you?'

'Well … there's Sadie and Martha to consider. I've never left them before and … what about my leaving you?'

'There's no need to worry about the girls. I'll be only too happy to look after them. After school, I'll let them help in the shop. You know how much they both enjoy doing that. And, as for leaving me – of course I shall miss you, but what is it they say about absence making the heart grow fonder?' He flashed a wicked smile.

'John Jenkins, I've said it before, and I'll say it again … you're one in a million! I'm that happy you chose to marry me and accept me and mine as your own.'

'Get away with you. Anyway you know only too well the feelings I had for you then … and now.' He gave an embarrassed cough. 'I'm sure your Frank would have had something to say if I hadn't made an honest woman of you, eh lad?' John winked at Frank.

Frank smiled. 'You're right there! I might have had to challenge you, a well respected butcher and businessman of the parish, to pistols at dawn for besmirching my widowed mother's good name!'

John, Frank and Mair all laughed aloud.

'You daft ha'peths,' Ethel admonished, as she struggled to suppress a laugh. 'And there was I trying to be serious.'

The sea was flat calm, but the air was bitterly cold. As they quietly stood in line for lifeboat number 10, Mair couldn't believe her eyes: the Boat Deck already had a noticeable list, tipping them at an angle. Was it possible? Could the ship actually be sinking?

'They build the biggest ship in the world and then they say, "It's so big there isn't anything that can make it go down," then along comes this iceberg and well, it's beyond belief,' a well dressed lady standing in line behind them said – she appeared to be alone and talking to no one in particular.

The ship's lights burned brightly, lighting up the spacious deck.

The Boat Deck, normally a restricted area for third-class passengers, a place where middle and upper-class passengers usually took an afternoon or evening stroll, was now full of people from all walks of life; lords, ladies and gentlemen, many having paid vast sums of money in order to be part of the *Titanic*'s maiden voyage, to ordinary working-class families, on their way to America in search of a better life.

Earlier Mair had peeked through the large entrance doors on the Boat Deck and saw a grand staircase and, towering above, huge glass chandeliers. Such opulence fair took her breath away. And now, just inside this entrance the ship's band was playing lively music, adding a kind of surreal party atmosphere to the whole proceedings. Above the ship's band came the loud hissing sound of distress rockets being let off at several minute intervals, lighting up the sky.

Mair couldn't believe the chaos unfolding around them. Passengers were milling to and fro, some desperately seeking relatives, women and children saying tearful goodbyes to their menfolk, not knowing when, or even if, they would see them again. They had all been told quite early on that there were not enough lifeboats to accommodate everyone. And, for now, the only men allowed onto each lifeboat were designated crew members, to take charge of the oars and tiller.

There could be no denying that this was really happening and the *Titanic* was in genuine trouble.

'It's fate. That's what it is,' Mair cried, unable to hide her increasing fear.

'Now whatever makes you think that?' Ethel asked, concerned that her young daughter-in-law might be losing control.

'It's fate!' Mair repeated. 'We shouldn't even be on board this ship! You know that our tickets were originally booked for us to travel on another American ship and if there hadn't been a coal strike, they would never have transferred us to the *Titanic*.... It's fate I tell you ... and we're all going to die!'

Catherine, upset by her mother's anguish, began to whimper.

'Please, Mair. Try to pull yourself together, you're frightening Catherine. We'll be fine. You'll see.'

'There's no way I can get into that lifeboat. I can't swim. Oh, no!' Mair cried out, her hands frantically clutching beneath her coat collar.

'What is it?' Ethel, seeing Mair's growing distress, feared she might drop Catherine. Ethel's arms went out. 'Mair, love, give Catherine to me and tell me what's wrong. Have you hurt yourself?'

'No. I've lost Rhiannon's locket! The one she gave me before she left for America. It was around my neck earlier, and now it's gone! Here, take Catherine … I've got to go back.'

'Go back? What, below deck? But we're about to be loaded into the lifeboat … it's madness even to think about going back.'

'I can't leave without the locket. Rhiannon gave it to me for "luck" before she left for America. She'd never forgive me if I lost it … it was her grandmother's. You stay in line with Catherine … I need to retrace our steps…. I'll be back before you know it.' She kissed her daughter and with that she was gone.

Minutes later Ethel, holding tight to Catherine's tiny hand, the toddler now fully awake and walking by her side, followed the line edging slowly towards lifeboat number 10. In front of her a young family that looked to be husband, wife and two small daughters, were saying their goodbyes. After helping his wife and children into the boat the man immediately turned and headed for the lower deck. 'I'll not be long … I promise,' he called before disappearing out of sight.

Ethel and Catherine, helped into the lifeboat by a friendly young crew member, took the seats next to the young family.

'I want my mammy,' Catherine whimpered.

'There, there, my love. Your mammy won't be long. I'm sure she'll be back with us before we know it,' Ethel whispered, as she cuddled the child closer to her, hoping with all her heart that her words were not simply a case of wishful thinking.

Though the lifeboat was less than half full, a fact that truly surprised Ethel, the boat began to slowly lower the sixty foot down to the freezing cold, unwelcome Atlantic Ocean.

The lifeboat dangled precariously about five feet from the Boat Deck above, the young man from earlier re-appeared holding a metal flask. He shinned down the rope then, stretching his arm out to his wife, handed her the flask. 'I thought the children might need some hot milk for the journey.' Seeing Catherine and Ethel seated next to them, he flashed a brave smile to his wife and children, 'Maybe you could share it with the little girl next to you,' he kindly suggested.

'Arthur, we love you so much,' the young woman cried.

'And I you,' he said, before instantly making his way up the rope and back onto the Boat Deck.

This act of unselfishness Ethel knew was borne out of the love of a devoted husband and father. The young man reminded her so much of her Frank and, for the first time she thanked God that Frank hadn't been able to make the journey.

She shook her head in disbelief. This tragic scene was so different from the one of only a few days ago, when the *Titanic* had left Southampton bound for New York. How vividly she still remembered the excitement she'd felt witnessing the pomp and ceremony, the brass band's loud rendition of patriotic songs and crowds of happy people waving them off, a scene repeated when the ship made a diversion to Cherbourg, France and Queenstown in Ireland, to take on immigrants, travellers hoping to start a new life in America, on what was expected to be a journey of a lifetime.... Who could ever have predicted this?

Ethel Jenkins looked on helplessly. Where was Mair? Why hadn't she stayed with them? Ethel pulled close the child left in her care. Catherine desperately clung to her, her piercing blue eyes looked bemused. No doubt, like everyone else, unable to comprehend what or why this was happening to them. Everyone in the lifeboat sat in stunned silence. No one spoke. They were all strangers – and strangers didn't speak to each other.

As the crew continued to inch the lifeboat ever closer to the sea, Ethel desperately looked up to the Boat Deck. It was getting further away by the minute, but there was no sign of Mair. The lifeboat hit the water and the crew members began furiously to row away from the *Titanic*, as if their life depended on it.

'We have to get away before the ship actually goes down. There's every chance she could drag us down with her,' the crew member in command of the tiller explained.

As they distanced themselves from the ship, although listing and with some ten storeys of her bow well beneath the waterline, the ship's lights still managed to burn brightly, and they could plainly hear the ship's band playing, right up to the final moment when the *Titanic* actually sank – entering the deep Atlantic ocean like a huge black torpedo.

Later, through the darkness they could hear people in the water calling out. It was heart-wrenching. But the crew refused to row back to help them. Long before dawn the cries stopped. By now, everyone in the lifeboat was shivering … waiting for dawn … and praying to be rescued.

Hours later, when they'd given up all hope, they were picked up by a large ocean liner called the *Carpathia*.

Chapter Two

A T 9 P.M. ON the evening of 18 April, Rhiannon Hughes and Gus Davenport, along with what must have been 10,000 other people watched as the *Carpathia*, carrying 705 survivors and with the *Titanic* lifeboats – thirteen in total – hanging over its port and starboard sides, sailed past the Statue of Liberty and proceeded to steam up-river. It was besieged by a flotilla of small boats carrying newspaper reporters, which pursued it to the White Star Line piers, where it lowered the lifeboats before returning to the Cunard Dock and finally unloaded the survivors.

Once the gangway had been run ashore, doctors, nurses and other medical personnel brought stretchers and wheelchairs on board to attend to the injured. Survivors who were considered able, and who could prove they had someone waiting for them, were allowed to leave. Others, in need of hospital treatment, were taken straight to New York hospitals. None of the survivors had to go through Ellis Island, as was the case for all other immigrants.

When the survivors descended the gangway, all of the pent-up emotion and anxiety was let loose in the waiting crowds of family and loved ones. Among the crowd were 500 women dressed in mourning, many of whom were crying for the 1,517 souls lost on the *Titanic*.

Gus Davenport had previously contacted the shipping line for information and had been duly furnished with a comprehensive list of all the survivors, those classed as missing and those lost at sea. He squeezed Rhiannon's hand as they anxiously waited for Ethel and Catherine to disembark.

Ethel Jenkins, with Catherine snuggled in her arms, walked down the long gangway and off the ship. It felt so good to at last be on land.

Although weary and feeling every bit her forty-two years, *terra firma* had never felt better. Earlier, as she stood on the Boat Deck of the *Carpathia*, staring out into the dark of the night she had thought how, under different circumstances, she would have enjoyed her first glimpse of the breathtaking New York skyline, the Statue of Liberty and the welcoming sight of the harbour – lit up like daylight and milling with thousands of people.

'Ethel! Over here! We're here!' Rhiannon shouted urgently, as Gus, holding her hand tight, fought his way through the crowds.

'Oh Rhiannon, Gus, it's so good to see you. What an ordeal. There was a time back there when—' Ethel gave a sob. The two women hugged, almost crushing Catherine between them.

The little girl uttered a brief cry and wrapped a small arm around Ethel's neck.

'Oh my poor love. I'm so sorry. Did we hurt you?' Rhiannon asked and her eyes welled with tears. Holding out both arms, 'Can I hold her?' she asked Ethel.

'Why, of course,' Ethel said handing Catherine to her. 'Catherine, look who's here. It's your Auntie Rhi. Your mother's dear stepsister.' Ethel managed to force an encouraging smile.

Rhiannon eagerly took hold of Catherine, and as she placed a gentle kiss on the child's cheek, finally gave way to the flood of tears she'd been straining to hold back. She stroked the soft light-brown curls. 'Oh my dear, dear child, you're the image of your mother,' Rhiannon cried.

Catherine's large blue eyes regarded her aunt with interest but she was clearly bemused by this tearful reunion. 'Where's my mammy?' she whispered. 'I want my mammy,' she said. Her heart-shaped face crumpled as she struggled not to cry.

'Here, let me have her,' Ethel said.

Reluctantly, Rhiannon handed the child back to her. 'I'm sorry. I didn't mean to upset her,' she said dabbing her eyes with a lace-edged handkerchief.

'I don't think it's anything to do with you. Ever since we were picked up by the *Carpathia* the poor lamb has been constantly asking for her mother. I'm afraid, by way of easing her distress, I kept telling her it wouldn't be long before we'd all be together again … I didn't know what else to say.' Ethel's eyes darted between Rhi and Gus, 'As neither of you have even asked about Mair, I'm assuming you must know what's happened to her. Please … tell me … is she all right? Have you seen or heard from her?'

'I'm afraid not. The shipping company issued us with a list of survivors – that's how we knew you and Catherine were safe—'

'What about Mair?' Ethel interrupted.

'I'm afraid she's been classed as missing.'

'Oh, please God … no!' Ethel sobbed.

Catherine's small hand wiped the tears from Ethel's cheeks.

Ethel caught her breath. 'Rhi, I begged her not to leave us, but she just wouldn't listen. I convinced myself that she'd been put onto a different lifeboat … I'll never forgive myself if—'

'Now we'll have no more of that,' Gus interjected 'We must keep our hopes up. There's every chance that Mair will still be found. I've asked the shipping company to notify us, as soon as they have any news. I think it best if we leave them to it and get you two safely to the Plaza Hotel,' Gus urged.

In Wales, the first John Jenkins heard of the disaster was the headlines in the *Daily Express*, 'TITANIC SUNK FEARED LOSS OF 1,500 LIVES. 675 RESCUED MAINLY WOMEN AND CHILDREN.' What followed for him were nights spent praying for Ethel, Mair and Catherine's safe return, and days spent trying to keep things as normal as possible for Sadie and Martha, Ethel's two young daughters.

On the morning of 17 April two telegrams were delivered to John's house. One was addressed to him informing him that Ethel was safe and well. The other was addressed to Frank. With his stepson billeted at Maendy Barracks, John felt duty bound to open it.

The commanding officer entered the barracks and marched straight over to Frank.

Frank immediately stood to attention along with the other nine recruits billeted in hut number 46.

'Private Lewis?' the officer called out.

'Yes, sir!' Frank answered.

'Stand at ease!' the officer ordered everyone.

Frank relaxed his position. 'Thank you, sir.'

'Private Lewis, this morning I received a letter from your step-father.' The officer now spoke in a much quieter voice.

Ever since the news had reached Frank about the sinking of the *Titanic*, he had been desperately waiting for news of his loved ones. The fact that John had chosen to write to his CO rather than directly to him did not bode well.

'Is it bad news, sir?'

'Your stepfather has asked me to let you know that he's received news that your mother, together with the child called Catherine, are both safe and well—'

'Thank God,' Frank interrupted. 'And ... Mair Parsons ... my girl-friend, sir?'

'I'm sorry, lad. I'm afraid she has been reported as "missing".'

Frank fell back onto his bed. 'When they say "missing" sir, does that mean they think she's probably d—?'

'It means exactly what it says. No more and no less. I think you should take heart from the fact that she's not among those listed as lost at sea.'

'Yes. Thank you, sir.'

'Your stepfather has requested if, under the circumstances, you may be given some compassionate leave ... and I agree.'

'Thank you, sir.'

'Yes. I have already put in an application to the quartermaster to sign you off with a month's leave on personal grounds. As of this moment, you are free to return home. I would, however, like to be kept informed and wish you and your family well.'

'Thank you, sir.' No other words would come.

Ethel was dressed in a smart pale-blue day dress – one of the four new outfits her husband had insisted on treating her to. 'You look as pretty as a picture', he'd said when he first saw her in this particular outfit. Ethel remembered how she'd blushed like a schoolgirl. There could be no denying that John had the knack of making her feel like a young girl again. Ethel scolded herself. So much had changed since that day. This daydreaming just wouldn't do, there were things to do – things that needed to be settled.

Ethel, after making a last check on Catherine, who was still fast asleep, hurried across the plush red carpet of the luxurious double bedroom with its elaborate silk embossed drapes. She gave a tap on the adjoining door, and entered Rhiannon and Gus's suite of elegant rooms at the Plaza Hotel. In her hand she clutched a letter delivered earlier by the hotel's bellboy.

'Good morning, Ethel. Such good timing. Room service has just delivered our breakfast. Where is Catherine?'

'She's fast asleep. I thought it best to leave her be for a little while. I've left the door ajar so that we can hear her if she wakes up.' Ethel raised the hand holding the letter. It was visibly shaking. 'I've just received this.'

'A letter – who's it from?' Rhiannon stood up from the breakfast table and crossed the room.

Ethel was struck by how beautiful Rhiannon looked, dressed in a long, cream silk housecoat. Only the dark shadows under her eyes told of her grief – her fear for Mair. She looked totally at home in the opulent surroundings – such a far cry from her humble Welsh valley beginnings. Ethel knew how proud her father, Dai, would have been of her.

'It's from the shipping company,' Ethel said, her voice full of emotion.

Rhiannon immediately offered her outstretched hand. 'Come and sit down. I'll pour you a cup of tea, and you can tell me what they have to say.'

Rhiannon's caring voice brought a lump to Ethel's throat. Ethel sat at the breakfast table, her face unable to hide her distress.

'Ethel, what is it? Is there news of Mair?' Rhiannon asked, her voice urgent.

'No, sadly, there's not a word about Mair. They want to know if – along with the other British survivors – I would like to be repatriated. Apparently there's a ship leaving for Southampton the day after tomorrow.'

'What! Why so soon? It's only been two days since the tragedy.'

Rhiannon spoke the truth. So far, all Ethel and Catherine had seen of New York was during the journey the night of the tragedy, when they'd been driven in a bright yellow taxicab – their first ever trip in a motor car – to the Plaza, a large, luxury hotel situated on Fifth Avenue in the heart of the city. Under different circumstances no doubt Ethel would have marvelled at the sights, the huge metal-framed bridges, the skyscrapers and the fact that even though it had been late at night the bustling city seemed to be full of more well dressed people of varying nationalities than Ethel had ever seen in one place.

'I'm so angry at the damn newspaper reporters. They are hounding each survivor and anyone connected with them. They have already singled me out. What was it the headline said? "SISTER OF BRITISH MUSIC-HALL STAR FEARED LOST AT SEA!" How dare they? Thank God Catherine's too young to read their scare stories. It's true what they say about newspaper reporters … what they don't know they just make up! If it hadn't been for them, we could have done so much together—'

'The truth is, Rhiannon, this waiting for news is killing me. Even without the reporters, I really haven't felt like doing anything other than stay close to the hotel.'

'Oh Ethel, I know it's terrible.' She wrapped her arms around Ethel's shoulders. 'But I'll not let them stop you registering with immigration. If you get Catherine up and dressed, I'll arrange a cab to take us straight after breakfast. Is that all right with you?' Rhiannon started toward the telephone table situated in the hallway.

'No! Please wait!' Ethel's voice sounded desperate.

Rhiannon stopped in her tracks.

'I-I'm sorry, Rhi. I didn't mean to startle you, only … look, Rhi, even before this letter arrived from the shipping company, I'd begun a lot of soul-searching and … I've come to the conclusion that *my* place is with the family back in Wales. I'm so worried about Frank and what he must be going through.'

'B-but … what about Mair?'

'Rhi, I don't want you to think that I'm giving up on her, but I feel so useless. Every day spent waiting and hoping is agony, and it can't be healthy for Catherine to see me like this day after day. I really think it's time I went back home.'

'I don't know what to say. This is the last thing I expected. It all seems so rushed.'

'Why delay the inevitable? I've got to go back sometime … it seems wrong to turn down the offer of free passage.'

'But wouldn't you rather wait until we know what's happened to Mair? Look, Gus has found out that some of the injured were taken to St Vincent's hospital here in Manhattan. He's there now. He felt it a good place to start our own search for Mair. Apparently, many of those rescued carried no identity papers. Ethel, I am determined to believe that Mair will be one of them.'

'I hope you are right. But I'll not be swayed. My mind is made up. I'm going home.'

'Oh Ethel, I'll be so sorry to see you go. How I wish I'd never sent Mair those damn tickets, if I hadn't invited her to come here then none of this would have happened. I find it ironic that the very locket I gave to her for luck appears to have brought her anything but. If only she hadn't gone back to look for it, she—'

'You mustn't think that way. I've spent nights churning over the "what ifs", and asking God why, when so many lives were lost, others were spared? I came to the conclusion that none of *us* are to blame. What happened that night was beyond our control.'

Rhiannon sighed, 'I'm sure you're right.'

'I keep going over in my mind how adamant Mair was about not going into the lifeboat. She couldn't swim, so being lowered onto the vast sea obviously terrified her. And well … while I don't doubt the loss of the locket … I have to ask myself if it gave her the excuse she needed to stay on board.'

'Surely not. She must have understood the urgency of the situation and wouldn't she want to get Catherine to safety?'

'Every night, as I pray for Mair's return, I take comfort in the fact that Catherine is safe and well…. Rhi, you do know how much I love her, don't you?'

'Of course I do. And it's plain to see that she loves you. You are as good as any grandparent to her.'

'I'm so glad you think that way. The thing is … I'd like to take Catherine back to Wales with me. I really think, at this present time, it would be the best thing for *her*.'

Rhiannon pondered for a while, disappointment darkening the shadows under her big brown eyes. 'I'm sure you're right. I often wonder what's going on in that little head of hers. One day her mother's there, the next she's gone! No, I'm in no doubt that the best place for her to be right now is with you, Frank and the family. I may be her auntie but the truth is, I'm almost a stranger to her.'

'So that's settled then. Catherine comes home with me.'

'Well this is it,' Ethel announced, as she and Catherine prepared to board the *Adriatic* – a liner from the Cunard fleet, bound for Southampton. She heaved a long sigh, 'Gus, promise me you'll let me know as soon as there's news of Mair.'

'I promise. Once we've seen you safely off, I intend to go back to St Vincent's. The hospital staff are on their guard. They've been told to trust no one. But we'll not give up, will we love?'

'No, I swear we won't,' Rhiannon said fiercely.

Gus enfolded Rhiannon in his arms. 'And then maybe you'll set a date, so that I can make an honest woman of you.' He placed a gentle kiss on her forehead.

'Be patient, my love. It'll happen one day. Preferably in Wales surrounded by friends and family … if Mair—'

'Rhi, I'll continue to pray every night for her safe return. I'm sure we'll all be together one day,' Ethel said.

'Oh Ethel, I do hope you're right. I'm so going to miss you. Just having you with us these last few days reminded me of the old days when my dad was alive. You were a treasure then … as you are now.'

Both women's eyes went directly to Catherine, who, clutching her new china baby doll, a parting gift from Gus, looked up at them and gave a smile. The child, dressed in a red velvet coat with black velvet trimmed collar and cuffs and matching floppy hat, looked as pretty as a picture, but her blue eyes kept darting around, constantly seeking her mother. The sight of the ship had made her uneasy.

'Thank you for trusting me to take her back, Rhi.' Ethel said, 'I know what a wrench it must be for you.'

Rhiannon nodded. 'Yes, it is. But I know you will look after her. I'll send lots of letters. I don't want her to forget me or … her mother.' Rhiannon looked pensive.

'I'll make sure she doesn't. Just you remember that you will always be with us in spirit.'

'Come on you two, I'm afraid it's time,' Gus announced.

After a last few tearful hugs and kisses, it was with mixed feelings that Ethel, with Catherine at her side, still holding tight to her doll, boarded the ship. As much as Ethel longed to be back with her beloved family, the thought of another long sea journey filled her with dread. Added to this, the fact that she was leaving New York without knowing Mair's fate deeply saddened her. In less than a week's time she would have to face Frank and try to explain once again how she and Mair became separated. One thing was certain, if the worst happened and Mair had indeed perished, Ethel vowed for as long as she had breath in her body to always be there for Catherine.

Chapter Three

MAIR PARSONS LAY in the darkness. She felt frightened and confused. She tried to open her eyes and failed. Where was she? Was she in a cave or maybe a long dark tunnel? Yes, that was it. She was in some kind of tunnel and there was a woman in black standing at the end of it – and behind her, a bright light. The woman was laughing! Mair instantly recognized her mother's coarse laugh.

'Mam, is that you?' Mair called out. 'Mam – Nellie? Please answer me!' Mair pleaded, but her mother just turned and walked away. Mair began to sob.

'There, there, it's all right. There's no need to be frightened. You're safe now. That's it. Try to open your eyes.' Mair heard a woman's friendly voice encourage her.

It took a real effort for Mair to open her heavy-lidded eyes, but eventually she succeeded. She felt awful. Her head ached, her lips felt cracked and sore and her throat as dry as sandpaper. Through blurred vision Mair became aware of a young woman standing over her.

'Well, hello there, how do you feel?' the woman asked.

'W-where am I? W-who are you?' Mair croaked, the brightness stinging her eyes. Her bleary eyes scanned the small room … white walls … white curtains … white bed linen.

'You're at St Vincent's hospital, and I'm your nurse. Here, take a sip of water.' With one hand supporting Mair's neck, the nurse placed a beaker of cold water to her lips.

Mair sipped the water, and as it gently slid down the back of her dry throat, it felt like honey.

'You've had a bad knock on your head. For the past few days, you've been drifting in and out of consciousness,' the nurse informed her.

'Well, nurse, what have we here?' a man's voice asked.

'Good morning, Doctor Hudson. I was just about to notify you that our patient has finally come to,' the nurse answered.

Aware of the doctor standing at her bedside, Mair squinted trying to get him into focus. He wasn't young. She was sure of that – a middle-aged friendly looking man with greying hair.

'It's good to see you awake at last,' the doctor said, his hand holding her wrist. The warmth of his hand felt comforting, and it took a while before Mair realized that he was just taking her pulse.

The doctor flashed a friendly smile. 'Your pulse is fine. For a while there, you had us worried. Now, if it's all right with you, I'd like to take a peek at those pretty eyes of yours.'

Mair didn't answer. She felt her colour rise and knew she was blushing.

If the doctor noticed, he hid it well. She watched him slowly remove a small magnifying glass from the pocket of his white hospital coat, which he proceeded to place over her right eye and then her left. 'Good. Everything appears to be returning to normal. Mind you, you'll probably have a beast of a headache for a few more days.... How is your memory? A bit foggy I suspect.'

'No – yes, I'm not sure. I keep having these weird flashes of memory that make no sense at all.'

'You're concussed. You suffered a slight trauma to the brain, and it will take a while to recover fully. Under the circumstances the memory flashes are quite normal. I'm going to give you a sedative. I'll come back later this afternoon, and we'll talk then,' the doctor said.

Mair tried to sit up but her head hurt. She grimaced.

The doctor gave a knowing smile. 'You rest up. I'll see you later,' he said, gently tapping the back of her hand.

Mair floated in and out of restless sleep. There was water … a lot of water … it was very dark … a beautiful staircase and above it a sparkling chandelier … music, lively, dance music … people were screaming....

When she did eventually wake up, she had no idea how long she had been asleep. Was it hours or was it days? What did it matter? The only thing that mattered to her was how much better she felt. Her pounding headache was nowhere near as bad and her vision had almost returned to normal.

'You're awake.' The nurse smiled. 'Good. I think it might be time for a bed bath, a change of nightdress, followed by a bite to eat and a long cool drink. What do you say?' she asked.

Mair heard her tummy rumble. 'Yes please. I do feel hungry, and so very thirsty,' Mair answered.

'That's a good sign. I can see we'll have you fighting fit in no time.'

It was just growing dark and the nurse had lit the night lights in Mair's room, when, as promised, Doctor Hudson returned to see her. Mair, by now well rested, freshly washed, fed and watered, felt almost human, and it surprised her how pleased she was to see him.

'Is this the same young gal I left earlier?' the doctor teased. 'You look so much better. Carry on like this and you'll be transferred onto the ward with the other female survivors, all well on the road to recovery.'

'Survivors ... from the *Titanic*, you mean?' Mair's eyes resembled those of a stunned rabbit.

'Yes, that's right. Look, I don't want you to become agitated in any way but, can you remember what happened to you?'

Mair nodded. There was another flash of memory ... she was aboard the *Titanic* travelling to New York ... another flash, then another, slowly it was all coming back to her, everything was beginning to fall into place. 'I can remember being aboard the *Titanic*, and it was ... sinking!' Mair had the sudden urge to tell all. 'There was a great noise – a hissing sound like hot coals being submerged in water. It was very cold on deck. Everyone was running around, "You have got to wear your lifebelt", someone said – clumsy big thing. A little girl was crying, "I want my mammy", was it Catherine?' She was growing agitated. 'Catherine! Where is she? I have to go to her! Is she still with Ethel? Are they both safe?'

'Please try to calm yourself. Who are Catherine and Ethel? Are they your relatives?' Doctor Hudson softly coaxed.

'Catherine is my 2-year-old daughter, of course!' Mair said more sharply that she intended. 'And Ethel ... well, Ethel ... is Ethel!'

'Catherine is your daughter, you say? And might I ask how old you are?' the doctor asked.

'I'm seventeen, if you must know.' Mair was getting angry. Then, seeing the shocked look on Doctor Hudson's face, she wished she'd lied about her age, but it was too late to change it now. Anyway who cared what the doctor or anyone else thought of her? She had far more pressing things to deal with. 'I need to know what's happened to my daughter and Ethel!' Mair declared.

'The truth is, I don't know. However, if you want me to find out, then I'll need a bit more to go on. What else can you remember?'

Mair gave a heavy sigh, 'I remember … an officer and two crewmen. They said, "You must get into the boat". They picked me up, I told them I needed to find Rhiannon's locket—'

'And Rhiannon is?' the doctor urged.

'Rhiannon Hughes. My sister, a famous music-hall star. I was on my way to see her with Catherine and Ethel. Anyway, these two men picked me up and threw me into the lifeboat. There were not more than fifteen of us in the boat….' Mair stopped, to catch her breath, 'I could hear the screams of people frantically calling to be picked up. The crewmen said we couldn't go back because, when the ship goes down, it would pull us down with it. So they kept rowing away. Through the darkness, I thought I heard someone call my name. 'Mair!' I heard. I stood up in the lifeboat. I remember how it rocked from side to side … that's when I fell and banged my head.'

'So your name is Mayre?'

The way the doctor spoke her name made Mair smile, reminding her of the way Walter Cahill, Aunt Florrie's American agent and friend of the family always pronounced it. At the same time, all the inner anger and frustration she'd felt earlier suddenly lifted from her.

'Yes … I'm Mair Parsons.'

Doctor Hudson offered an outstretched hand. 'Well, Mayre Parsons, I'm very pleased to meet you, and I promise I'll do all I can to reunite you with your loved ones.' His voice was warm and reassuring.

Mair smiled and shook his hand. 'Thank you, doctor.'

The next day Mair, out of danger and on the road to recovery, was transferred to the ward with the other female survivors of the *Titanic* tragedy. Her allotted bed was next to a young woman who was lying on her bed with a small baby wrapped in her arms. The woman had dark rings under her eyes from lack of sleep.

'How old is the baby?' Mair asked.

The young woman looked up. 'She's nine weeks old.'

'She's so young. Is she all right?'

'Yes. Thank you, we're both fine. I was only brought here because I fainted. When we disembarked in New York, I went straight to the shipping office to see if there was any news of my dear husband.' The woman shook her head and clutched the baby so tight it whimpered. 'I left him behind. "Women and children first", they said.'

Mair's heart went out to her. 'Yes, I know. My little girl went into a boat with her grandmother, we became separated and then I had a knock to the head.'

'I'm sorry. Do you know what happened to them?' the woman asked.

'No. Not yet. I'm desperate to find out.'

'I'm not certain what's best – knowing or not knowing. When I asked at the office I was told that my husband's name was on the list of those who perished – lost to the Atlantic Ocean … it's so unfair! He was only twenty-two with everything to live for. We were meant to be starting a new life in America. Now I don't know what's to become of me and the baby.' She began to sob and her distress transferred to the baby who started crying.

'Here, let me take her,' Mair offered.

The woman frantically shook her head. 'I know you mean well, but I can't bear the thought of being parted from her. I'm afraid to let her out of my sight.'

'You don't have to. Look, if you hand me the baby, I'll sit with her in this chair next to your bed. If you want to close your eyes and get some sleep, I promise I'll not move.'

The woman stopped crying and stared into Mair's eyes. 'You promise?'

'I promise.' Mair said, as she gave a friendly smile.

Reluctantly the woman handed over the tiny child and as Mair took her in her arms, she was reminded of the time when Catherine had been that small. She longed for news of her daughter and Ethel and prayed that God would keep them safe. She sat in the chair, her charge safely wrapped in her arms.

'Thank you,' the woman said, 'I really do feel exhausted. I can't remember when I last slept.'

'Then close your eyes. We'll still be here when you wake up.'

The woman gave a deep sigh, and, closing her eyes, she whispered, 'Well maybe just for a few minutes.'

After a little while a senior nurse walked over to Mair. 'Thank you. I saw what you did. It was so good of you to help. We're short staffed and as you can see we're rushed off our feet.' The nurse softly brushed the back of her hand on the baby's cheek. 'Her mother must have really trusted you. We've tried several times and she refused to give the little one to us. The way you gained her trust shows you to be a caring person – you'd make a good nurse.'

Mair felt heartened by this. It was the first time anyone had said she might be good at something.

Gus rushed into Rhiannon's dressing room. For once he didn't knock.

'Rhi! Mair's been found!' He crossed the room.

Rhiannon was seated at her dressing table, in the process of applying her stage make-up, but she immediately stopped what she was doing and stood up. 'Oh Gus, please tell me she's all right. I couldn't bare it if—'

'You don't have to. Mair's alive and well and what's even more amazing – she's here in Manhattan.'

'Thank God. But I don't understand. Why wasn't she listed as a survivor?'

'When the crew of the *Carpathia* rescued her from the lifeboat, she was unconscious; they had no way of knowing who she was. Then, when the ship docked, she was taken by ambulance to St Vincent's Hospital. When she eventually came to, she kept calling for Nellie, her mother – that's the only name they had to go on.'

'Nellie. Why on earth would she call for her? After what that woman did to her, I'd have thought Nellie would have been the last person she called for.'

'Well, she *was* concussed and suffering from memory loss. Thankfully, she's recovering. Mind you, it's taken until now for her to remember who she is and why she's in New York.'

'I just hope and pray that this tragic episode with the *Titanic* doesn't push her over the edge. She's already endured so much in her young life.'

'I know and I think it might be wise if we tread carefully for a little while – ease her back to full health.'

'Gus, can we go see her? I've hours to spare before my next show.'

'There's no need. She's on her way here. They were preparing to ship her back to Southampton. But she was adamant she wanted to come to you.'

Chapter Four

FRANK LEWIS, WHILE still on compassionate leave from Maendy Barracks, stared across the Jenkins' kitchen table at Catherine, who, having just finished her breakfast, was busily playing with her wooden building bricks. As far as he was concerned Catherine *was* his daughter; with the same blue eyes and light brown hair – a perfect miniature of her mother – and he loved them both so very much.

He looked over at his own mother, relaxing in her easy chair in front of the open coal fire. Since returning from America, he couldn't help but notice how much older she looked; her hair now streaked with grey, her face lined and dark rings under her eyes ... surviving the *Titanic* tragedy had definitely taken its toll.

Many a time both he and John Jenkins had tried to broach the subject ... but Ethel had made it perfectly clear. 'I don't want to talk about it. We're safe, and as far as I'm concerned, there's nothing to talk about. That's what I told all those reporters who bombarded me with questions the day our ship docked in Southampton, and the same when the man from the *South Wales Echo* called ... in my mind they were no better than wolves baying for blood!'

The biggest change of all was how Ethel, having been a regular chapel-goer, could no longer bring herself to attend, leaving it up to John and Frank to take the girls. The previous Sunday, John had tried hard to get her to attend Sunday Service. 'Come on, love, the men from the Pontbach Male Voice Choir will be there, you always enjoy them,' he'd coaxed.

'Yes, Mam. We all know how much you love to hear them sing all the Welsh hymns. Come with us, please,' Frank pleaded.

'No, son. If you don't mind, I'd rather not. I seem to have fallen out with God ... and if I was to enter His house of worship, I'd feel a hypocrite. No, you and John take the girls and go. I'll be fine.'

That was only yesterday. Today his mam, always an early riser, had already prepared a hearty breakfast for her husband John who liked to be at his butcher's shop for seven o'clock, and then did the same for Frank's sisters, Martha and Sadie, before they left for school.

In comparison, Frank, Catherine and Ethel's breakfast was a more leisurely affair. Although he wished it was under different circum-stances, he welcomed being on leave of duty. It meant he could spend more time with Catherine, and in so doing, give his mother a short respite in caring for her. For while his mother never complained, looking after an energetic 2-year-old took a lot of time and patience. He just hoped Mair appreciated his mother's total commitment to Catherine as much as he did.

There was a knock on the door.

'I wonder who that could be,' Ethel said.

'To find that out, do you think we might have to go answer the door?' Frank teased his mother.

Ethel shook her head and gave a loud 'Tut-tut, I know that. I was just thinking aloud. That's all.' She made to get up from her seat.

Frank gently touched his mother's shoulder. 'You stay put, Mam. Catherine and I will go, won't we, *cariad*?'

'Yes, Daddy.' Catherine eagerly raced ahead down the narrow passageway.

There was another knock – this one more urgent. 'Frank! There's a telegram for you,' Jones-the-post's voice called out.

This caused Frank to stop dead in his tracks. His heart sank. Could this be the news he'd been dreading?

'Catherine, come on back. You go sit with *Mamgu* Ethel, there's a good girl.' Frank tried to sound normal; he didn't want to alarm the child, but his mind was in turmoil imagining the worse.

Catherine, as strong-willed as her mother, pretended not to hear. 'Come on, Daddy,' she called, turning to take his hand and lead the way, 'let's go see the postman.'

'Frank, come on, man,' Jones's voice was growing impatient. 'There's a telegram for you. It's from Am—'

Frank opened the door.

'And about time it is, too. A telegram's arrived from America, addressed to you,' the postman gushed as he handed it to Frank.

'Thank you,' he said, gingerly taking the telegram from his old friend since schooldays. 'Thanks. I've never had one of these before.' Frank, keeping Catherine close, turned to head back inside.

'Aren't you going to open it? You may need to reply. Look I've brought my pad and pencil just in case. My mam, the postmistress, told me I had to come quick … it's news about your Mair, see?'

'About Mair, you say?' Frank flashed Jones a quizzical look, hoping to see a hint of the telegram's contents, but the postman's face gave nothing away.

'Well go on, man, open it,' Jones urged.

Frank reluctantly let go of Catherine's tiny hand and slowly tore open the telegram…. He read the message: GOOD NEWS. MAIR FOUND SAFE AND WELL. SHE'S WITH ME AND GUS IN NEW YORK. I WILL KEEP YOU INFORMED. LOVE RHIANNON.

Frank re-read it, just to be sure, before letting out a loud, 'Thank you, thank you, Lord!'

His uncharacteristic outburst brought Ethel rushing to the front door. 'What is it, son?' Ethel asked.

Before answering, Frank turned to lift an excited Catherine up in his arms. 'It's wonderful, *cariad*. I didn't mean to shout so loud. But, it's good news, see?' He waved the telegram in the air. 'Your mammy is safe and well.'

'Mammy!' Catherine shouted and her blue eyes shone.

'Thanks be to God!' Ethel cried out.

'Will there be any reply, then?' Jones asked.

Frank shook his head. 'No. But I can't thank you enough for bringing us such good news.'

'You're welcome,' the postman answered and, with a doff of his cap, sitting astride his pushbike, he headed back to the post office situated on Ponty Square.

'I'll go straight next door to John's shop and give him the good news,' Ethel declared.

'Yes, Mam, you go tell him that our Mair is safe and God willing, she'll soon be returned to us.'

Frank placed a tender kiss on his daughter's cheek and pulled her to him. 'Catherine, my lovely – your mammy is coming home.'

Catherine threw her arms around his neck, 'Yippee! My Mammy's coming home!' she squealed with delight.

Chapter Five

'ALL RIGHT, I know when I'm not wanted! I can't believe that you're sending me away! A few weeks ago you thought me dead. Now here I am alive and well, and all you want to do is send me back to Wales. Why?' Mair pleaded.

'Mair, be reasonable. You've been in America for the month we'd planned. In three days' time my contract here in New York comes to an end and Gus and I are booked to travel across country for the next leg of the tour. So you see it's just not practical for you to stay on. Anyway, I'd have thought you would be eager to be reunited with Frank and Catherine. Just think how much that poor mite must be missing you,' Rhiannon tried to reason.

Mair knew perfectly well what her sister was trying to do. She was hell-bent on making her feel guilty. Mair was having none of it. She dismissed this argument out of hand.

'So once again and true to form, you're pushing me away. Just like my mother, you can't wait to be rid of me, can you?' Mair challenged.

'That's not fair. What Nellie did to you was—'

'What?' Mair demanded. 'Her leaving us to go to Cardiff with her fancy man or allowing him to—' she stopped in mid-sentence. Mair still found it hard to speak about what had happened to her. Instead, hell-bent on making Rhiannon squirm, she completely changed tack. 'When your dad married my mother, you said it made us sisters.'

'And it did. We are. No one can change that.'

'So tell me, *sister, dear*, if that really is the case, then why, when we were in Cardiff, why did you let Nellie take me from you?' Mair heard her voice rising, but for some reason she couldn't control it.

'That's not fair. It wasn't my fault. After all, she is your mother.' Rhiannon argued.

'Oh, silly me. I almost forgot. Nothing is ever *Rhiannon Hughes's* fault, is it?' Mair couldn't believe how cruel her words sounded. She hadn't meant to say what she had – it just came out. What was happening to her? Could it be that the knock to her head had affected her more than she had first thought?

'When we went to stay with Aunt Florrie, we both knew it was only a short-term arrangement,' Rhiannon reminded her.

'Oh yes, yet another music-hall star that couldn't wait to be rid of me, it's not just her talent you've inherited, eh? And where's the great Florrie Grayson now?'

Rhiannon gave a heavy sigh, the hint of sarcasm in Mair's voice not lost to her. 'The last I heard she was on tour in Australia. And, I'd like to remind you that—'

'What? That I managed to lose your grandmother's gold locket aboard the *Titanic* – you always boasted how it was Florrie's parting gift to you.'

'No. The locket was the furthest thing from my mind. I was just going to point out that when Aunt Florrie left Cardiff, she was abandoning me too,' Rhiannon argued.

'But don't you see? You had everything, the locket, your stage career and even Gus Davenport. What did I have? Now let me see … oh yes, a baby, born out of wedlock, and a man who would ask me to marry him out of pity.'

'That's not true! Frank loves you. You're twisting everything. I think you're just looking for a way to get out of facing your responsibilities. I know you've had it hard. But Frank's a good man and Catherine—'

'You're right.' Mair nodded her agreement. 'Frank is a good man. He's far too good for the likes of me, eh? And although I'm in no doubt that both he and Catherine would be better off without me … you win. I'll do as you ask. I'll return to Wales, if only to get away from you. Don't look so shocked. You should be happy that you're finally rid of me.' As soon as she'd said the words Mair wanted to scream out 'Sorry, Rhi', to tell her sister that she didn't mean it and that she really did love her – but the words just wouldn't come.

*

'Gus, it was awful.' Rhiannon was upset. 'She said such cruel things. Do you think I should go and make up with her? Her ship sails for Southampton today. I really don't want us to part like this.'

'I think it best if we leave her be – at least for the time being. I've spoken to Doctor Hudson. He warned me that this might happen. Mair has suffered a trauma to the brain. He told me how this often causes a change in behaviour and in some severe cases it can completely change a patient's personality. He believes that once she's reunited with her family and friends in Wales, she'll make a full recovery.'

'I suppose there's nothing I can do. I will have to trust his judgement. It just doesn't seem right for us to part like this.'

'Look, in a few months' time, when your tour has ended, we'll take a holiday, a trip to Wales. Time enough for Mair to sort herself out and for you two to make your peace.'

'I hope so. And a holiday in Wales would be grand…. Gus, can we at least make sure she has enough money to tide her over until then?'

'I've already seen to that. I've arranged with the ship's captain to present her with a hundred and fifty pounds and to tell her it was a gift from us. That should see her all right for a while. I also included a list of dates and venues of your American tour – to ensure she can always contact us.'

'Thank you, my darling. I can always rely on you to do the right thing.'

'All part of the service, ma'am. Just you remember I'm always here for you – willing and able to satisfy your every need,' Gus teased, as he gently swept her in his arms and carried her to their four-poster bed.

Chapter Six

FRANK LEWIS WAITED patiently on the quay at Southampton for Mair's ship to dock. He'd booked a room for the night at a small bed and breakfast establishment where he and Mair could spend the night and catch up on lost time. He'd missed her. When his mother and Catherine returned from America without her, it had been a bitter blow. For a while, he thought he'd never see her again. Every night he thanked God for saving his mother and Catherine and prayed for Mair's safe return.

When he received the telegram from Rhiannon, with the news that Mair was indeed safe and well, he knew his prayers had been answered. Frank had hoped to receive a letter from Mair – but none came. He longed for news of her return to Wales. As the days passed, with still no news, Frank couldn't understand the delay.

'You have to be patient,' his mother had said.

'I know, Mam. But I just want her back with us, so much.'

Two long weeks later another telegram arrived....

> MAIR ABOARD THE ADRIATIC ARRIVING AT
> SOUTHAMPTON DOCKS MON 20 MAY 1912.
> I TRUST YOU WILL BE THERE TO MEET HER.
> LOVE RHIANNON.

'Are you all right, son?'

'Yes, Mam. It's just, well ... I've longed for this news and, now it's come, I'm frightened. Mair's been through so much. I need her to know I'll always love and support her.'

'I'm sure she knows that, son. But there is only so much any of us can do. Mair is stronger than you think. She will always be her own person.'

'All I want is to make her happy. To give her and Catherine the life they deserved. I love her so much, Mam. I'd marry her tomorrow.'

'I know you would.'

'The truth is ... I'm not sure she feels the same about me. I keep asking myself, why hasn't she written? Why hasn't she tried to get in touch? Is it because she doesn't care for me any more?'

'You have to stop tormenting yourself like this. There can be any number of reasons for her not getting in touch. The main thing is – she's coming home, and all your doubts and fears will be answered.'

'I hope so. One thing's for certain, when she arrives in Southampton, I intend to be there waiting for her.'

'That's right, son. You go to Southampton and bring her back home to us.'

The *Adriatic* docked in Southampton at 4.30 on the afternoon of Monday 20 May 1912. During the nine-day journey from New York harbour, Mair had had plenty of time to think about her future.

Over the years she had trained herself to put Nellie, Harry Stone and ... what that horrible man had done to her, to the back of her mind. To pretend it never happened. And, for the most part, it worked. Of course there were occasions, usually sparked by the way Catherine sometimes looked at her, when the horrible memories came flooding back. After all, Catherine was living proof – a constant reminder. Mair often questioned how such a sweet and beautiful child could be the product of something so ... so ... evil.

If Mair was being honest with herself, she felt more than a little apprehensive of what lay ahead. She was seventeen and, until recently, couldn't remember a day when she had put herself first, there always seemed someone else to care for and to worry about. When she was younger it had been her mother, Nellie, then her stepfather and Rhiannon, and now Catherine and Frank, constantly on her mind – constantly expecting her to 'do the right thing', to be a good girlfriend and mother. Well, now she had the chance to change all of that. Having recently cheated death, she vowed to take charge of her own life – to become a free spirit.

To achieve this, during her trip from New York, Mair had decided on a course of action, one that would need her inner strength and determination to succeed. What she ultimately needed to do, was to grow up and act like the strong young woman her stepfather, Dai Hughes, would have been proud of. It was the only way.

The time had come for Mair to think of her future. And, thanks to Gus Davenport and Rhiannon, her dear, dear sister, she held in her pocket a new found wealth to start her on her way. To afford respectable digs, a place of her own and to begin the search for her mother … Nellie Parsons – the only person who could provide an end to the whole sordid episode and to help Mair get on with the rest of her life.

Mair's thoughts went back to the way she and Rhi had parted. She felt awful. The last thing she'd wanted was to fall out with her sister, and she wished they could have parted on better terms. Mair knew she'd said some dreadful things to Rhiannon, things she hadn't really meant to say, things said in the heat of the moment. The fact that she had been hurt by Rhiannon's eagerness to see her return to Wales, was no excuse. She vowed to write her sister an apology so that they might get back on friendly terms – but not until she'd settled everything with Nellie.

Something told her that if Rhiannon knew of her plan, she'd do everything in her power to dissuade her.

After what seemed like an age, the passengers of the *Adriatic* began to disembark. Frank instantly spotted Mair. As he watched her walk down the steps onto the pier, he thought how beautiful and smart she looked, dressed in a brown skirt and coat, cream striped blouse with a brooch pinned at the neck and on her head, a straw hat trimmed with dried flowers.

His face lit up – Mair was actually here! 'Mair,' He called as she came towards him. As soon as she was close enough, he swung his arms around her. 'Mair, my lovely girl. I can't begin to tell you how good it is to have you back with me. I've missed you so much.'

'It's good to see you too, Frank.' She sounded genuinely pleased to see him. 'I wasn't sure if you would be here to meet me. I thought you'd be tied up with your regiment. Tell me, how's Catherine? Is she all right?'

'Catherine's fine. I left her at home. My mam thought it too long a journey to bring her with me, but I know she can't wait to see you.'

Mair nodded. Frank sensed she was about to say something and then changed her mind.

'Come here. Give us a *cutch*.' He cuddled her to him and kissed her long and hard.

He couldn't fail to miss the way she reacted, allowing him to kiss her, yet not responding and, was it his imagination or had she pulled away from him? As he gently placed his arm around her to walk from the quay, he scolded himself for the way he'd pounced on her. Little wonder she'd pushed him off. The thing was, she looked and sounded so different. In the six weeks since she'd been away she seemed to have grown up so much. She looked so damned attractive, and yes … she aroused him, a feeling, up to now, he'd always managed to keep in check.

'How come you're not busy playing soldier back at Maendy Barracks, then?' Mair asked.

Ignoring the hint of sarcasm in her voice, he flashed a warm smile.

'When the news came that you were "missing", my commanding officer arranged for me to have a month's compassionate leave. Then when we heard that you'd been found safe and well and were on your way home, he extended it so that I could be here to meet you.'

'A pity they couldn't have given you the time off to travel to America with me, eh? It's almost as if I have more worth dead than alive.'

Frank couldn't fail to notice how different Mair was from the last time he'd seen her and not just in her looks and demeanour – even the way she talked had changed, everything she said seemed to have a bitter edge to it. It made her sound a lot older than her seventeen years.

'Now, don't talk so daft. Look, I know what a long journey you've had, so I booked us a room for the night in a boarding house close by. I'm sure you'll feel better after a good night's rest.'

The Seaways boarding house was close enough to walk. Frank led the way, carrying Mair's single carpetbag with one hand and tenderly holding her hand with the other.

Mair dreaded the task ahead of her, but she knew it had to be done.

Their room, although small, was clean and comfortably furnished.

It had a double bed, a wardrobe, a washstand, complete with a large china jug and washbowl and situated in the bay window, a small table and two chairs, Frank ordered a pot of tea for two and a plate of cold meat sandwiches.

'You look tired,' he said, taking her hand. 'I've so many questions.... What happened to you the night of the disaster? How did you become separated from my mother and Catherine – what possessed you to risk your life for a locket? I want to know about your time in hospital and, most importantly, if you are fully recovered. But this can all wait until you are well rested.' He made to lead her towards the double bed.

Mair didn't move. She stayed put as if glued to the spot, her eyes staring at the bed. She didn't speak, there was no need. Her look of terror said it all.

Frank put an arm around her, 'Mair, love, please don't look so worried. It's not what you think. I did try to get us separate rooms but this was the only room available. I promise you, all I want to do is lie beside you to *cutch* you – to hold and cuddle you, just like we used to back home in Ponty. I give you my word ... Mair, you do trust me, don't you?' Frank looked hurt.

She felt awful. She knew he was speaking the truth. Back home in Ponty, they had slept in the same bed on a few occasions, but there had been nothing but a loving embrace between them.

'I'm sorry, Frank. I didn't mean to hurt your feelings. Of course I trust you. I'm just being silly. I'm tired. That's all.' She gave a long sigh, and felt the weight of the world on her shoulders.

After removing her coat and shoes, she lay on the bed. Frank lay down beside her and, keeping a respectable distance, draped his arm around her. He began to softly kiss the nape of her neck. 'I've missed you so much.' He moved closer, 'I don't know what I'd have done if—'

'Frank! Stop it!' Mair sat bolt upright in the bed.

'What is it? What's wrong? I wasn't going to—'

'Yes, you were. When we first started courting and you asked me to marry you, I told you then that I didn't think I'd ever be able to – to be intimate with you.'

Frank moved off the bed. 'And I'll tell you now what I told you then, I understand and accept it. I can wait for as long as it takes. All I wanted then and now was to take care of you and Catherine.'

Mair's eyes welled up with grateful tears. 'And believe me, you have. What you did, taking me on, even though you knew I was shop-soiled goods, opening your heart not just to me but to Catherine—'

'It was easy. I loved you both then, as I love you now. Nothing else matters.'

Mair hadn't banked on it being this hard, but she knew she'd come too far to stop now. 'But it's not fair on you! Frank, we're not even married, and yet you care for us as well as any husband or, in Catherine's case, father – with none of the obvious benefits. You're a warm-blooded man and it's only natural that you should want ... well ... you know? You deserve more – more than I can ever give you.' Mair sat on the edge of the bed, her eyes staring into his, pleading with him to agree with her.

Frank shook his head. 'Why not let me be the judge of that? And you're wrong. I have so many benefits. I have a beautiful young woman whom I love and who has agreed to be my wife, a gorgeous daughter who looks so much like you, that she makes my heart flutter every time I see her.' Frank leant down and placed a soft kiss on her forehead. 'So you see I do have a lot to be thankful for. And tomorrow I shall take you home to Ponty. Everyone is so looking forward to seeing you, especially Catherine.'

Mair stood up, and brushing past him, walked across the room. 'Well, she, like the rest of them, might have a long wait,' she announced.

Frank was puzzled. 'I don't understand. What do you mean?'

'Frank, I'm not coming back to Ponty with you. Tomorrow morning I'm leaving.'

Frank's shocked expression said it all. For a while, he just stood in front of her opened mouthed, rendered speechless. After what seemed like an age, but in fact was only a few seconds, he regained his compo-sure. 'Now let me get this straight. When you say you're leaving, what do you mean exactly?'

'Frank, please believe me when I tell you that I didn't take this deci-sion lightly. On the trip from New York, I had a long time to think about the future. I came to the conclusion that getting married would be a big mistake; we'd be marrying for all the wrong reasons. You want to right a wrong that was none of your doing. And I wanted to feel safe. Frank, ever since I was a little girl you've always looked out for me—'

'But you don't love me! Is that it?'

'No – yes, oh Frank, I do love you, but not the way someone should love a future husband. I love you as a true friend, who I know will always be kind to me. You're a good man, but it's never going to work. If surviving the *Titanic* has taught me one thing it's how quickly life can be snatched away from you. For years I've been quite content to sit back and accept the way things were. Well, not any more. I intend to take charge of my own life – and if that means walking away from you and even from Catherine, then so be it.'

'Forgive me. You see, I'm finding it hard to take in what you're saying. Even if I were to accept your illogical reasons for wanting to leave *me*, I can't believe that you actually intend to walk away from your only daughter! Especially as you know what it's like to be abandoned by your own mother.'

'Yes, I do. I can still remember the day my mother ran away with Harry Stone, leaving Dai Hughes, my stepfather, to care for Rhiannon and me.'

'So, knowing first-hand how it felt, how can you even think of doing the same to Catherine?'

'But that's just it. The day my mother left us I was relieved. It meant Dai, Rhi and me could be happy…. With Nellie gone there'd be no more awful arguments.'

'We don't argue.'

'No? What do you think we are doing now, then? And worse it'll get if you make me stay. I know how much you and your family all love Catherine.' Mair bit her bottom lip. The thought of leaving the one pure, sweet and innocent thing in her life tore at her heart. She told herself she had to be strong. 'It's for the best. Catherine needs the stability of a caring family. Trust me, you'll all be so much better off without me. After all is said and done, I *am* my mother's daughter.'

'There's no denying Nellie Parsons was a bad 'un,' Frank agreed.

'Exactly,' Mair interrupted, 'have you never heard the saying "An apple never falls far from the tree"?'

'I don't believe what I'm hearing!' Frank put his head in his hands.

Mair hated herself for putting him through this – she so wanted him to understand why she was doing it.

'Frank, during my time in hospital, I kept having this dream about my mother – she was standing in the distance. I called out to her, but she just kept laughing at me … goading … telling me what a bad daughter I was, and what a bad mother I'd turned out to be.'

Frank looked up and stared at her, his eyes pleading. 'Mair, love. Please listen to me. You've had a bang on the head and your mind is obviously playing tricks on you,' he argued.

'That's as maybe, but it felt so real. That's when I knew I just had to find her. I need to know why she always hated me, and why she continues to haunt my dreams – my nightmares.'

'Leaving us, running away like this, is not the answer. It's been almost three years since you last saw or heard from Nellie and Harry. They could be anywhere in the world.'

Mair flashed him a look of defiance. 'We both know better than that, don't we? I still remember the day you went looking for them at their digs in Cardiff and found they'd done a runner. If I'm not mistaken a neighbour told you then that they'd headed for London.'

'He said he *thought* they'd gone to London … London's a big place. It might have just been a red herring. They knew that if I could have found them, I'd have—'

'But you didn't,' Mair pointed out. 'You – we – let them get away!'

'Oh believe me, I was sorely tempted to follow them, but I decided they were not worth the trouble it would cause. You mustn't let what they did haunt you for the rest of your life. I've tried to help you get through it – to help you forget—'

'Forget! Forget what? The fact that my own mother stood by and watched her fancy man auction me off to the highest bidder for sex? Forget it? I don't think so!'

'Look, if you'll come home with me tomorrow, I promise I'll make some inquiries. I've heard the Salvation Army do a lot to help trace long lost relatives. They might be able to give us a lead as to Nellie's whereabouts, what do you say?'

'No! I've already waited too long. I need to do this now!'

Frank gave a deep sigh and wearily shook his head. 'I can't believe how much you've changed. You've always been strong-willed, but the Mair who left me just weeks ago would never have even thought of leaving us, she—'

'Forget the young girl you thought you knew and loved. I've changed and it's time for you to do the same!'

They carried on with the discussion well into the night. Frank desperately trying to persuade her to stay, treading the same ground over and over and over again, pleading with her, until Mair could take no more. In the end there was only one thing for it ... she feigned sleep.

She felt Frank's hand brush a strand of hair from her forehead before he kissed it.... 'That's right, my love. You sleep. I'm sure you'll feel different after a good night's rest.' Frank cuddled down beside her and before long he was fast asleep.

Mair waited until she was sure that Frank was in a deep sleep before she quietly slid out of bed. And, still wearing the same clothes as the day before, she picked up her small carpetbag and crept out of the room.

Chapter Seven

WITH A HEAVY heart, Mair made her way to the railway station. It was a fine day. Although late May, there was still a cool feel to the morning, and she was glad of her short coat.

Under different circumstances Mair might have relished the fact that she was back in England and heading out on a new adventure in London. But instead she endeavoured to shake the nagging doubts from her mind, telling herself over and over again that she was doing the right thing. This was something she just had to do.

Arriving at the station she duly purchased a one-way ticket to Waterloo Station in London. As she boarded the train she made the decision to use the three-hour journey to focus her mind on a plan of action. The first thing she needed to do when she reached London was to find herself somewhere to stay – a small hotel or boarding house would do, nothing too fancy just as long as it was clean and respectable. And now, thanks to Gus and Rhiannon's generous gift of a hundred and fifty pounds, she had enough money to tide her over for a long while to come.

It had crossed her mind to leave some of the money back at the boarding house with Frank along with a note explaining that it was her contribution toward Catherine's keep. But, knowing how proud Frank was, she decided against it. Instead, she vowed to write to Ethel and explain why she had felt the need to leave Frank and Catherine and travel to London. Ethel had always been so good to her. She of all people deserved an explanation. She would also send some money towards Catherine's keep. Mair was sure Ethel would accept it in the spirit it was given – Ethel would understand.

After she had found suitable accommodation, she would set about finding Nellie and Harry Stone. During last night's long discussion with Frank, he had mentioned the Salvation Army's work in finding lost relatives. This had to be a good place for her to start her search. She had long since given up the idea of finding her actual attacker ... all she knew about him was that his name was Jake and without a surname ... she realized how hopeless it would be.

Comforted by this thought she settled into the leather-backed carriage seat. Last night's discussion with Frank had drained her and there could be no doubt that the lack of sleep had begun to take its toll. Realizing she could no longer fight the inevitable, she closed her heavy-lidded eyes.

The loud noise of the carriage buffeting as the train came to a stop awoke her.

'Waterloo Station!' Mair heard a station guard announce.

Mair stood up and, after straightening her clothes, reached for her valise and prepared to leave the train. Through the haze of steam expelled from the engine she stepped off the train. The station was much busier than she could ever have imagined. Many people from all walks of life rushed to and fro with a purpose; everyone seemed to know where they were headed and what they had to do to get there. Everyone, that was, except Mair, who amid all the hustle and bustle felt completely out of her depth – lost in a sea of strangeness and totally alone. Panic rose like bile and settled in her throat.

'Are you all right, Miss? Do you need some assistance?' a station guard, who looked to be in his early twenties, asked.

'No ... yes, please. I'm looking to find accommodation. A small hotel or guest house, maybe?' Then seeing the questioning look on his face she added, 'I'm all alone, but I do have funds.'

The guard gently pulled her to one side. And in a whispered voice said, 'I hope you won't mind me saying, Miss, but if I were you, I wouldn't broadcast the fact that you're on your own and carrying money. London's full of opportunists; thieves, vagabonds and the like, just waiting to pounce on lone travellers like you.'

Mair couldn't believe her stupidity. How many times had Ethel or Frank and before them Rhiannon, warned her to keep her own council?

'Thank you. I'm sorry. I just wasn't thinking.'

The young guard flashed a friendly smile. His kindness warmed her, proof that there were *some* good people still to be found.

'Now, accommodation, you say?' He scratched his chin. 'I'm afraid I can't help you there ... but I know of those who can.'

Breathing a sigh of relief, Mair prompted him to continue.

'Do you see those two ladies over there?'

Mair looked to where he was pointing. 'Those dressed in long coats and shaking collection tins?' Mair asked.

'Yes, that's right, Miss. They're from the Salvation Army. Every day they come collecting for charity and the like – every day except Sunday that is. On Sunday they meet up with the Salvation Army band to sing and march on the streets, spreading the word of God. I'm sure they'll be able to help you.'

Mair couldn't believe her luck, she hadn't been in London more than five minutes and she'd already found people from the Salvation Army.

'Thank you, that's very kind of you.'

The guard doffed his cap. 'All part of the service, ma'am. By the way, the name's Albert Stubbs. If you're ever passing this way, come say hello.' And with that he turned and went about his business.

As Mair approached the two ladies she couldn't help but notice how severe they looked; their plain faces pinched and disapproving. One looked to be in her mid-twenties and the other, the one who seemed to be in charge, a lot older. Both wore their hair strained back under military-style bonnets, wearing not even a touch of make-up, their skin as pale as alabaster.

'Excuse me,' Mair said nervously.

'Yes, what is it, my dear?' the older woman asked, her voice much softer than her stern outward appearance would suggest.

'The st-station g-guard over there said you m-might be able t-to help me.'

'Where are your travelling companions?' the woman asked.

Mair took a deep breath in an effort to control her nerves ... 'I'm alone and looking to find suitable accommodation. The guard said you could—'

'How old are you, child?'

'I'm seventeen.'

'Rather young to be travelling alone. May I ask what brings you to London?'

Mair wondered if this might be a good time to mention Nellie, and how she hoped to find her, but she decided against it – now was not the time. 'I'm here on family business,' Mair heard herself say. Then, remembering the guard's warning, leant closer to the woman and whispered, 'If you do know of somewhere for me to stay, I *can* pay my way.'

'I'm glad to hear it. You'd be surprised the number of young girls … and boys, who arrive penniless, believing the streets of London really are paved with gold…. Anyway, enough of that, I think it's time for introductions. I'm Sister Agnes and this is Sister Ruth,' she said, gently touching the younger woman's arm.

Sister Ruth turned and flashed a warm smile before turning back to continue shaking her collection tin at passers-by. 'Please help the poor and destitute, please give a small donation to help the homeless on the streets of London,' she pleaded, her voice soft, her sentiment obviously genuine.

'And you are?' Sister Agnes asked.

'Mair – Mair Parsons and I'm from South Wales,' Mair proudly answered.

'Pleased to meet you,' Sister Agnes said, her outstretched hand gently shaking Mair's hand. 'You've travelled all the way from South Wales today?'

'N-no, today I've come from Southampton. Mind you, before that I spent days travelling by ship from New York to Southampton.'

'My goodness, quite the little globe-trotter…. I'd be interested to hear about your long journey. I sense you might have an interesting tale to tell. However, I'm sure there'll be time for that later. Right now, we should be thinking of getting you some refreshment.' She promptly turned to Sister Ruth. 'Sister Ruth, be a dear and take yourself over to the refreshment table and purchase a cup of hot sweet tea for young Mair here.'

'Of course, Sister Agnes,' the young Sister enthused as she eagerly made her way to the refreshment table – a table laid with flowers, teapots and various items for sale, situated in the centre of the platform. Once there she joined the small queue of waiting customers.

'She'll not be long. Now, regarding your accommodation. I have to say that at first, with you being all alone in this great metropolis, I had it in mind to take you back with us to the women's refuge but now … having spoken to you and seeing that you are obviously not destitute, I've changed my mind. I have a friend who just happens to own a respectable boarding house for young women. Her clients are all trainee nurses. I'm sure you would be most welcome and comfortable there. How does that sound?'

'It sounds lovely to me, thank you.'

Sister Agnes looked up at the station clock situated high above the entrance to the station. 'In under an hour – two o'clock to be precise – Captain Johnson, our respected brigade leader and protector, will arrive to escort Sister Ruth and me back to our base at the women's refuge situated on Blackfriars Road. On our way, we usually call in at our local Salvation Army mission hall to check on their progress. The captain is never late. He prides himself on his punctuality. So, if you wouldn't mind waiting until then, I'll be happy to take you and introduce you to the proprietor of the establishment I mentioned earlier.'

'I'd like that. I really don't mind waiting.'

'Good. Now, do you see that wooden settle over there in front of the booking office?'

Mair nodded.

'Well, when Sister Ruth brings you your tea, you take yourself over there and rest up awhile. Sister Ruth and I will carry on shaking our collection tins until Captain Johnson arrives.'

At precisely two o'clock, a tall, middle aged man arrived dressed in a dark serge military style suit, his jacket sporting six shiny brass buttons with purple and gold braid strategically placed on both shoulders and hat-trim. He approached Sister Agnes and Sister Ruth. Their greeting was warm and friendly and, after a brief exchange of pleasantries, the small group turned and headed in Mair's direction.

'Mair, dear, this is Captain Johnson,' Sister Agnes smiled.

Mair stood up, almost to attention.

'How very pleased I am to meet you, my dear,' Captain Johnson enthused.

'Thank you, me too,' Mair politely replied.

'Sister Agnes has briefly explained your immediate needs, and I whole-heartedly agree with her choice of accommodation by way of a solution. If you like, we could take you there right now. The sooner we get you fixed up the better. I assume this is yours?' Captain Johnson reached down and picked up Mair's carpetbag.

'Y-yes, but it's all right. I can carry it,' Mair offered.

'I'm sure you can. However, how would it look if a big strong fellow like me was seen to stand by and watch a slip of a girl carry her own carpetbag? Why I'd be the talk of the brigade! I'm sure you wouldn't want that on your conscience, now would you?'

'No-no, I d-didn't mean t-to—'

Captain Johnson gave a loud belly laugh, interrupting her apology, this in turn sent the two sisters into a fit of laughter, their laughter so infectious Mair, having realized the big man was teasing her, joined in.

When the laughter eventually subsided, Sister Agnes shook her head. 'Captain Johnson, what are we to do with you? Sorry, child, it's just his way,' she explained.

Captain Johnson placed a gentle hand on Mair's shoulder. 'It's not just my way. It is God's way. You looked so very serious. I thought a bit of light-hearted laughter might just break the ice. God knows how it works every time. Come now, let's make a move.'

Captain Johnson led the way and Mair followed. Closely flanked on either side by Sister Agnes and Sister Ruth, they left the station. Mair found herself surrounded by such warmth, kindness and love that suddenly she felt safe in the knowledge that these were her new-found friends, and she was no longer alone.

Outside the station, the weather was cloudy but fairly warm; the air filled with smoke billowing from a large factory across the way and a pungent stench of dirty drains. Mair's first impression was of a rather noisy and unwelcoming place and if the people on the street – hawkers with their wooden wheeled carts rattling along, men on bicycles and several women flower sellers – were anything to go by, this was a poor area and nothing like the London she had heard and read about.

Led by Captain Johnson the small troupe turned immediately left and proceeded to walk a hundred yards to the end of the row before making another left turn on to York Road. It was a long road of terraced properties, but they had only passed a few houses when Captain Johnson came to a halt, stopping outside a large Victorian house called Grange House. Mair inspected the four-storey building with eight windows, two on each floor, with arches picked out in red brick. On the third floor a large wrought-iron balcony matched the gate at the front of the building, leading to both the front door and also down to the basement.

'Sister Agnes, if you would like to take our young charge into the boarding house,' he said, offering her Mair's carpetbag, 'Sister Ruth and I will go pay a visit to the Duke of York public house, and rattle our collection tins.' He pointed to a tavern some distance away. 'I'm always both saddened and warmed by the good people who frequent these ale houses, spending as they do such a large part of their weekly wage on hard liquor, yet still managing to find a few coins for our cause to help the poor and needy – if for no other reason than to appease their own conscience. We bless and pray for their salvation and for them to one day see the error of their ways.'

'Amen,' the sisters said in unison.

Mair watched as the captain and Sister Ruth headed down York Road in the direction of the tavern, just managing to avoid a horse and carriage and a couple of male cyclists. Mair's eyes suddenly became transfixed by their destination, instantly recognizing the tavern as the type of establishment her mother and Harry Stone used to frequent with their cronies back in Cardiff. For all she knew, they could both be sitting in there now, swigging ale, laughing and joking – totally oblivious of her existence, not caring if she was alive or dead. One thing was certain, where Nellie and Harry were concerned, the captain and the Sister were on a hiding to nothing; no amount of tin rattling would see either of them give a penny to charity. Mair knew from first-hand experience that they didn't have a charitable thought between them and, as for appeasing their conscience … what conscience?

Mair wondered how Nellie and Harry would react if she were to just walk in on them. She was tempted to cross the road herself and find out. She almost did it – she so wanted to have her say, to finally have it out with Nellie and hopefully bring an end to the part of her life that continued to haunt her.

'Are you all right, my dear? You look as if someone just walked over your grave.'

Mair didn't answer. Afraid to speak, afraid she might be tempted to bare all to Sister Agnes, aware of how easily one word could lead to another, and another, and another. No! She scolded herself. Now was not the time. Although her meeting with Nellie and Harry Stone was long overdue, it would have to wait for a little while longer. Anyway, the chances of them actually being in the first London pub she'd come across, were slim to say the least. She needed to think of a quick excuse – a little white lie.

'Sorry, Sister. Honestly, I'm fine. It's just that everything is so different and … so strange,' Mair answered.

'And no doubt, with it being your first time in London, a little intimidating?'

Mair simply nodded her agreement. So far, she was finding the streets of London even more frightening than those in New York.

Opening the gate, Sister Agnes proceeded to climb the four well-scrubbed steps, leading to the high-glossed black painted front door of the boarding house. Mair followed. She watched the Sister lift the heavy brass door-knocker and knock once … then twice. A few moments later the door was opened by a fair-haired young girl dressed in a grey dress and highly-starched, white pinafore and hat.

'Why, Sister Agnes, how nice to see you,' the young girl said.

'And you, Violet. We've called to see Mrs Turnbull.'

The girl called Violet held the door open, revealing a long hallway with black and white floor tiles and pale cream embossed wallpaper stretching up to the high ceiling with an alabaster freeze and ornate centre rose.

'Come on in, Sister. If you'd like to wait in the living room, I'll let the Mistress now that you're here.'

As the maid led the way into the pleasantly furnished living room, her easy manner was comforting. It seemed a very friendly establishment. Mair's eyes were drawn to the large bay window looking out over the street below. It was late afternoon and, apart from the rattle of a single horse-drawn carriage over the cobbled road, very quiet.

The living room door opened.

'Sister Agnes, what brings you here? I wasn't expecting you until later this evening,' an attractive middle-aged lady asked.

Mair thought how elegant she looked dressed in a skirt of lavender blue and a white high-necked blouse with an attractive green, white and violet brooch pinned at the neck. During Mair's recent journey from New York, she had encountered many ladies wearing similar brooches – she later found out that it signified allegiance to the Suffragette movement: 'Give Women Votes'. Green stood for hope, white for purity and purple for dignity.

'Good afternoon, Ada. I've come today to introduce to you, Miss Mair Parsons.' The Sister beamed a smile in Mair's direction. 'This young lady made herself known to me at Waterloo Station earlier today. She was travelling alone and in need of suitable accommodation. I immediately thought of your establishment.'

Ada Turnbull cast a quizzical eye at Mair. 'Well, as it happens, I do have a vacant room that would suit but – Waterloo Station, you say?'

'Yes, apparently she'd travelled from New York to Southampton and then on to London,' Sister Agnes offered.

'That's a long way for anyone to travel, especially a young woman and – travelling alone?'

Mair instantly sensed Mrs Turnbull disapproval and, fearful of being refused accommodation, decided to speak up in her own defence. She turned to face the two women. 'Mrs Turnbull, if I may explain? Sister Agnes, I'm sorry I didn't mention this earlier – it's not something I like to talk about. You see, I was a passenger on *RMS Titanic* and as a survivor of that dreadful tragedy, the American authorities organized my repatriation to England. They simply issued me with my one-way ticket from New York to Southampton, aboard the *Adriatic*, a Cunard liner. I had no choice but to accept it. I can assure you that under normal circumstances, I would never have chosen to travel alone.'

For a while both Sister Agnes and Mrs Turnbull stood in shocked silence.

'The *Titanic*,' Sister Agnes exclaimed. '*You* were actually a passenger on its maiden voyage?'

'Yes. I was travelling with a friend and her daughter,' Mair lied. She wasn't prepared to bare all, not just yet. She quickly added, 'We were on our way to visit my sister who lives in New York.'

'Oh, you dear girl. What about your friend and her daughter?'

'They are both fine, thank you. They were repatriated a month ago. Unfortunately, I had suffered a bump to the head and needed to spend time in hospital. Then later, my sister nursed me through convalescence. The authorities wouldn't let me travel until they felt I was in good health.'

'I trust that you are now fully recovered?' Mrs Turnbull asked. Her voice was suddenly full of compassion.

'Yes, thank you. Although I must say the last few days' travelling has left me feeling very weary.'

'I'm sure it has. However, nothing a good lie down on a comfy mattress wouldn't put right. If you'd like to follow me, I'll take you to your room.'

Mair nodded her head and smiled. She hadn't planned to use the *Titanic* or her head injury as a bargaining tool, but as they say – needs must.

'Well, now that I can see you're settled, I'll be off. I need to find Captain Johnson and Sister Ruth. We're due back at the refuge,' Sister Agnes said.

'Yes, Sister, you get yourself off. I assure you that your charge is safe with me. Will you be making your usual call this evening?' Ada asked.

'Yes. I thought I might call on my way home from the refuge, if that's all right with you?'

Ada nodded her approval. 'Sister, I shall look forward to it. You know you're always welcome.'

The Sister smiled. 'Thank you, Ada. And Mair, if you feel that you're up to it, when I return, perhaps you and I could have that chat I spoke about earlier? I was right when I said I thought you had an interesting tale to tell.'

Mair turned and smiled. She so looked forward to meeting up with Sister Agnes again. For a moment she had feared that, having found accommodation, Sister Agnes might think her job done and not want to keep in touch. 'I'd like that, Sister. In fact, I may have need of your expertise and advice regarding a personal matter – the reason for my being in London.'

'Oh, I do love a mystery, don't you, Sister?' Mrs Turnbull piped up.

'These days, I only like the ones I can solve! I'll see you both later.' And with that, Sister Agnes turned and left.

Mair's room was one of three on the second floor, a comfortable, well furnished room with a magnificent mahogany-framed double bed and matching bedroom suite; wardrobe, chest of drawers and dressing table. In the far corner – shielded by a delicately painted screen – stood a marble washstand.

'Bathroom facilities for this floor are at the end of the hall,' Mrs Turnbull informed her. 'I have six double letting rooms in all. I usually try to get two girls sharing each. And, if you stay on, there may come a time when I shall ask you to do the same. But for now, I'm quite happy for single occupation. The other three rooms are on the floor above.' Mrs Turnbull cast her eyes toward the high ceiling.

There was no lift and, as grateful as Mair was to have found such comfortable accommodation, she was glad not to have to make the steep trek up to an attic room.

'Supper is at 6.30. The dining room is just off reception. My residents tend to be all nurses or hospital trainees who work shifts. Consequently I'm not always sure how many there will be for supper. The girls do try to keep me informed, but the hospital rota can change daily. Now you get some rest. I'll see you later.'

Mair looked around the room – her new home. It felt strange and, at the same time, oddly exciting to have made this huge step. Part of her wondered how she would cope without the support of Gus, Rhi, Frank and the Jenkins family. She prayed to God that Catherine would not think too badly of her.

In an effort to take her mind off such thoughts, Mair proceeded to lift her carpetbag up onto the high feather bed and unpack her clothes carefully in the wardrobe. Her undergarments were placed in the chest of drawers, her accessories – handkerchiefs, lace collars, cuffs, shawl and brooch – in the dressing table drawer.

Satisfied with her efforts, Mair lay on the bed to rest. It had been a long day, and she still had to face being introduced to her fellow residents at dinner. She hoped they were friendly and would welcome her being there.

*

It was with much trepidation that Mair entered the dining room, to see three girls seated at a large mahogany table with Mrs Turnbull at the head of it. The young maid called Violet, was standing at a long sideboard laden with various meats, a big round of cheese, bread and cakes. She flashed a friendly smile in Mair's direction then, with ladle in hand, began stirring a large tureen of soup.

'There you are, my dear,' Mrs Turnbull said in welcome. 'Come on in. You're just in time. Young Violet here was just about to serve us soup and bread. Nothing like a nice bowl of Cook's homemade soup, that's what I say.'

Mair hesitated.

'We don't bite, honestly. I'm Kitty Slater. You can sit next to me if you like,' the pretty girl, with auburn hair and a sprinkling of freckles on her cheeks, offered. She was dressed in what Mair instantly recognized as a nurse's uniform.

'Well done, Kitty.' Mrs Turnbull praised. 'This is Mair Parsons, and she's come to stay with us for a while.'

Mair slowly made her way to the empty seat next to Kitty. 'Hello, Mair. As I said, I'm Kitty, and across from us are two of the three 'Js' – on the right, there's Jenny and next her, Josie. There is another one called Jane, who's still on duty at the hospital – their names can make you a bit tongue tied sometimes.'

'Welcome!' the two 'Js' said in unison.

'Thank you. There's kind you are,' Mair smiled.

'Where are you from, then, ducky? You've got a funny accent,' one of the Js asked.

'I'm from South Wales. Back home it's the way we all talk,' Mair answered defensively.

Kitty smiled. 'Well, I think it's a nice accent. It's much better than your cockney one, Josie.'

'We can't all have a posh Surrey accent like you, *Lady* Kitty, now can we?' Jennie returned.

Kitty shook her head. 'Mair, as you can see, we don't stand on ceremony here. We all know how it feels to be away from our home and loved ones and thrust among strangers.'

'But, under my roof, I'm proud to say, strangers soon become friends! Isn't that right, girls?' Mrs Turnbull prompted.

All three girls vigorously nodded their agreement.

'Are you one of us?' Kitty asked.

'I don't understand – in what way?'

'In the, are you a nurse, way?'

'Me? N-no, I don't work in London. I'm just here on family business.'

'What family business would that be then?' Kitty asked.

'I bet she's here to seek out a long-lost lover … oh, how romantic,' Josie offered.

'Don't be silly, she's far too young for that. No, I think she's come to London to claim the fortune bequeathed by some old dowager!' Jenny exclaimed.

'N—' Mair was just about to deny both.

'That's enough!' Mrs Turnbull interrupted. 'We'll have no more fanciful speculations. Mair's business is her own. Do you hear? What will she think of us?'

Silenced and admonished, the girls all looked embarrassed.

Mair smiled in the direction of Mrs Turnbull by way of a thank you for her timely intervention.

'Don't look so sheepish, you lot. I'm sure Mair hasn't taken offence. Have you, Mair?' Mrs Turnbull asked.

'No. Of course not,' Mair assured them.

'Mrs Turnbull, may I serve the soup now?' the maid asked, 'Cook will be fearful angry with us if we let it go cold.'

'Yes, Violet, you're right. Serve the soup. It's time to eat.'

Over supper the mood lightened and they all settled into general chit-chat about the weather, the girls' shift-work timetable and how good Cook's soup tasted. Mair agreed. It was delicious. She hadn't realized how hungry she really was.

After a dinner of a platter of cold meats and pickle, Mair returned to her bedroom. She lay on top of the bed. The feather mattress felt so comfortable and so … welcoming. It had been a long day; she had travelled to London, found the Sisters of the Salvation Army and with their help settled in digs and made new friends.

As pleased as she was with her achievements thus far, the guilt she felt for abandoning Catherine, and the way she'd left Frank sleeping like a baby in the Southampton boarding house, kept nagging at her.

There was a part of her that wondered if Frank might come after her, follow her to London. Mair was sure he'd guess where she was headed. She'd said as much during their argument the night before. She hoped he wouldn't. She didn't want to be the one to get him into trouble with his regiment. Mair knew how much he loved being in the army, and *she* was secretly proud of what he had achieved in leaving the valley to better himself. What a pity she couldn't bring herself to tell him, eh?

Mair shook her head ... there was another more selfish reason why she didn't want him to follow her. She needed him to be there for Catherine. Frank had always been a constant in Catherine's life – Catherine loved him as the father she believed him to be. Mair also knew that Frank loved Catherine as a daughter. She trusted him to do the right thing and to always look out for her.

Chapter Eight

IT WAS DUSK. Frank was on the last leg of what had seemed like an endless journey from Southampton to his home in Ponty and as the horse-drawn charabanc travelled up Oxford Street toward Ponty Square, it passed John Jenkins' butcher shop and the family home next door. Frank spotted his mother standing on the doorstep, her familiar and well-worn black and white Welsh shawl draped around her shoulders. As soon as she saw him, she began waving, while at the same time standing on tip-toe – no doubt straining for a glimpse of Mair. Her puzzled look spoke volumes.

Frank stepped off the charabanc and, taking a deep breath, he headed toward his mother – and home. Throughout the long journey, as much as he longed to see his family, he had been dreading this moment. The moment when he'd have to admit that Mair had left him.

The first thing his mother did was open her arms, such loving, welcoming arms, it almost reduced him to tears. 'It's so good to see you, son,' Ethel enthused, her arms holding him that tight he could hardly breathe.

'You too, Mam.' Frank kissed her tear-stained cheek.

'Frank, love, where's Mair? What's happened? Didn't she arrive? Wasn't she on the ship?' Ethel asked, finally releasing her grip.

'Mam … Mair arrived in Southampton as planned, but now she's gone.' He breathed a sigh of relief, at last the truth was out.

'Gone? What do you mean gone? Gone where?'

'It's a long story. Let's go inside,' Frank urged.

Almost immediately Ethel turned and, leading the way down the hall, entered the welcoming kitchen.

Much to Frank's surprised relief, only his mother appeared to be at home. He'd been expecting and dreading a welcoming party.

'Where is everyone?' Frank inquired.

'John and the girls have taken Catherine for a walk up Carn Mountain. Your charabanc was a good half hour late. I feel I've been stood on this doorstep for ages. I didn't want to miss being the first to see you and Mair.'

'Oh, Mam. Whatever am I going to tell Catherine? I promised to bring her mammy back home.'

'I have to admit that, since you left, "seeing her mammy" was all she could talk about.'

'Well, Mam, in Mair's own words, "she and everyone else might have a long wait".'

'I don't understand. Where has Mair got to? Is she ill or what?'

'No, not ill exactly ... confused and misguided? Certainly.'

'*Duw, duw*, whatever next? Come and sit yourself down, son. You look done in. I'll put the kettle on, and you can tell me all about it over a nice cup of tea.'

Later, as they sipped the freshly-brewed tea, Frank poured his heart out to his mother. He told her everything that Mair had said – everything except the fact that they still hadn't slept together. But he knew that his mother was a shrewd woman, and as he and Mair had been living with her for the past few years, albeit in separate bedrooms, it crossed his mind that she might have guessed. Although, he wouldn't know if she had – his mother would never discuss anything as personal as her son's bedroom activities – or lack of them.

'Well, I never. Gone off to London in search of Nellie, you say? The girl must have taken leave of her senses – the result of that bang on the head she had the night of the *Titanic* tragedy, no doubt. What happened that fateful night has left its mark on all of us survivors ... although it would seem some more than others.'

'I think you might be right. She's obviously not thinking straight. Although I have to say, she did look healthier than I'd ever seen her, so beautiful and so ... grown up. Oh, Mam, this morning when I found her gone, I raced to the railway station. I just knew, after what we'd discussed, where she'd be headed. But the train for London had already left. I was torn between following her and coming back home. I couldn't bear to think of Catherine waiting and watching for us to arrive.'

'Now don't you go tormenting yourself. You made the right choice. I'm sure when Mair discovers how futile her trip to London is, she's bound to see sense and head on back to us.'

'I do hope you're right. But in the meantime, what am I going to tell everyone – especially Catherine?'

'Well, if I take my John to one side and tell him the truth about what's happened, I think it best if you just tell Catherine and the girls that the ship has simply been delayed with, say, engine problems, and that Mair is still with Rhi and Gus in America. Under these circumstances, I'm sure God will forgive a lie told to save a child's feelings.'

Chapter Nine

THERE WAS A knock on the door.

'Miss Parsons,' a girl's voice called, then again, louder, 'Miss Parsons!'

Mair awoke in a cold sweat. She'd had another nightmare – night after night the same nightmare: the *Titanic*; her mother's laugh. When would it end? Darkness surrounded her. She felt frightened and confused. Where was she? Someone had called out her name. But who? And what did they want with her?

'Miss Parsons, it's Violet. Sister Agnes asked me to let you know that she's downstairs in the parlour waiting to see you. I've brought you a candle,' the girl informed her.

Violet? Sister Agnes? The names took a second to register with Mair, then it came to her ... she was safe ... Sister Agnes had brought her to Grange House ... Violet was the maid. Mair gave a sigh of relief. 'Thank you, Violet. Please, come on in.'

The door opened. Violet, with candlestick in hand, the candle's amber glow flickering brightly, walked towards her.

'Sister Agnes said, she thought you'd probably dropped off to sleep. Shall I leave you be? Or do you want me to lead the way downstairs?' Violet asked.

Mair slid off the bed. 'N-no, it's all right. I really want to see Sister Agnes. Just wait there, while I wash my face and brush my hair. I'll not be long.'

Mair slipped behind the painted screen hiding the washstand. Minutes later she emerged and, with brush in hand made her way to the dressing table mirror to tidy her hair.

'If you don't mind me saying so, Miss, I think you have such lovely hair, long and shiny and so different from my dull mousy-brown curly mess.'

'Thank you. But, with my hair as straight as pokers, what I wouldn't do for a few natural curls.'

Violet smiled. 'Why is it, we're never happy with what we've got, eh?' Violet didn't wait for an answer, instead she turned and headed out the door. 'If you'd like to follow me, I'll show you to the parlour.'

Mair entered the front parlour, an elegant spacious room decorated in shades of green and gold. Sister Agnes and Mrs Turnbull sat together on the heavy brocade sofa, Mrs Turnbull busy, holding a teapot aloft, pouring tea into fine porcelain teacups.

'Oh, there you are, Mair, dear,' Sister Agnes beamed. 'I trust you are well rested?'

'Yes, thank you, Sister.'

'I hope the room is to your liking and the bed comfortable?' Mrs Turnbull inquired.

'My room is lovely. I've never had a double bed to myself before.'

'Well, you enjoy it. Sister Agnes and I are sharing a pot of tea. Why don't you come and join us?' Mrs Turnbull motioned to the easy chair next to them. 'Please, take a seat.'

'I hope Violet didn't disturb you, child, only you did say there was something you wished to talk to me about … something about you needing my help?' Sister Agnes inquired quizzically.

'Yes. That's right. I'm sorry if I kept you waiting, I fell asleep, I didn't realize the time.'

'Not at all, my dear. Ada and I often meet of an evening for a chat. I only live just around the corner from here. We've been neighbours for years,' Sister Agnes volunteered.

'Here's your tea, child,' Mrs Turnbull said, handing Mair a fine porcelain cup and saucer.

Mair took it and smiled gratefully. As she sipped the tea her thoughts went to Ethel Jenkins back in Ponty – how Ethel would have loved this tea set. For the first time in ages, Mair was overcome by a feeling of homesickness. She struggled to hold back the tears that threatened.

'There's no need to apologize or upset yourself, child. You're among friends now,' Sister Agnes assured her, leaning over to pat Mair's hand. 'Just sit back and enjoy your tea, we'll talk later.'

They sat in comfortable silence, until Sister Agnes turned to Mair. 'Well now, why don't you tell me how I might help you?'

Mair's eyes went from Sister Agnes to Mrs Turnbull and then back again. She felt embarrassed – confiding in Sister Agnes was one thing, but her landlady?

Mrs Turnbull stood up and gave Mair an obliging look. 'If we're all done, I shall take the tea tray back to the kitchen. I promised Cook I'd go through this week's accounts with her. I'll leave you two on your own to have your little chat.'

'Thank you, Ada, I'll see you before I leave for home,' Sister Agnes said as Mrs Turnbull left the room.

Sister Agnes indicated for Mair to join her on the sofa. 'Now child, in your own time....'

'Sister Agnes, before I start, I want to thank you for your help in finding me this accommodation. Meeting you like I did, well, I feel it was a sign.'

'In what way, child?'

'Before arriving in London, I already had it in mind to seek out someone from the Salvation Army. I couldn't believe my luck when the station guard pointed you out on the platform of Waterloo Station.'

'I see. So, if it was your intention to contact the brigade ... may I ask why?'

Mair took a deep breath. 'Sister Agnes, I came to London in search of a woman called Nellie Parsons. She ... she's my mother.'

'Oh my dear child, you mean your mother is lost to you? For how long?'

'For nearly four years. I was just thirteen when she up and left Cardiff with her f—' Mair was about to say fancy-man, but didn't want to shock Sister Agnes, 'with a man friend,' Mair continued. 'I was told by a neighbour that they were heading for London. I'm afraid that's as much as I know.'

'If all this happened when you were thirteen, why have you waited until now to look for her?'

'It's a long story. Let's just say my mother and I have unfinished business.'

'And you think we at the Brigade might help you find her?'

Mair nodded.

'I see. My dear, I don't wish to pry, only, you mention your mother … what about your father?'

'I never knew my real dad. I was seven years old when my mother married Dai Hughes – a kind, hard-working man, a widower with a 10-year-old daughter, Rhiannon. He treated me like his second daughter and gave me the love of a real father. He insisted I attended school and he taught Rhiannon and me good manners. He encouraged us always to hold our heads high.'

'And I can see what a credit you are to him. You conduct yourself admirably. He must be very proud of you.'

Mair gave a heavy sigh. 'I'm afraid not long after my mother left us to be with Harry Stone, Dai was killed in a mining accident.'

'I'm so sorry. However did you and your sister manage without him?'

'We were forced to leave Ponty, our small mining village and went to live in Cardiff with Rhiannon's Aunt Florrie – Florrie Grayson the great music-hall star. Rhiannon has followed in her footsteps and is presently appearing at the Colonial Theatre in New York.'

'The person you were on the way to see in New York when the *Titanic* tragedy struck?'

'Yes, that's right. Sister, every day I ask myself repeatedly, why, when so many passengers aboard the *Titanic* lost their lives, was I saved? Since the tragedy I've been haunted by nightmares.'

'I would think, my dear, that having been involved and survived what must have been such a terrible experience, this is to be expected.'

'Sister, you don't understand. In every nightmare, I see Nellie amid the turmoil on board the *Titanic*. She's always there, standing at the end of a tunnel, laughing and telling me what a disappointment I've been to her. Yet Nellie was never on the *Titanic*!'

Sister Agnes put a comforting arm around her. 'There, there, Mair.'

'If you're to help me find her, then there's something you have to know….'

'Go on, child. I'm here to listen if you want to unburden yourself.'

'The thing is … when Nellie and Harry were living in Cardiff, he put her to work as … a prostitute.'

'A prostitute, are you sure?' Sister Agnes looked disturbed.

'I'm sorry, Sister. I didn't mean to shock you.'

'My dear child, I assure you, whatever you say, you'll not offend my senses. During my work at the refuge, I see many such women, most of whom are destitute and used by their pimps. These men are evil procurers who live off women's earnings – women who give their trust to these men. I'm sorry to rant on so, it just makes me angry.'

'The night Nellie left Ponty, I overheard her tell Dai that she was looking for a better life. Sister, I know Nellie was no angel, but to become – what she has become? I think you could be right. I know she loved and trusted Harry Stone, and he let her down.' Mair couldn't believe how easy and right it felt to defend Nellie.

'So you think, if they are in London, he would have her likewise employed?'

'Yes, I do.'

'Tell me, child, why do you insist on referring to her as Nellie and not Mother?'

'I no longer think of her as my mother. To me, she is just Nellie Parsons. A woman who let me down in a way no mother should – a way so dreadful, I'm too ashamed to tell you. As far as I'm concerned, she gave up the right to be called Mother a long time ago. As I said – she let me down.'

'It sounds to me as if ultimately your mother let herself down, by allowing herself to become a used woman and … a lost soul. Well, I'm up to the challenge of finding her. We at the Brigade are in the business of saving souls.'

'Sister Agnes, I'm afraid, where Nellie Parsons concerned, her soul was far beyond saving a long time ago.'

'If that is the case then our refuge might be a good place to start to look for her. Working girls, as they like to be called, are a sisterhood – where everyone knows everyone else. If Nellie worked the streets of London, then I'm sure one or more of the women at the refuge would have heard of her. Tomorrow evening when I visit the refuge, I shall make some inquiries.'

'Sister Agnes, would it be all right if I came to the refuge with you?'

'Oh dear, I'm afraid it is no place for a young girl like yourself.'

'Not even if I'm accompanied by you and Captain Johnson?'

The Sister pondered for a while. 'I shall put your request to the captain. This coming week we have an extremely busy schedule. However, I'll do my best to arrange for the captain to meet you here at Grange House on Friday evening – on our way back from Waterloo Station. Ultimately, the decision for you to visit the refuge will lie with the captain. On Friday he can let you know what he decides.'

'Thank you, Sister. I shall look forward to seeing you both then.'

The next morning Mair went down to breakfast – she'd had a fairly good night, only once waking up with the sweats … the *Titanic* … her mother…. Mair wondered if there would ever be a time when she would be nightmare-free.

She entered the dining room and was much surprised to find her landlady breakfasting alone.

Ada Turnbull looked up from the table. 'Good morning, my dear. I trust you slept well?'

Mair smiled, and decided it was easier to tell a lie than have to explain her nightly turmoil. 'Yes. Thank you, Mrs Turnbull.'

'Come take a seat,' her landlady beckoned.

'Where is everyone?' Mair asked, as she sat down at the table. 'I hope I haven't held you up. I'm not late am I?'

'No – no, your timing is perfect. I'm alone because the other girls had an early start at the hospital this morning. Cook sent them off with a nice bacon sandwich each. Tell me, child. What, if anything, do you plan to do today?'

'I thought I may go for a walk. Maybe get to know the area.'

'Well, you've certainly a nice morning for it. There's not a cloud in the sky. I can't believe we're almost into June.' Ada Turnbull gave a deep sigh, 'I'm sure that the older I get, the faster the months seem to fly by.'

Mair smiled, 'That's exactly what my friend, Ethel, used to say….'

'You must miss your friends and family.'

'Yes, this is the first time I've ever been on my own. It feels strange not to have them to confide in.'

'Well, if it's any consolation, I'm a good listener – as are Sister Agnes and Captain Johnson.'

'Thank you. You have all been so very kind to me.'

'I know I speak for us all when I say, you're welcome. Now, eat your breakfast before it goes cold.'

After breakfast, Mair returned to her room in much better spirits and decided the time had come to sit at her dressing table and write to Ethel.

Dear Ethel,

You're probably wondering why I didn't come back home with Frank to be re-united with Catherine.

Ethel, I need you to know that my decision to leave her with you and the family was the hardest I've ever had to make. While you may not agree with what I've done, I need you to tell her as often as you can that I really do love her. I would never have left her behind if I hadn't felt safe in the knowledge that she'd be loved and well looked after in your care. That's why, in my heart, I know it's for the best.

Frank has probably told you my reason for coming to London. If surviving the Titanic taught me one thing it was how fragile life is. And made me determined to make something of my life. To achieve this, I need to find Nellie and put old ghosts to rest.

Please believe me when I say it was never my intention to hurt or mislead Frank. I really did love him, and in my own way I still do. It wouldn't have been fair to keep him hanging on – to give him false hope. I just had to walk away – to prove to myself that I was strong enough to put my life in order.

The money enclosed is toward Catherine's daily care ... the love you all show her is priceless. I thank you from the bottom of my heart. I send this with love to you and the family, and hope you won't think too badly of me.

Mair.

Mair decided that her letter to Rhiannon would have to wait. At least until she had news of Nellie and Harry Stone. She couldn't risk her sister's intervention in trying to dissuade her from her task.

Then, placing her straw hat on her head, she reached for her fawn shawl, handbag and gloves, and left the room. Once outside Grange House she took a deep breath. Mrs Turnbull had been right, it was a lovely day.

During the next four days in London, as she walked the surrounding area of Lambeth, she soon realized the massive task ahead of her ... akin to finding a needle in a haystack. She came to the decision that, realistically, her only hope of ever finding Nellie lay with the captain and Sister Agnes.

She remembered how Frank had tried to warn her about how futile her trip to London would be ... she hoped he wouldn't be proved right.

It was Friday evening. Mair sat in the parlour, accompanied by Ada Turnbull, waiting patiently for Captain Johnson and Sister Agnes's arrival. Ada Turnbull had been told of Mair's predicament.

'I do think, as your landlady, Ada should be told,' Sister Agnes had advised, 'at least in part, of your reason for being in London.'

Although not entirely happy, Mair didn't want the Sister to think she didn't trust her judgement in such matters. 'If you think it's for the best then I'll do what you say,' Mair agreed.

'There's no need for you to say anything. I'll simply say that you really wanted her to know, and that you asked me to tell her. I thought to give her a slightly edited version of the facts. Suffice to say that you have come to London in search of your dear mother who has disappeared and that we at the Salvation Army intend to seek the help of the women at the refuge in the hope of finding her.'

Mair smiled and nodded her agreement.

Sister Agnes had been of the mind that, by taking Ada Turnbull into her confidence, she would become a trusted ally. And it worked.

Earlier that day Mrs Turnbull had come to Mair's room.

'Mair, dear, I just wanted you to know how I wish you all the luck in the world in finding your mother. One thing's for sure – being under the protection of Captain Johnson and Sister Agnes, I know you couldn't be in safer hands.'

'Thank you, I'm sure you are right.'

'I believe they're calling to see you en route from Waterloo Station. If you'd like to come to the parlour at around four o'clock, I shall, with you permission of course, sit with you and keep you company.'

'Thank you. I'd like that.'

Captain Johnson, Sister Agnes and Sister Ruth arrived at Grange House around 3.30 on their way to the refuge.

'Sister Agnes has explained to me your quest to find your mother, and your wish to accompany us to the refuge this evening,' the captain said.

'Yes, that's right. Sister Agnes seems to think there's a strong chance that someone at the refuge might have heard of her. I'd like to see for myself.'

'Are you really sure you want to do this? The refuge is quite an intimidating place, filled with sad and destitute women, all fighting to survive. Women who are no longer welcome in society – it seems they offend our sense of decency. However, we at the refuge believe that, with the Lord's help, they can turn their lives around,' Captain Johnson's voice was filled with passion.

'Are you really certain, this is what you want to do, Mair?' the Sister asked.

'Yes, I really want to come with you.'

Captain Johnson put a friendly arm around Mair. 'Very well, but I don't want you raising your hopes too high. Now, come on, let us be on our way.'

'Mair, I don't mean to offend, but here … take this,' Mrs Turnbull said, handing her a large, fawn-coloured, knitted shawl. 'I thought you might like to wear it in place of your lovely coat? 'Ada Turnbull looked somewhat embarrassed.

'Why, thank you, Ada. I think your suggestion a sound and very wise one,' Sister Agnes said. 'The women at the refuge might not be as eager to help, if Mair appears to be too well dressed.' She helped Mair remove her coat and she draped the warm and more practical shawl around her shoulders.

Chapter Ten

THE WOMEN'S REFUGE was situated on Blackfriars Road in the area of Southwark, a good fifteen minute walk from Grange House, up Westminster Bridge Road and across St George's Circus, which meant that it was getting on for 4.30 when they arrived.

The Army shelter was a big, clean-looking building, fronting the street, with two large doors above which a bold notice declared 'The Salvation Army Shelter for Women' and boasted 'Clean comfortable beds and a safe haven'. Mair inspected the list.

1) A mug of hot tea and two slices of bread and dripping ... One Penny
2) Bath and wash house (a change of clothing optional) ... One Penny
3) A bunk for the night, with clean bedding ... Two Pence
4) A bed with clean sheets and a soft pillow ... Four pence

Captain Johnson made for one door, Sister Agnes the other. 'The shelter is divided into two separate wings. A mother and child unit, where Sister Ruth and I are headed, and the women's unit – Sister Agnes's pride and joy. You go with her. I strongly advise you not to leave her side. May God go with you.' And with that he entered the first door closely followed by Sister Ruth, who turned and mouthed a 'Good luck'.

Mair nodded. She was eager to go inside and start asking questions about her mother.

A tall, heavily-built man approached from the opposite side of the road. 'What do we have 'ere, then?' He stood barring their way to the door of the shelter. He turned to Mair, 'What's a pretty thing like you doing with this bloody do-gooder, eh?' The man took a bottle of gin from the inside pocket of his dirty jacket. 'Fancy a little swig, eh?' He made to touch Mair's arm.

Mair immediately pulled away. 'Leave us alone.'

Ignoring her, the man tried to move closer, 'Trust me. You'll not get even a whiff of the hard stuff in there. The people who run it are a lot of bible-punching, non-drinking, hypocrites. They're against what they call "the evil of drink", yet it doesn't stop them shaking their collecting tins in ale houses all round London, eh?' he sniggered.

Mair edged away.

He made a grab for her hand, 'Why don't you come with me? My digs are just around the corner, I've got plenty more of this,' he said, pushing the bottle of gin under her nose. 'Come on, you know you want some!'

Sister Agnes placed herself between them, forcing him to let go of Mair's hand, 'Be off with you, you brute! You ought to be ashamed of yourself, standing in wait all the time, holding up strong liquor as a final temptation for the poor women seeking refuge,' the Sister admonished.

The man gave a dirty laugh, 'Some of these women are desperate for a swig of gin ... some of 'em will do anything for it. Some will even—'

'Well, this time, there's no one for you to tempt,' Sister Agnes interrupted. 'So clear off before I call for assistance.'

'All right, keep your hair on. I'm going.' And with that he headed off down the road.

'I'm sorry about that, my dear,' Sister Agnes said briskly. 'I'm afraid the world is full of such unscrupulous fellows. I hope he didn't offend you, too much.'

'If it had been left to me, I'd have—'

'You're obviously not used to such lurid behaviour, whereas I see it every day.'

Mair checked herself. Had it not been for Sister Agnes's timely interruption, Mair was about to say, 'I'd have given him a real mouthful of abuse,' after all, when she and Rhiannon worked at the Empire Theatre in Cardiff, they had to deal with stage-door Johnnies nearly every night. Instead she felt it wise in this instance to simply nod in agreement.

They finally entered the refuge. The first thing that hit Mair was the noise of chattering women, all appearing to speak at once; a raised voice here, a swear word there, closely followed by admonishment. Then her senses were overcome by the strong smell, reminding her of washday back in the valley, a mixture of green wash soap, carbolic and boiling water.

They entered a large room lined with long trestle tables and wooden settles. The room was full of women of all ages, shapes and sizes, most were shabbily dressed, some scratching for fleas. Mair shuddered.

'There are so many of them,' she said. 'Are they all...?

'All prostitutes? Yes, most of them are. And I'm afraid to say it's only a matter of time before the few who still manage to get a day's work here and there, charring or skivvying for a few pennies a day, succumb to the temptation.'

'How many women are there?' Mair asked.

'We house two hundred and fifty women and children at any one time – it saddens me to say that it's full to capacity every night.' Sister Agnes shook her head sorrowfully. 'This shelter is the only one of its kind in the country. We aim to give them shelter and support until we can hopefully find a family member to take them in.'

Sister Agnes led the way and Mair followed. As they passed each group of ladies Sister Agnes's greeting was warm and everyone seemed friendly towards her. She questioned each one in turn to discover if anyone had heard of Nellie Parsons, but to no avail. They moved from group to group, and Mair was shocked by how young so many of the women were – some looked even younger than she was herself.... Suddenly, Harry Stone's words, echoed in her mind: 'There are men who will pay good money for a young virgin.' Maybe some of these young girls had been auctioned off for sex too, only they hadn't been lucky enough to have a Frank or Rhiannon or Gus or Ethel in their lives to rescue them.

After about half an hour with still no luck, Sister Agnes moved on to a much older crowd of even louder and more unkempt women.

'Good evening, ladies. I trust I find you well and in good spirits?' the Sister asked.

'A bit lacking in spirits, I'd say,' a very large woman called out. 'Could do with a little nip of gin if you're offer'ng.'

This caused the other women to laugh aloud.

Sister Agnes just ignored them. 'Ladies, I'm here to ask your help. We're looking for a woman called Nellie Parsons – I believe she worked the streets, has any of you ever seen or heard of her?'

The women huddled together whispering, then one of them said, 'Go on, Peg, you tell 'em.'

A tall woman, who looked to be in her late thirties with an unkempt mop of red hair, stepped forward. Although her clothes were worn and in need of a good wash, the cut of them spoke of better days.

'Nellie Parsons, yes a few of us know that evil, gin-swigging old bugger. The last time I saw her, she was sleeping rough under the Embankment.'

Mair took a deep intake of breath and felt her pulse race. 'Are you sure it was her?'

'I'm as sure as my name's Peggy Perkins! What's it to you anyways?'

Mair clutched the woman's scrawny wrist. 'When you saw her, was she with a man called Harry Stone?'

'If that's the flash-bugger she used to hang around with, then rumour has it, he upped and left her and buggered off to France with some rich piece,' Peggy told her.

From the back of the room a woman's voice called out, 'Was he your hubby, love? What, did he up and leave you for a bit on the side? Is that why you're here?'

Mair tried to hide her distress.

'Peggy? You say you last saw Nellie at the Embankment – and when exactly was this?' Sister Agnes asked.

Peggy forced her fingers through her matted hair to scratch her head. 'Mmm … six months … maybe a year. Come to think of it I haven't seen – or sniffed – the dirty old cow for ages.' The woman gave a loud cackle, her mouth wide open to reveal a mouthful of black teeth. Then turning to face the others, ''Ave any of you lot seen her lately?' she asked.

The women all shook their heads.

'Thank you, Peggy, at least we know she was definitely here in London. It's a start. If you think of anything else, you know where to find me,' Sister Agnes smiled. Then, turning to face the other women, she said, 'Thank you, ladies. We'll be leaving you now. Enjoy the rest of your evening.'

'Are you all right, Mair?' the Sister asked when they were in the hallway.

Mair nodded, trying to compose herself. It had come as a shock to hear the way the woman called Peggy spoke of Nellie. 'Yes, Sister. What does "sleeping rough" actually mean?'

'It means exactly that. Many of the women you see here are forced to sleep on the streets. There are many areas in and around London, favoured by "down and outs", destitute men and women. Under the Embankment, the one Peggy mentioned, is well known to us and one we often visit, offering the women, for just a few pennies a night, safe shelter at the refuge. But we are under no illusion what they have to do to earn that money.'

In Mair's eagerness to come face to face with Harry and Nellie, she had never considered how destitute Nellie might have become. Seeing and hearing how low these women had sunk, filled her with … not just pity … but compassion. She checked herself and felt the heat of her anger for her mother start to fade. After all this time, was it possible for her to begin to feel sorry for Nellie?

'Do you think Nellie might have slept here at the refuge at some time?'

'It's possible. Mind you, there are some that can't … or won't admit they need help.'

They were just about to leave when Peggy came after them, 'Sister Agnes! I'm not sure if this'll help, but, as Nellie Parsons more than liked a drop of gin … she used to be a regular up at the Crown and Cushion – I'm sure the regular punters there would know a thing or two. Mind you, if I was you, I'd not go alone – they don't like strangers nosing about.'

Sister Agnes turned to Mair. 'I think it might be a good idea to ask Captain Johnson what he thinks, don't you?'

'The Crown and Cushion? I know it well. It's not far from Grange House, and an establishment we visit often. Sister Ruth has been known actually to fill a collection tin in one evening,' the captain boasted. 'Mind you, that's on a Saturday night when the customers are in a generous mood.' He rubbed his chin, as if pondering his options then, taking a fob watch from an inside pocket, he checked the time. 'It's just after seven. It might be a good idea to head over there before I have my supper.'

'What? Visit the Crown and Cushion tonight, you mean?' Mair hadn't expected that.

'Yes, that's right. If, as you say, no one has seen your mother for six months or more, then it's quite possible she may have moved out of London. The sooner inquiries are made, the better, isn't that right Sister?'

'Yes it is, Captain. We know from experience how difficult it can be to trace someone once the trail has gone cold.'

'I hadn't thought of that. Well, I'm ready if you are. How far do we have to go to get there?' Mair asked, adjusting her borrowed shawl around her shoulders.

'We – no, I'm sorry, child. Maybe I didn't make myself clear. I think it best if, at least in the first instance, I visit the Crown and Cushion on my own. I'm well known to the landlord and customers alike and they're used to me inquiring about one or more lost souls. They might not be so forthcoming if a stranger were in their midst.'

'But—'

'Mair, you really have to trust the captain's judgement on this. We shall head back to Grange House. And be assured, if anyone can find out about your mother – it's the captain.'

Captain Johnson brought out a small notebook and pen. 'Right … Nellie Parsons and Harry Stone,' he wrote, 'and the couple probably arrived in London from Cardiff some four years ago, you say?'

Mair nodded.

'That's all I need to know. You leave it with me. Sister Agnes, you two be on your way back to Grange House. Sister Ruth, you can also head off home. Good night, ladies. I'll see you all tomorrow.' And with that he doffed his hat and headed down the road.

Mair and Sister Agnes arrived back at Grange House at around eight o'clock to find Ada Turnbull sitting in the parlour awaiting their return.

'Come in, come in, Agnes, Mair, please, take a seat,' Ada gushed as Violet showed them into the parlour. 'I instructed Cook to have the kettle on the boil and hot crumpets at the ready for your return. Violet, you can let Cook know that they've arrived.'

'Yes, Mrs Turnbull,' Violet said.

Ada waited until the maid had left the room and the door firmly closed behind her, before asking in a voice quietened almost to a whisper, 'Well? How did you get on? Was there any news of your mother?'

With a nod from Mair, by way of giving her permission, Sister Agnes quickly updated Ada on the events of the evening. It hadn't gone unnoticed to Mair how both Mrs Turnbull and Sister Agnes talked of her 'mother' when referring to Nellie. Mair didn't argue the point. It was the truth, after all. A fact Mair could no longer deny.

'Well, that's good news, isn't it? At least you know that your mother was actually in London,' Ada enthused.

Mair nodded. 'I suppose so. My only concern is that, as it is such a long time since anyone has seen her, she might have moved on.'

There was a tap on the door and the maid entered carrying a tray laden with a freshly brewed pot of tea, the bone china tea set and a plate of hot buttered crumpets.'

'Thank you, Violet. If you'd like to serve Mair first—'

'No thank you, Violet. I'm really not in the mood. If it's all right with you, Mrs Turnbull, Sister? I'd rather go straight to my room.'

'Of course it is, child. We don't mind at all, do we Ada?'

'No … in fact, why don't you get Violet to fill you a hot bath, and afterwards I'll get Cook to make you up a nice mug of cocoa and a light supper.'

'I don't want to put anyone to any trouble.'

'It's no trouble, Miss,' Violet insisted. 'I could even put a few lavender crystals in the bath water – and you wouldn't be hesitating if you'd tasted Cook's hot, milky cocoa before, I can tell you.'

'Well, thank you. I'd like that.'

At 8.30 the next morning Mair woke feeling refreshed after an uninterrupted night's sleep – nightmare-free for once. As she entered the dining room, she asked herself if this might have had anything to do with her search for Nellie. Whatever the reason, she felt better for it.

'Good morning, stranger,' 'Kitty jibed. 'We missed you at supper last night, didn't we, Jenny? We both had the night off and were going to ask you to join us in a game of charades.'

'Yes, we did. Mind you, I told Kitty how I saw you leaving with the Sister and Captain Johnson,' Jenny boasted.

'You're not thinking of joining the Sally Army are you?' Kitty asked.

'No, not really, Sister Agnes—'

'Sister Agnes and the captain are simply befriending Mair, that's all,' Ada Turnbull intervened.

'What, helping her with her "family business", is that what you mean? It all sounds mighty suspicious to me.'

'That's as may be, Kitty. But, as I told you before, Mair's business is no concern of yours. I'd have thought you'd both be much better off tending to your own business – you still haven't delivered an up to date hospital rota.'

'I'm sorry, Mrs Turnbull. I know that, as of tomorrow, I'm 8 p.m.–6 a.m., Jenny's got the 4 a.m.–2 p.m. I'll have to check on the others, but I promise to write the rotas when I get back from my 12–8 p.m. shift today.'

'Thank you. Without it it's so hard for Cook to plan her menus.'

With the subject now changed, thanks to Mrs Turnbull's clever intervention, Mair felt sufficiently relaxed to enjoy her breakfast of light and fluffy scrambled eggs, hot buttered toast and a pot of freshly-brewed tea.

Breakfast was almost finished when Violet entered the room. 'Mrs Turnbull, Captain Johnson has arrived and has asked to see both you and Miss Parsons,' she announced.

'Thank you, Violet. If you'd kindly show him into the parlour, Mair and I will join him there shortly. You might also ask him if he'd like a pot of tea and some biscuits.'

Mair immediately stood up. 'Mrs Turnbull, if the captain has called to see us this early in the day … do you think he…?'

'He's what?' Kitty asked.

'Kitty, will you stop looking for intrigue where there is none? Captain Johnson is simply making a social call, nothing more, nothing less. Now, if breakfast is finished I suggest you two get yourselves off to the hospital – it wouldn't do to be late, now would it?'

'No, Mrs Turnbull, we're on our way.'

Mrs Turnbull nodded her approval. 'I'll make sure there is a hot drink and a light supper waiting at the end of your shift.'

'Thanks, you're a landlady in a million,' Kitty gushed.

'Goodbye, Mair. We'll catch up with you tomorrow.' Jenny said, flashing Mair a friendly smile.

'And good luck with your "family business",' Kitty added, obviously unable to resist having a last dig.

'Thank you,' Mair answered, but she wondered how long she could keep the truth from them.

When both girls had left the room, Mrs Turnbull turned to Mair.

'If you're ready we can now go and meet the captain.' But when she looked at Mair's face, she asked, 'Are you all right, my dear?'

'Yes – no, oh Mrs Turnbull, I'm really not sure. I suddenly have this awful feeling of foreboding.'

'Now don't you go thinking the worst. Let us just wait to hear what Captain Johnson has to say.'

Minutes later they entered the parlour to find, not just Captain Johnson, but Sister Agnes also sitting in wait.

Mair looked from one to the other – their solemn faces sent a feeling of dread rushing through her. 'Captain … Sister? What are you both doing here so early?'

'Mair, dear, I have only just arrived.' Sister Agnes's voice was more than a little shaky. 'The captain kindly sent a messenger to my home … I came as soon as I heard.'

'Heard what? Captain Johnson, what's happened?' Mair demanded.

'Please, take a seat, child. I'm afraid the news is not good.'

Mair's legs felt like jelly, afraid to move a muscle in case she fell over. 'If it's all the same to you, I'll stand. Why the solemn faces? Surely, the news can't be that bad? Nellie's up and left London, is that it?'

Sister Agnes stood up and walked across to Mair. Gently she put a friendly arm around her, holding her, supporting her. 'No it's not that, child,' she softly said.

'Then what is it? Captain Johnson, please tell me!' Mair urged.

Captain Johnson took a deep breath. 'Last night, as planned, I went to the Crown and Cushion public house. Once there I made inquiries regarding Nellie Parsons, first with the landlord and then with the customers. Much to my surprise, one of the customers was none other than the man called Harry Stone—'

'Harry Stone was actually there?' Mair interrupted, her voice sounding incredulous.

The captain nodded his head. 'Yes, and what an aggressive, angry man he turned out to be. He demanded to know what business I had with Nellie Parsons. I explained that I was making inquiries on behalf of her daughter, a fact he seemed to find amusing. That was when he told me—'

'Told you what?' Mair urged.

'I'm sorry, child … but he told me that your poor mother is … dead.'

'Dead? That can't be true … she is too young to … Harry Stone is lying! A spiteful lie! It's so typical of him.'

'I'm afraid it's the truth. It was backed up by a couple of female customers who apparently knew her … fellow ladies of the night.'

Mair reached for the back of the nearest chair to steady herself. Sister Agnes's arm tightened around her. 'Come sit down, child.'

This time Mair did as she was asked. She shook her head in disbelief. 'When? How?'

'It happened over a year ago, a dreadful accident by all accounts. It appears that she was run down by a horse and carriage outside the New Gaiety Theatre on the Strand in central London. Apparently eyewitnesses said she didn't stand a chance.'

Mair gave a deep sob, and dropping her head in her hands, gave way to tears.

Chapter Eleven

I^T WAS SATURDAY morning in Ponty. Ethel had put Catherine down for her morning nap and, taking advantage of the pleasant late May morning, decided to wash the red-cardinal-painted front doorstep. She had just finished when Jones-the-post approached and handed her two letters.

'One is for Frank and the other is for you,' he said, adding, 'Frank's has an army stamp and looks to be official … while yours, I'm sure you'll be pleased to hear, is from Mair. I recognize her writing, see,' he boasted.

'Thank you, Eric,' Ethel said, smiling to herself as she watched him ride away, sure in her mind that many folk, outside the valley, would think it nosy for the postman to so closely examine private letters. But in the valley it was regarded as just taking a friendly interest. There was no malice attached to it – so no one ever took offence.

For a while Ethel stared at both letters, faced with a dilemma. She decided to hide the one from Mair and quickly placed it in her apron pocket. The fact that Mair had chosen to write to her and not to Frank, she knew would hurt his feelings. Much better to keep the letter to herself – at least until she knew what Mair had to say.

Ethel entered the kitchen to find Frank busy polishing his army boots.

She handed him his letter, 'Jones-the-post just delivered this. It looks to be important.'

'Thanks. I can see by the stamp that it's from my regiment.' Setting his boots aside, he opened the letter and proceeded to read it.

'What does it say, son?' Ethel asked.

'I'm afraid it's the orders I've been expecting. My CO has requested my immediate return to Maendy Barracks.'

'Well, as you say, lad, we all knew it was coming. I think your commanding officer, in giving you such a long period of compassionate leave, has been so understanding – you be sure and thank him from me.'

'I will, Mam. It's just, I feel awful leaving you to cope with Catherine on your own.' He shook his head, 'It's going to be such a wrench to leave her. You know how upset she was when Mair didn't come home…. I couldn't bear for her to think that I've abandoned her too.'

'Frank, now you listen to me. You're a soldier. And when you signed up, you made a commitment. It's your job and we are all so very proud of you. I'll explain it to Catherine. Trust me, she'll be fine.'

'But it doesn't seem fair on you. You have enough to do, without having to run around after Catherine. I've seen what a handful she can be.'

'Now, don't you give it another thought. Catherine's home is here with us. She's part of the family, and we all love her. I know John will agree with me when I tell you to get yourself back to your unit. We will all still be here when you next come home on leave.'

'Thank you, Mam. I don't know what we'd do without you. I hope Mair appreciates what you and the family do for the love of Catherine, as much as I do.'

They heard Catherine stir upstairs. 'Daddy … *Mamgu* Ethel,' she called out.

Ethel started to rise from her easy chair in front of the hearth.

'You stay there, Mam. I'll go. In fact, I think I might take her for a walk and treat her to a penny ice cream at Luigi's.'

'You do that. You go and enjoy some time with her while you can. I'll put my feet up for a spell.'

Frank entered his bedroom and saw Catherine standing in her wooden-framed cot at the bottom of his bed. His eyes were drawn to his mother's wedding photograph. Mair stood off-centre, her eyes shining with happiness. The photograph was strategically placed on the wall opposite the Catherine's cot, looking down on the child as she slept. A constant reminder of what her mother looked like. 'Daddy, I come out,' she beamed at him, with both arms reaching for him.

'Yes, my lovely. I'm going to lift you out right now.'

As Frank walked over to the cot his eyes fixed on the beautiful child – he could see her mother in her; her light-brown hair, gleaming with health and her blue eyes so full of life. Catherine was his little girl. He loved her so much and couldn't bear to think of the day in the future when she would find out that he was not her real father. When Frank gave his name to Catherine, it seemed the most natural thing to do. His plan had been to marry Mair, the love of his life, and for the three of them to live as a family. He hadn't expected to have to wait until Mair was twenty-one and now, with Mair having gone off to London…?

'Daddy,' a restless Catherine urged, now jumping up and down in her cot.

'Yes, there, there, your daddy's got you.' Frank swept her up in his arms. 'Now, for being such a good little girl, Daddy's going to take you for an ice cream, what do you say to that?'

Catherine caught around his neck and crowed with delight.

With Frank and Catherine safely out of the door and heading down the street, Ethel reached into her apron pocket for Mair's letter. She had hoped that the letter might contain news of Mair's homecoming, but on reading it, she soon realized nothing could have been further from the truth – Mair's mind seemed fixed on staying in London to find her mother.

Ethel had always thought of Mair as a troubled child. She remembered the day Mair and her mother, Nellie, first arrived at Dai Hughes's front door. Ethel, who lived next door, had been cleaning her doorstep, with Frank looking on. They had both witnessed their arrival. Nellie had come in answer to Dai's advert in Joe Luigi's shop window for a suitable person to look after his daughter, Rhiannon, while he was at work down the pit.

Ethel had always had a soft spot for both Dai and Rhiannon. Dai had lost his young wife to scarlet fever, leaving him with Rhiannon, Dai's pride and joy.

The day Dai took Nellie and Mair in, he must have known how wide-open he made himself to valley gossip. Nellie was well known in the valley and had, what some would call, a dubious reputation – especially where men were concerned. A reputation not helped by the fact that she'd given birth to Mair out of wedlock, when she was barely sixteen. It came as a great shock to friends and neighbours alike when Dai proposed marriage, thus making 'an honest women' of her, although everyone in the valley felt the marriage was doomed to failure. Sadly they were proved right when Nellie ran off with a travelling salesman called Harry Stone. At the time, Ethel could only imagine how 12-year-old Mair must have felt. For although genuine, Dai and Rhiannon's love must have been poor comfort for a mother's abandonment ... a fact which only made what Mair was now doing, even more unbelievable.

Ethel stared at Mair's letter. What was Mair thinking of? Catherine might be only a small child, but she still missed her mother. Ethel struggled to understand Mair's reasoning. Her mention of Frank in the letter cut Ethel to the quick. She knew how much he loved the girl – he would be heartbroken if he knew how final Mair thought their parting to be. As Ethel held the generous sum of money 'towards Catherine's keep', a sum she would hold in safety for the child's needs, she decided it best to keep the contents of the letter, and the address where Mair was now living, to herself. At least for the time being.

Chapter Twelve

MAIR STRUGGLED TO get through the next few days. Her mother, Nellie Parsons, was dead. After all the anger that had burned inside her for years, it surprised Mair how deeply sad this news made her feel. The irony of the situation was not lost on her – once again her mother had escaped a final confrontation. There would be no answers now. She had wasted so much time and energy hating her mother, blaming her for letting her down. When in truth all Nellie Parsons had done was to fall for the wrong man, a man who she ultimately loved and depended on. So much so that, in order to be with him, she had turned her back on her own daughter – and away from her responsibility.

Mair knew that for the sake of her own sanity, she needed to draw a line under that particular chapter of her life, but there was still the matter of unfinished business.

She often wondered if, in choosing to come to London, she had done exactly the same thing to Catherine. How would her actions affect her? Would it be a case of history repeating itself? All the time there lurked in Mair's mind the thought that Catherine would be better off without her. She wondered what Rhiannon would think, when she found out. Mair gave a heavy sigh … she could delay it no longer; the time had come to write to her sister. She opened the dressing table drawer to retrieve the list that been attached to the gift from Gus and Rhi, with the dates and venues for Rhi's American tour. As she checked the list she saw that as of 1 June 1912 Rhiannon would be appearing at the New Theatre, Boston and on 20 June at the Palace Theatre, back in New York. Mair didn't know how long her letter would take to get to America, so she decided to send it to the Palace Theatre in New York.

Dear Rhi,

I don't know if Frank, or Ethel, have already been in touch and told you but either way, I know it will come as a shock to you to find out that, having travelled from New York and docked safely at Southampton – and yes, Frank was there to meet me – I made the decision not to return with him to Ponty. I decided to travel on my own to London in search of Nellie and Harry.

I didn't want to write to you earlier, because I knew you'd do your utmost to stop me – as did Frank – but my decision was made. Although, I'm afraid, my search turned into something of a wild goose chase – I can almost hear you say "I could have told you that". What none of us knew is that Nellie is dead! A fact that was discovered by my newly-made friends, Captain Johnson and Sister Agnes of the Salvation Army.

Apparently, Nellie was abandoned by Harry and worked as a prostitute on the streets of London but she fell on hard times. Sometime last year she was tragically run over by a horse and carriage outside the New Gaiety Theatre. She died instantly. As for Harry Stone – he's still somewhere in London.

Rhi, I'm sorry. Sorry for all the hurtful things I said before I left. I didn't mean them. It was just my way of striking out at you. I guess you knew that – you and Gus's generous gift proved your forgiveness. Thank you both.

You'll be pleased to hear that Grange House, where I am staying, is a respectable establishment run by Mrs Ada Turnbull, and only takes in young ladies. I think I shall stay on in London for a little while longer. I've made such good friends and while I miss Catherine so very much, I know Frank and Ethel will look after her. I've already sent Ethel some money toward Catherine's keep.

Rhi, I've been so lucky having you as a sister. Please give my regards to Gus. Like you, he'll always have a special place in my heart.

Please write to me, I'd so love to hear your news.

Your loving sister,

Mair

When the news of Mair's mother's death reached Grange House, Ada Turnbull took it upon herself, having first checked with Sister Agnes, to inform the rest of the household. And in the days that followed everyone in turn – Cook, Violet, the three Js and Kitty – offered Mair their condolences. Kitty even apologized to her....

'I'm so sorry, Mair, for being such a nosy cow, and for making all those snide remarks regarding your "family business". To have lost your mother in such a way must be really terrible. I'd like to make it up to you. I do hope we can still be friends.'

Mair nodded her head. 'It wasn't entirely your fault. You weren't to know. I just didn't want everyone knowing my business. That's all. And yes, I'd like it if we could become friends.'

'Good, I'm so glad. Now, if there's anything I can do for you, you just ask,' Kitty said.

With her letter to Rhiannon well on its way to America, Mair settled down to write another, this one addressed to Ethel Jenkins in Ponty.

Dear Ethel,

I do hope this letter finds you all well. I must say, I didn't expect to be writing to you so soon after my first letter, only, I thought you and the family would like to hear the shocking news I recently received of my mother's death.

It happened last year. I'm afraid she died in sad circumstances – destitute and alone on the streets of London. A fact I would never have found out, had I not been helped by Brigade Captain Johnson of the Salvation Army. He made inquiries on my behalf and found Harry Stone, who told him of Nellie's sad end. I believe they were not together when she died.

I feel numb and don't really know what my next move should be. I have allowed what happened to me all those years ago to cloud my life but I realize the time has come to let it go. I know you'll be pleased to hear that I'm working towards that end. Frank was right when he said London is a big place. I miss you all so very much, especially my dearest Catherine. Please give her a big hug and kiss from me.

Love,
Mair

'What will you do now, child?' Sister Agnes asked the next night, when she called at Grange House.

'I'm not sure, Sister. I suppose the sensible thing to do would be for me to go back home to Wales.' Mair wanted to tell Sister Agnes about Frank and Catherine, but she felt too ashamed. How could she ever justify the way she had left them both?

'If I were you, I'd take a little longer to consider my options. You've had a terrible shock, and it's bound to take a while for you to come to terms with it.'

Mair nodded her agreement. Sister Agnes always seemed to have Mair's best interests at heart. She wondered if the Sister would feel the same way if she knew the truth about Frank and Catherine.

Over the next few days Mair did as the Sister advised and considered her options. It was a black time for her but now she had come to a decision.

The next morning, she breakfasted in her room – a luxury afforded her by Mrs Turnbull, 'You have to rest up, after having had such a shock, it's the least I can do,' she'd insisted. Mair, keeping her bedroom door slightly ajar, patiently waited to catch Kitty on her way down to breakfast.

'Kitty, Kitty,' Mair called in a whisper.

'Mair, what is it? Are you all right?' Kitty asked, poking her head around Mair's bedroom door. Off duty and out of uniform, Mair thought how pretty she looked in her aqua-blue day dress and with her auburn hair pinned back in a chignon.

'Kitty, please come in and close the door behind you.' Mair urgently beckoned with both arms. 'I need to ask a favour.'

'What sort of a favour? I meant what I said … if I can help in any way—'

'Well … I need to get to St Thomas's hospital. I've been thinking of making inquiries to join the Red Cross. I do believe they are stationed there,' Mair confided.

'Yes, they are. I see them most days … and what a great idea. Look, I'm working 8 p.m.–4 a.m. for the next four nights, so it would be no trouble to take you there. You just have to tell me when.'

'Thank you … what about tonight?' Mair asked.

'Tonight is fine with me. But are you sure you're up to it?'

'If I don't do something soon, to take my mind off what's happened, I'll go mad.' Mair hoped Kitty wouldn't question her motives for, while she had indeed been intending to do some voluntary work, spurred on by Sister Agnes, her more urgent reason for wanting the direction to St Thomas's was that she'd overheard the captain mention how the hospital was situated close to the Crown and Cushion public house.

'I can understand that. So, tonight it is then. We'll leave straight after tea.'

'Kitty, I'd prefer it if this could be our little secret. I don't want Sister Agnes or Mrs Turnbull fussing over me. I know they mean well but—'

'Say no more. It'll be our secret.' Kitty seemed pleased to be party to a bit of secrecy.

Mair had given this course of action a lot of thought. While her mother's death had, in a way, denied the reunion Mair had wanted, she still had a score to settle with Harry Stone. She was determined to visit the Crown and Cushion and confront him. It was the only way she could finally lay her ghosts to rest. This was something she had to do for herself – no hiding behind the captain, the Sister, Mrs Turnbull or anyone else, for that matter. This quest was hers and hers alone.

It was just after 7.30 when Mair, dressed in a white blouse, a navy skirt and jacket and a small brimmed navy felt hat, pulled on her lace-up leather boots and quietly left her room. She crept down the stairs and out the front door.

She and Kitty had arranged to meet a few yards down the road. Mair didn't want anyone, other than Kitty, to know of her intention to leave the house that night. As was expected in early summer it was a mild evening. And, with the local factory closed for the night, its chimney no longer polluting the air, there was little or no smog. She looked up to the sky where bright twinkling stars would soon be visible and hoped the same stars were shining down on Catherine and the family in Ponty.

York Road was unusually free of traffic. Only one hansom cab travelled in the opposite direction, its horse's hoofs eerily echoing in the darkness as it clip-clopped on the cobbled road.

'I'm over here, Mair,' Kitty whispered.

'Thank goodness you're here. This is the first time I've been out at night since my arrival at Grange House.'

'Come on, we'd better get a move on,' Kitty urged. 'It's a good fifteen minute walk to the hospital. I don't want to be late for work.'

As they approached the entrance to St Thomas's hospital, Mair's eyes were drawn across the way to Westminster Bridge Road and the large old building Captain Johnson had visited a few nights before. She read the huge black-lettered sign stretching across the front of the building – Crown and Cushion. Mair tried to hide her excitement.

'I must say, this is the happiest I've seen you look in days. Maybe, finding something new to do to take your mind off, well, you know what, *was* a good idea after all.'

While part of her felt guilty for keeping the real reason of her trip a secret, especially from Sister Agnes, Mair knew that, if she were to tell anyone of her plan to confront Harry Stone, they would try their hardest to stop her. Her heart was racing.

'Thank you, Kitty, I appreciate your help.'

'Right then,' Kitty announced, 'This is the hospital's main reception area. Will you be all right from here on in? I'm afraid I need to report to Matron before heading off to work on the ward.'

'Yes, you go. I'll head over to the information desk and make some inquiries about the Red Cross.'

'And after you've done that, will you be able to find your way back to Grange House?' Kitty asked.

'Yes, of course. It's not far, so I'm sure I'll be fine,' Mair assured her.

'Well, just don't leave it too late to head back. Mrs Turnbull will have my guts for garters if anything untoward were to happen to you.'

'Now what could possibly happen to me? As I said, I'll make some inquiries then be on my way, so don't worry.'

'All right, if you say so. Good luck. I'll catch up with you at breakfast tomorrow.' And Kitty turned and left.

First things first – the Red Cross. Mair walked over to the information desk situated at the right of the reception area.

It was nearing eight o'clock when Mair, taking a deep breath, entered the Crown and Cushion. The tavern was much busier than she had expected. It smelled of cigarette smoke and spilt beer. Slowly she began to push her way through the crowd of rowdy drinkers, mainly men, though a few women with sad eyes were among them.

'Well, now what have we here, then?' a man's loud voice called out.

'The young filly is here looking for me, isn't that right, my dear?' another man jibed.

'Get away with you. This one's far too young for the likes of you … she's here looking for me, go on, tell 'em, my lovely,' a younger man urged, as he made to touch her arm.

Mair pulled away. 'Leave me be!' she demanded.

'You can all leave her be!' someone bellowed from the back of the room. 'I know that girl. Her name is Mair Parsons, She's Nellie's daughter. She's here looking for me, aren't you?' The man's voice came closer, and sent a shudder through Mair.

Mair looked across to see Harry Stone staring directly at her. He hadn't changed much – a little older, with a noticeable beer-belly – but he still dressed like Jack-the-lad: dark serge trousers and waistcoat, a grey cotton twill shirt and black, well worn, bowler hat. Her whole body began to tremble. She had waited so long for this moment … now what?

'I must say, Mair, you've turned into a damned good-looking young woman. With more than a striking resemblance to your mother – when she was in her prime, that is. It's as if I'm seeing her ghost.'

'Nellie's daughter or not, you'd better tell her that we don't take kindly to strangers poking their noses where they're not wanted,' a woman's voice called.

As the crowd moved to surround her, Mair struggled to breathe … what had she walked into?

Suddenly Harry Stone made a grab for her wrist. Mair attempted to pull away but his grip was too tight. He began leading her out of the tavern.

'Let go of me! Where are you taking me?' Mair demanded.

'Away from these nosy buggers, somewhere where we can be alone.'

'Go on, Harry, you lucky bugger, you. Go on, give her a poke for me while you're at it,' a drunken lout shouted after him.

'Who are you trying to kid, Jack? Why, you haven't got a good poke in you – you're just a drunk with a limp dick,' a woman's voice chided, causing the rest of the crowd to erupt into raucous laughter.

Ignoring his drinking cronies, Harry Stone made for the door and led Mair down a dark alleyway situated alongside the pub. Mair continued to struggle, in an effort to set herself free.

'Let me go, you brute,' she protested, trying her hardest to kick out at him. She felt her right boot connect with his shin.

'I can see who you follow. Your mother was as wild and no doubt as pig-headed as you. If she hadn't got it in her daft mind to stop working and go back to Wales, I'd still be earning a few bob from her.'

Mair stopped struggling. 'What? She actually said she wanted to return home?'

'Yeah, the ungrateful cow said she hated everything about London … the fog … the filth … the punters. Mind you, by then she'd found more than a taste for the gin bottle,' Harry sniggered.

'And who could blame her? Having to do what you made her do, would send anyone to drink. I'll never forget what you made me do—'

'Is that why you've come here? Are you still holding some sort of grudge for something that happened years ago?' Harry challenged.

'What did you expect? I was still only thirteen when you auctioned me off to the highest bidder for sex. You ruined my childhood.' Mair had the urge to scream and to hit out at him, but, much to her surprise she managed to control her emotions. She needed to stay calm, *needed* to have her say.

Harry shrugged his shoulders. 'It was simply a matter of supply and demand. And you were *almost* fourteen … old enough in my eyes. My mate, Jake Brewer – he was the man who took you – he happened to be looking for a commodity … I was selling one. It was business – nothing more nothing less.'

While his matter-of-fact tone of voice made her blood boil, she made a mental note of her attacker's name.

'So that's all I was, a commodity? Have you no conscience? Is that how you thought of Nellie, was she "just a commodity"?'

'You don't know anything about me and Nellie. We used to be good together. I looked after her, I did. I gave her a roof over her head, nice clothes to wear … that was before the ungrateful bitch thought she could just up and stop working the streets. Well, I showed her.'

'What did you do to her?' Mair demanded.

'I threw her out. That's what I did. I thought it would teach her a lesson, show her what side her bread was buttered.'

'What happened to change your mind?'

'Well, I met this other woman, see. She was moving to Paris, France, no less. She wanted me to go with her. Well, I'd have been a fool not to, eh?'

'So you left N— my mother to fend for herself?'

'Serves the silly bitch right. She shouldn't have upset me with all her talk of going back to Cardiff – there was no way I could go back there, too many people chasing me for money.' He gave a loud laugh.

'If you'd let her go back home then, there's every possibility she might still be alive. She loved you … how could you?'

'Oh, so you're blaming me for her death now, are you?'

'Well, if the cap fits!' Mair spat.

'I think it's time you heard a few home truths, my girl. Oh, yes, you may be right, in the beginning Nellie probably did love me but come the end, she loved the gin bottle more. Do you really believe that, had she gone back home to Wales, everything would have been different … that she would have miraculously changed into the fairy-tale mother you obviously wanted her to be? It would never have happened. The truth is, Nellie Parson's died as she lived … in the gutter!'

'I hate you, you bastard, you! Harry Stone you truly are a wicked, wicked man!' Mair hit out at him, her arms raised and, with both fists clenched, she pounded his chest.

Harry Stone threw his arms around her, pulling her close, his wet mouth seeking hers. Mair struggled to pull away but, once again, his grip on her was too tight. 'I do love a girl with a temper … it reminds me of my Nellie. How does it go? "Like mother like daughter?" Well there's only one way to find out.' Harry pushed her with such force against a brick wall that her hat fell to the ground and she banged her head … it sent a shooting pain from the back of her head to her temples. She felt his knee pressed against her groin, and his hand fumble her undergarments, his open mouth slobbering, sucking at her neck.

It all came rushing back to her. The horror of it. The last time she'd felt this vulnerable and afraid. That time when the man, the one she now knew was called Jake Brewer, paid Harry one hundred guineas for the right to rape her. She vowed then to always carry a knife at her side to stop it ever happening to her again ... but since she'd felt so safe with Frank, she no longer kept it.

As Harry continued groping her, trying to force her legs apart, she swore she would die rather than give in. 'Stop it! You bastard, stop it!' she screamed. She bit and raked her nails across his face and smelled the blood, his or hers, she didn't know. Pain still pounded in her head.

'You heard the lady. Get off her,' a strange accented voice ordered.

The next thing she knew, Harry Stone was being torn from her, so violently that he lost his balance and fell to the ground.

'I'm up for a fight, if you are,' Mair's rescuer goaded Harry. 'Only I warn you now, I've won many a prize in the boxing ring back home in the Highlands of Scotland.'

Harry Stone scrambled around in the dirt searching for his bowler hat, looking so frightened. As Mair watched him grovel on the ground, she finally saw him for the pathetic coward he truly was. Brave when it came to abusing women but against another man...?

'As far as I'm concerned you can have her. She's not worth fighting for. Only be warned; she fights like an alley cat,' Harry scoffed, wiping a hand across his blooded face.

Mair watched as Harry Stone turned tail and ran down the alleyway and into the darkness. As far as she was concerned, she never wanted to see or hear of him or, for that matter, Jake Brewer, ever again.

The fact that her mother had wanted to return home to Wales filled Mair with a mixture of sadness and hope ... hope that towards the end, after such a pitiful life, her mother was finally at peace. With this in mind, Mair vowed, in the future, not to think too badly of her mother. With her mother dead and Harry Stone, at long last, out of her life forever, she could now make a fresh start and look to the future.

'Let me get this for you,' the man said, bending down to retrieve her hat from the ground. As he handed it to her, he gently took her arm and led her to stand beneath the street gas-lamp situated opposite the alleyway.

'Are you all right, Miss...?' he asked.

'Parsons ... Mair Parsons. And yes, I'm fine now thanks to you.'

'My name's Andrew Baxter ... Doctor Andrew Baxter,' the handsome, dark haired, young man held out his hand. His eyed fixed on her. He looked to be a good few years older than her.

'Pleased to meet you,' she said, shaking his hand. 'And thank you for coming to my rescue.'

'You're more than welcome. Tell me, who was that awful man?'

'His name is Harry Stone. He was a "friend" of my mother's. It's a long story, but he's no longer anything to do with me.'

'I'm glad to hear it.'

'I really can't thank you enough. I dread to think what might have happened if—' Mair shuddered. It didn't bear thinking of.

'I'm just glad I happened along when I did. As a duty doctor at St Thomas's hospital, I was on my way to work when I heard the skirmish coming from the alleyway. As soon as I saw a man attacking a young woman – a young woman who, I have to say, seemed to be doing a splendid job in fighting him off, I felt I had to intervene.'

'And thank goodness you did.' Mair said.

'As you can probably tell from my accent, I hail from Scotland. And if I'm not mistaken, you are from Wales.'

'Yes, that's correct. I come from a small mining village in South Wales.' Mair offered.

'And what brought you to London?'

'I had family business to attend to,' she said, continuing with her well-practised answer.

'Business connected with the dreadful man who attacked you?'

'Yes. I'm afraid so. As I said, it's a long story and ...' Mair hesitated.

'And anyway, it's none of my business?' Andrew Baxter interjected.

'No, I didn't mean—' Mair began to shake her head, but soon stopped when a shooting pain to her temple caused her to wince. She raised her hand touch the back of her head to see if it was bleeding.

'Let me have a look,' her rescuer said, gently taking her head in his hands and tilting it to the side. 'It doesn't look too bad. No blood, although there is a nasty lump there. You'll live,' he joked.

She forced a smile, feeling dizzy. She needed to lie down.

He seemed to read her mind. 'Where are you staying in London?'

'I'm staying at Grange House on York Road. I really should be heading back. I wouldn't want to cause my landlady to worry about me.'

'I understand. But I refuse to let you risk making the journey alone. Not after such a bump to the head. Look, there's a hansom cab. Let me hail it. I'll take you straight to your door … my treat.' He didn't wait for an answer. She watched him raise his hand, beckoning the horse-drawn hansom. He handed her inside and within a few minutes they were outside Grange House.

'Dr Baxter, how can I ever thank you.'

'Well, I would very much like to see you again.'

Mair felt her colour rise, it was obvious to her that he liked her. 'I - I …' she didn't know what to say.

'Look, as luck would have it, I have tomorrow afternoon off. What say I call for you here? There are so many places of interest I'd like to show you – one being the Florence Nightingale Museum, annexed to St Thomas's Hospital. Although tomorrow I'd like to take you on a little excursion north of the river Thames, and afterward maybe you would let me take you out for high tea.'

The thought of being taken out for the afternoon by such an attractive gentleman filled her with excitement. 'Thank you. I'd like that. Only, I will have to present you to my landlady – Mrs Turnbull always insists on checking gentlemen callers.'

'And I say, quite right too. I shall look forward to meeting her.' He gently shook her gloved hand. 'Until tomorrow, two o'clock.' Then raising his head, he gave a nod to the horseman, sitting atop the driving seat, instructing him to move off.

Chapter Thirteen

IT WAS CLOSE to nine o'clock when the front door opened to reveal a welcoming committee for Mair, made up of Mrs Turnbull and Sister Agnes.

'Mair, my dear, thank goodness you are safe and well,' the Sister said in a rush of concern.

'I must say, it's not often one of my girls arrives back with a gentleman in a hansom cab. I trust you are going to explain yourself, young lady,' Mrs Turnbull curtly demanded.

Mair, realizing there was no way she could wriggle out of giving an account of where she'd been and what she'd been doing, decided it best to tell these two caring women the truth.

'Mrs Turnbull, Sister Agnes, if we might go inside, I will explain everything.'

Without another word, Ada Turnbull led the way into the parlour and, once she and the sister were settled on the sofa, Mair sat in the armchair opposite them. After taking a deep breath, she began to relay the events of the evening. She left nothing out – not even her cunning subterfuge in enlisting Kitty's help to show her the way to St Thomas's and ultimately the Crown and Cushion.

When she had finished, the two women just stared at her in shocked silence.

Mair felt the need to clarify her actions. 'You have to know, that it was never my intention to deceive any of you. I really have been thinking of becoming a Red Cross volunteer, but I also had to find a way to confront Harry Stone. The other evening Captain Johnson mentioned how he'd found him at the Crown and Cushion ... I knew if I told either of you of my plan – you'd have both tried to stop me.'

'And knowing the outcome and what that dreadful man tried to do to you, we'd have been right to do so,' Mrs Turnbull pointed out.

'When I think of you entering that place on your own, my blood runs cold. The fact that everyone stood by and watched him drag you from the premises and down an alleyway ... well, what can I say?' Sister Agnes shook her head in disbelief.

'I say, thank goodness for your rescuer. And if I ever get the chance to meet Dr Baxter, I shall be only too pleased to thank him in person,' Mrs Turnbull said.

'As a matter of fact, he's calling here tomorrow. He asked to take me out for afternoon tea,' Mair blurted out.

Mair couldn't help but notice the disapproving look on her land-lady's face. 'I see, and you have agreed?' her landlady inquired.

'On the understanding that he comes to Grange House to present himself to you first – and only then if he meets with your approval,' Mair quickly assured her.

'And at what time is he intending to call for you, my dear,' the sister asked.

'He said he'd call for me, at two o'clock.'

'In that case, I shall look forward to meeting this doctor. He certainly does sound like an admirable young man ... but one can never be too careful. What do you think, Agnes?' Mrs Turnbull looked to the Sister.

'You're quite right, Ada. I'm just sorry that, with my duties at Waterloo Station, I can't be here to support you in your decision. However, you know how I trust your judgement in these matters.'

'Mair, you've had a long and disturbing day. Get yourself off to bed. I had Cook make you up a sandwich and some milk. It's on the table in the dining room. Take it up with you when you go,' Mrs Turnbull instructed.

Mair spent a restless night, tossing and turning, reliving repeatedly her skirmish with Harry Stone and the coincidence of the way Dr Andrew Baxter just happened to be passing. All of this intertwined with the excitement of seeing the doctor again. The thought of actually being taken out by him made her heart flutter. There could be no denying her attraction to him, and she wondered whether he felt the same.

That night Mair had difficulty sleeping and after tossing and turning for what seemed like hours, she decided to get herself out of bed and sort out what she would wear for her planned outing with Dr Andrew Baxter. She only had two smart outfits, both bought for her by Rhiannon in New York; all the lovely clothes that John Jenkins had treated her to before she left Wales had sunk with the *Titanic*. She had thought to replace them out of the funds Rhi had given her, but it didn't feel quite right to spend it on new outfits. She could put it to better use – especially when there was Catherine to think of.

At around 4.30 there was a light tap on the door. 'Mair, are you in there?' Kitty's voice whispered.

Mair opened the door.

'I'm sorry if I woke you. I've just finished my shift at the hospital, and I thought that, before I take myself off to bed for a well earned rest, I'd make sure you arrived back safely last night. I felt awful leaving you to your own devices.'

'Don't be silly. I couldn't sleep. You see, I have a confession to make.'

'Of course, sleep can wait for a while longer, I just love confessions.' Kitty entered the room and flopped herself onto the bed. 'Well come on, tell all,' she urged.

Mair related exactly the same story as she had done the night before and when she had finished, she caught Kitty's hand. 'Kitty, I'm sorry I didn't confide in you. It was something I really had to do. Please say that we're still friends.'

'Well I won't say I'm not mad at you … because I am. If you'd told me, and could have waited until my next day off, I would have been only too pleased to go with you … safety in numbers and all that.'

'I know. But it's done now, and I do feel so much better for it.'

'I'm sure you do. I'd have done the same if some blackguard had abandoned *my* mother.'

Mair nodded. She didn't feel the need to tell Kitty the full story of why she hated Harry Stone so much. That was in the past. From now on, she must think only to the future.

'So does that mean we're still friends?' Mair urged.

'Yes, of course we are. But only on the understanding that there are no more secrets between us!'

'I promise.' Mair caught around Kitty and gave her a hug.

'So ... Dr Baxter was your knight in shining armour?'

'Yes. I dread to think what might have happened had he not intervened. He was very kind to me.'

'Oh yes, our Dr Baxter is well known for his bedside manner,' Kitty smirked.

'So, you know him?' Mair asked, oblivious to the hint of sarcasm in Kitty's voice.

'Well, to be precise, I only know *of* him. I often see him visiting patients on my ward. Trust me, his reputation precedes him.' Kitty made a husky sound as if clearing her throat, and in a low whisper added, 'in more ways than one.'

Mair didn't hear her last sentence, so answered, 'I can believe that. I bet he's an excellent doctor. He certainly looks to be a fine young man.'

Kitty didn't respond. Instead she looked toward the wardrobe. 'So tell me, why are your clothes hanging on the wardrobe door?'

'I'm trying to decide what to wear this afternoon. I really want to look my best.'

'Why? What's so special about this afternoon?'

'Dr Baxter has arranged to call for me at two o'clock. He's taking me for afternoon tea.'

'Is he indeed? And what did Mrs Turnbull have to say about that?'

'She said she can't wait to meet him. She wants to thank him for rescuing me. Kitty, why the glum face? I'm that excited and happier than I've been for ages. Please say you're happy for me too.'

Kitty shook her head. 'Of course I am. Just promise me that you will take things slowly ... and be sure and tell me *all* about it,' she joked. 'And if you're interested, my choice would definitely be the brown skirt and cream striped blouse. The navy is far too formal, and if I'm not mistaken, you wore that one yesterday?'

'Yes. I did. Thank you, Kitty – the brown and cream it shall be.'

'Good. And then you could finish the outfit by wearing your cream straw hat and fine woollen shawl.'

Mair nodded. 'Thank you, Kitty. You're such a good friend.'

It was just coming up to two o'clock. Mair, too excited to sit down, gazed out of the bay window, looking up the street in anticipation of Dr Baxter's arrival. It was a fine day and Mair was now suitably dressed in her brown skirt and cream striped blouse with only the top button left undone – she missed not having her gold locket. It would have looked just right with this outfit. But sadly that, along with all her clothes and all those lost souls, was somewhere on the bottom of the ocean. She shook herself; today was no time for sad memories. Soon she would be 'walking out' with an attractive young gentleman – or was she being too presumptuous?

Within minutes a hansom cab pulled up outside and Andrew Baxter stepped down. He was dressed in a light tweed jacket, waistcoat and trousers, high collar cravat, highly polished boots and sported a wide brimmed soft brown trilby hat. Mair smiled to herself when she realized how her brown outfit perfectly matched his. She watched as he stretched up to the driver and handed him some money for the fare. Then he turned and proceeded up the steps to the front door.

Without even waiting for him to knock Mair made to leave the room to greet him, but at that precise moment, Mrs Turnbull entered the room and stopped her dead in her tracks.

'Mair, it really doesn't do for a young lady to appear too eager when receiving a gentleman caller,' Mrs Turnbull admonished. 'I suggest you take a seat and wait for him to present himself in a proper manner.'

Mair did as she was told. She didn't want to risk upsetting her landlady. She was only too aware that Mrs Turnbull had it in her power to thwart her afternoon excursion. There was a loud knock on the door. Once again, Mair was about to get up from her chair.

'You stay where you are, my dear. I've already instructed Violet to show Dr Baxter into the parlour, as soon as he arrives.'

And then, as if on cue, the parlour door opened and in walked Violet followed by the doctor.

'Dr Andrew Baxter,' Violet announced.

'Thank you, Violet, that will be all,' Mrs Turnbull commanded.

Violet, after bobbing a small curtsey, obediently left the room.

Mair struggled to suppress a giggle.

Andrew Baxter walked across the room. He didn't even give a sideways glance in Mair's direction, but headed straight toward Mrs Turnbull.

Ada Turnbull stood up and offered her outstretched hand. 'Dr Baxter, I'm Ada Turnbull, Miss Parsons' landlady and as she has no family in London, I like to think, her protector.'

'Mrs Turnbull, I'm so pleased to meet you. Miss Parsons made it quite clear to me last evening that, especially where gentlemen callers are concerned, you have strict, and in my mind, sensible, house rules.'

'Quite. I believe one can never be too careful. Although I must say, in your case after having saved my charge from … well, who knows what, and then bringing her safely back to us in a hansom cab, I thank you and welcome you to Grange House.'

'No thanks necessary, Mrs Turnbull, it was my pleasure. And I have to say, that Miss Parsons, even before my intervention, was giving a good account of herself. The brute attacking her was not having everything his way.' He flashed Mair a warm, friendly smile.

Mair smiled back. When he first entered the room, she had felt hurt by his lack of recognition – now she saw the sense and reason behind his action. His coming to Grange House was all about gaining Mrs Turnbull's trust and approval, and from what Mair could see, his charm offensive had already won her over.

'Yes, Dr Baxter. I, like you, soon recognized in Mair – Miss Parsons – a young woman of strong character, someone not to be trifled with.'

'And if I'm not mistaken someone, not unlike yourself – a suffragette, am I right?' Andrew Baxter's eyes went to the green, white and violet brooch pinned to the collar of her day dress.

Mrs Turnbull automatically reached up and touched the brooch – her suffragette talisman. 'Yes, and I'm proud of it. I strongly believe that women should have the vote. And I intend to support the suffragette movement until they do.' She looked across to Mair. 'And if you ever want to join our cause, my dear, you just let me know. We are always on the lookout for young women with spirit, who can stand up for themselves.'

'Thank you, Mrs Turnbull. I shall keep it in mind. Although I'm not sure I could go as far as some of your members,' Mair said.

'I have to admit we do have a few extremists in the group. You will come across this in all walks of life. Is that not so, Dr Baxter?'

'It is indeed, Mrs Turnbull,' the doctor agreed.

Mair still wasn't at all sure. Her thoughts went back to 1 March – she remembered the date because it was St David's day in Wales, long before her fated journey to New York, when John Jenkins had read a piece from the *Daily Herald* reporting on how two suffragettes, imprisoned for breaking the windows of some important buildings in London, had gone on hunger strike.

'My dear Mair, this is no time to be day dreaming. I was led to believe that Dr Baxter has come to take you out for the afternoon. So what are you waiting for?'

Mair stood up. Andrew Baxter immediately walked over and, taking the shawl from her hand, gently placed it around her shoulders. His touch sent a shiver up Mair's spine. She felt her colour rise, but thankfully neither he nor Mrs Turnbull appeared to notice.

Andrew Baxter offered his hand to Ada Turnbull. 'I must say it's been a pleasure meeting you, Mrs Turnbull. And my sincere thanks for giving your permission for me to accompany Miss Parsons on an afternoon excursion. I promise to take good care of her and have her back at—'

'Dinner is at 6.30 sharp,' Mrs Turnbull interrupted. 'I'd appreciate it if you could have Mair back by then. I have already informed Cook of the numbers expected for dinner. She, like me, abhors waste, and with Mair getting back too late for dinner last night – I really don't want it repeated.'

'I understand. I promise to have her back well before 6.30.'

'Thank you. Now, it's already gone 2.30, if you don't get a move on, the afternoon will be over.'

Once outside Grange House, Andrew Baxter gave an exaggerated sigh of relief. 'At last, I thought we'd never be on our way. Your Mrs Turnbull is quite a force to be reckoned with. I would much rather be her friend than foe.'

'Her bark is much worse than her bite,' Mair offered.

'I'll take your word for it.'

'Well, she obviously liked you. You had her wrapped around your little finger.'

'It's my boyish charm,' he joked.

They both laughed.

'I thought we might take a hansom straight to Waterloo Station, and from there, if you're in agreement, we could catch the underground railway, across to the City of Westminster. What do you say?'

Mair gave a gasp of excitement. 'I say, that sounds just great.'

With one arm raised and the other gently touching her elbow, he proceeded to hail a hansom cab. Minutes later they had arrived at Waterloo Station where the smog was a thick yellow, the colour of gas lamps.

'I'm afraid the thick smog is caused by the sulphurous clouds gushing from the chimneys of industry this side of the river,' Andrew Baxter explained.

On leaving the hansom, the doctor led her the short distance across the cobbled street. The street bustled with hawkers pushing wheel-barrows across the road, weaving their way in and out of the oncoming traffic. Mair couldn't help but notice how many young street urchins, boys and girls were standing on corners. Some were selling small bunches of dried flowers, but others were begging from passers-by. Mair wondered who they were and if they had families to care for them. It made her feel sad.

'This way,' the doctor said, leading her down some steep steps to below ground.

'Where are we going?' Mair asked, trying to conceal the apprehension in her voice.

'We're going to catch an underground train, an ingenious rail system, the first in the country to run on electric cable and built to travel beneath the streets of London. They're called tube stations.'

'Are they safe?' Mair asked.

She wasn't at all comfortable being so far down into the bowels of the earth, with the air as dank and musty-smelling as unwashed drains. It reminded her of how her stepfather, Dai Hughes, had explained the conditions down the colliery mine shaft. She knew too well how often the timbers gave way and shafts fell in. But when she saw the ease with which Andrew Baxter and the other travellers, appeared to be taking the surroundings in their stride, she tried to relax and follow their lead.

A small two-carriage train sat on a narrow track with its doors open. Andrew Baxter took her hand and gave it a gentle squeeze. 'Come on, where's that spirited young woman of yesterday evening? Just think of it as an adventure. This is a new and exciting mode of travel and one I'm sure Mrs Turnbull and her suffragettes use regularly.'

Mair nodded and smiled. To feel his hand holding hers, momentarily took her mind off her fear. So, taking a deep breath, she allowed him to lead the way into the small wooden-slatted carriage. Its high-backed seating accommodated only four passengers either side. It was lit by just one electric light – the new invention. Mair suddenly felt claustrophobic, fearful of being buried alive. Instantly remembering her *Titanic* ordeal, she wondered what was worse, to drown or to be buried alive? Her fears were not helped when Baxter felt the need to tell her how the tube actually travelled through a tunnel that passed *under* the River Thames. 'Such a wonderful feat of engineering,' he exclaimed.

Mair was thankful that the journey was short and quick and breathed a sigh of relief when the tube train made a scheduled stop at Bank station.

Andrew Baxter stood up. 'This is where we get off. It's close to the Embankment and Charing Cross and the City of Westminster.'

They left the tube station and climbed the steep flight of steps out from the dank smelling near-darkness and into daylight and *almost* fresh air, for even above ground there was still the lingering stench of dirty drains.

'Have you been this side of the river before, Mair – Miss Parsons?' he asked.

'No, Dr Baxter, this is my first time.'

'Please, my name's Andrew. Dr Baxter sounds so terribly formal, don't you think?'

'Well yes, it does a bit,' she agreed.

'That's settled then. And I shall call you Mair. It's such a pretty name – almost as pretty as the girl who owns it.'

Mair felt her colour rise.

With his arm once again softly touching her elbow, Mair let herself be led by Andrew, who insisted on giving a running commentary on all the names of the places and buildings they passed along Victoria Embankment, as she marvelled at the vastness of the River Thames, and how busy it was with cargo and pleasure boats vying for position. She wondered if this was the same Embankment where her mother had slept rough. And if so, had she too been taken aback by such a splendid sight? She shook off such thoughts. Today was to be a new start ... no more looking back. 'It'll only give you a crick in the neck', as Ethel would say.

'Please say if I'm walking you too fast,' Andrew said.

'No, I'm fine. Mind you, I'm so glad I chose to wear my comfortable leather boots.'

'Comfortable and yet still fashionable – you chose well.' He flashed a warm smile.

They continued on, and were soon passing a row of ancient buildings, all larger than any she had seen before. They continued up to Horse Guards Parade, where Andrew assured her the King's own regiments could often be seen. Then, onto Parliament Street where she was given her first glimpse of the Houses of Parliament – it simply took her breath away. This was the London she'd previously only read about. Next they came to Trafalgar Square, it was so grand and ornate with its large fountain and two statues of lions flanking the steps. And the pigeons, hundreds of them, being fed by passers-by. It was almost too much for her to take in.

'Well, that's the end of this, your first tour. I'm sorry if it's been a bit of a long walk for you, I just wanted to fit in as much as I could. What did you think of it?'

'I'm practically speechless. I never expected it to be so big and so beautiful.'

'As a visiting Scot, I just love it here in London. That's one of the reasons I jumped at the chance to work at St Thomas's hospital. There's so much history here. Next time I'll take you to see Buckingham Palace and perhaps one of the museums.'

Mair caught her breath. He had actually said 'next time' which surely meant he intended to ask her out again. This thought pleased her very much. It was getting on for 4.30 when, having dodged the busy traffic all weaving in and out of each other – trams, charabanc, horse-drawn carriages, hansom cabs and motor cars – to get across the Strand, they entered Lyons Corner House. It was full of elegantly dressed folk, all enjoying tea. A waitress soon showed them to a small table in the window, and after taking Andrew's order of tea for two, she left them alone.

'Now, tell me. I want to know all about you. I already know why you came to London, but do you intend to stay? Are you seeking employment?'

'Well to be honest with you, I did think that in the short term, I might enrol as a Red Cross volunteer. I do have sufficient funds to last me a while. Although I would really like to train as a nurse but, without a reference, I'm afraid—'

'A reference you say? Now, that may be something I can help you with.'

Chapter Fourteen

D R ANDREW BAXTER, true to his word, had sent a letter to the matron at St Thomas's hospital, putting Mair's name forward as a possible trainee auxiliary, claiming to be a friend of the family. 'A little white lie never hurt anyone,' he assured Mair.

During the two weeks that followed, Andrew Baxter was a regular visitor to Grange House, using his days off to show Mair more of the sights of the City of Westminster, and also, when he was doing a night shift at the hospital, he would call to take her for afternoon tea at either the Lyons Corner House or the Kardomah Café. This was usually followed by a stroll around Regents Park, before hailing a hansom cab, which would drop him at the hospital. He'd now taken to giving her a farewell kiss on the cheek, before instructing the cabbie to return Mair to Grange House and, to appease Mrs Turnbull, always before 6.30.

The more Mair and Andrew saw of each other, the deeper her feelings had become. She also believed, because of the way he smiled at her, the way he caught her eyes in his glance at every opportunity, that he had feelings for her. She wondered if she and Andrew were destined to fall deeply in love, and if so, would this mean her uprooting to live in Scotland? And most of all – was it what she wanted? What about Catherine … and Frank? There were so many unanswered questions. Mair scolded herself for letting her mind run away with such fanciful thoughts. She and Andrew were just friends, nothing more and nothing less.

When there was still no news from the matron at St Thomas's hospital, Mair made the decision to enrol as a Red Cross volunteer, and was welcomed with open arms. In the beginning she was tasked with preparing refreshments for Red Cross nurses or folding linen and packing food parcels to be distributed around the world. Then, having proven herself a good worker, she was invited to accompany nurses and other volunteers, visiting the poor and infirm at workhouses in and around London. On these occasions Mair often bumped into Sister Agnes, who was also a regular visitor to the workhouses in the area.

It was nearing the end of June when a letter finally arrived from St Thomas's requesting her to report to the matron's office for an interview.

The interview went better than Mair could have expected.

'Miss Parsons, I already know a little about you from Dr Baxter, whom I believe to be a friend of your sister and her theatrical manager in New York.' She looked to Mair for conformation.

Mair simply nodded and said, 'Yes, that's correct, Matron.' No harm in a little white lie, Andrew had said.

The matron smiled. 'Dr Baxter is an excellent doctor – though a little headstrong and a mite too popular for his own good. No one can deny what an asset he is to St Thomas's, we're so lucky to have him on our staff, if only for a short while.'

Mair was a little taken aback; she had never even considered how long Andrew Baxter had worked in London or, for that matter, how long he intended to stay.

'Anyway,' the matron continued, 'Dr Baxter told me all about your recent ordeal aboard the *Titanic*. I cannot imagine the dreadful scenes you must have witnessed. He said that you had a knock to the head and were in hospital suffering concussion. However, he also assured me that you are now fully recovered. I trust this is so?'

When Mair had told Andrew of her *Titanic* ordeal and her stay with Rhiannon and Gus, she never expected him to use the information to support her reference … it put her in such an awkward position.

'Yes Matron. The initial reason my friends invited me to stay with them here in London was to aid my recovery – and I'm pleased to say it worked.' Mair crossed her fingers – yet another white lie.

'I'm glad to hear it. Tell me, Miss Parsons, are you in gainful employment at the moment?'

'No. Although, I have recently enrolled as a Red Cross volunteer.

But if I were fortunate enough to be accepted as a trainee auxiliary nurse, my time with them would be limited to any days off I might have,' Mair assured her.

'That's very admirable. It certainly proves a willingness to care for others. Now, if you're accepted for training, there will be no monetary cost to yourself. This course, like many others, is funded by the Florence Nightingale Trust,' the matron proudly told her. 'Now, during the initial six-week training period you will be expected to live in, here at the hospital. Do you have a problem with that?'

'No problem at all, Matron. I know my friends at Grange House will understand and give me all the support I need.' Mair made a mental note to have a word with Mrs Turnbull.

'The support of family and friends is a proven asset to success. As I said, the training is intensive. At the end of the six weeks you will need to sit an examination. If you pass, you will be accepted as a trainee auxiliary nurse ... fondly known as a "Nightingale Nurse".'

At no time during the interview did the matron question Mair's age. With her eighteenth birthday – the requisite age for trainees – only a few months away, she felt it was not worth mentioning.

Ten days later Mair was informed by the matron that the position was hers, and instructed to report for training on Sunday 4 August. She found she had mixed feelings. On the one hand, she felt elated that she had been accepted, safe in the knowledge that, if she worked hard, a career in nursing could be her future. On the other hand, it would mean that all thoughts of returning to Wales would, once again, have to be shelved. Over the past few months she felt she'd won a small battle – able to move on with her life, no longer plagued by the shame of the past. Yet she still carried with her the guilt of abandoning Catherine, believing as she did that it made her no better than her own mother – just like Frank had said it would. Was she someone Catherine would be better without?

With her place now secured, Mair approached Mrs Turnbull, to tell her the good news and to ask if it was possible to move back into her room after the six-week training period.

'Well, first of all, let me say how very pleased I am for you. You deserve some good news at last. And yes, after your six-week training, I'll be happy to welcome you back as a guest. Everyone here is so very fond of you. However, I'm afraid I can no longer afford you the luxury of having a double room to yourself. I did explain when you first arrived that in the future you might have to share.'

'Of course, I understand. But who would I share with?' Mair asked.

'I thought … maybe Kitty? This morning I received news that Jenny, Kitty's room-mate, has to return to the Midlands. Sadly, her mother has been taken ill, which means that Jenny is needed to care for her father and her four young siblings. I thought that if Kitty were to move in with you, her twin room would then become free. What do you say?'

'I think it's a splendid idea,' Mair said with enthusiasm.

'Good. I shall have a word with Kitty.'

On 14 July a letter arrived at Grange House addressed to Miss Mair Parsons. It carried a postmark from New York, USA. Instantly Mair recognized the writing as Rhiannon's and her hand shook with both excitement and anticipation as she struggled to open it.

Dear Mair,

When Gus and I returned to New York on 20 June, I was pleased to find your letter waiting for me at the Palace Theatre. I, like you, felt saddened by the way we parted. We both said things we regret – I suppose it's what sisters do. I am so pleased that you made contact again. I think of you every day, not just as a sister, but as a true friend. That said, I cannot deny the disappointment I felt to find out that, instead of returning home with Frank to be reunited with Catherine and the family, you decided to go off to London on what, I too would have believed to be a 'wild goose chase' in search of your mother and Harry Stone.

I was truly sorry to hear of her death. Yet I am relieved to hear that you have your newly-made friends from the Salvation Army and what sounds like a caring landlady to help you through it. I admit there was no love lost between Nellie and myself, but I would never have wished the poor woman such a sad end. To think of her being knocked down by a horse and carriage just yards away from the New Gaiety Theatre where I was then appearing – my name up in lights and visible to all, made me think that she may have been on her way to see me. Was it her intention to seek you out – to make peace with you? I like to think so. After all, people have been known to change for the better. I do hope this thought gives you some comfort. Mair, I need you to promise me that you will stay away from Harry Stone ... let your mother's death be the end of it. I suggest you get yourself home to Wales.

The good news is that, with my American tour almost at an end, Gus and I plan to return to Britain on 20 December. We have booked an overnight stay at The Grand Hotel, Southampton, before heading to Wales. Our first stop is Cardiff, so that Gus can finalize my contract at the Empire Theatre – I'm to top the bill of an eight-week variety show, due to start Monday 3 February, at the end of the pantomime season. As usual, we shall base ourselves at the Angel Hotel. After that we intend to head for Ponty, to see Ethel and the family in time for Christmas and ... our wedding!

Yes, I've finally agreed to let Gus make an honest woman of me. It would make me so happy if you could be there to welcome us home and to join in the celebrations.

Your loving sister,
Rhi

Rhi's letter, while giving Mair food for thought, definitely lifted her spirits. Was it possible? Could she return home?

She decided to banish such thoughts from her mind, at least until she completed her training at St Thomas's. If the worst were to happen, and she failed to qualify, then she would have no other option than to return to Wales. She wondered how Andrew Baxter would feel about that.

July was the hottest since records began, and it was a relief when it gave way to August.

At around eight o'clock on Saturday 3 August – the night before Mair was due to report to the hospital for training – Dr Andrew Baxter called at Grange House.

Mrs Turnbull and Sister Agnes were in the parlour sipping a glass of cordial, when they heard a knock on the front door. This was followed by a light tap on the parlour door. Violet entered and behind her, Andrew Baxter.

Without waiting to be announced, he brushed past Violet and crossed the room to where the two ladies sat.

'Good evening, dear ladies. I apologize for calling uninvited. I've only just left the hospital and, as I was passing, I wondered if I might have a quick word with Mair – Miss Parsons?'

'Well, Dr Baxter, I do believe that at this present time Mair is busy packing, in preparation for her move into nurses' quarters tomorrow. I'm not sure if—'

'I do understand,' Andrew Baxter interrupted, 'I promise I'll not keep her long. I just wanted to wish her luck, that's all.' He pleaded – with a look of desperation on his face.

Mrs Turnbull pondered for a while. 'Oh, very well. Violet, would you go and inform Mair that she has a visitor, please?'

'Yes, Mrs Turnbull,' Violet answered, as she turned and left the room.

For a little while an awkward silence filled the room – both ladies staring at Andrew Baxter as he fidgeted with the watch and chain attached to his waistcoat pocket.

It fell to Ada Turnbull to break the silence. 'You seem a trifle agitated, Dr Baxter. I do hope there isn't anything wrong.'

'No, everything's fine. It's just that, as I haven't seen Mair since last Sunday, I realized I hadn't wished her luck for tomorrow ... although I'm sure she'll not need it. I do have every faith in her.'

'I agree. I think she'll make a wonderful nurse,' Sister Agnes said. 'I've had occasion to see her at work as a Red Cross Volunteer, ministering to the poor and infirm – she's such a caring, sensitive young woman.'

'I'm sure we all appreciate her qualities.' Dr Baxter flashed a broad smile in the direction of both ladies.

There was a tap on the door.

Mair entered and, on seeing Andrew, her eyes lit up.

'Andrew – Dr Baxter, what a lovely surprise. I wasn't expecting to see you this evening. Is anything wrong?'

'No – everything is fine. I was just explaining to Mrs Turnbull and Sister Agnes that, as I was passing, I thought I might call and wish you good luck for tomorrow.'

Their eyes met, and Mair instantly sensed that he wanted to say more. 'Thank you, that's very kind of you.'

Again an awkward silence. Mair watched Andrew's gaze go from Ada Turnbull to Sister Agnes then across to herself. It was apparent to her that he had something to say – something that was for her ears only.

'Well, now that's done, I'll be on my way,' he said.

'And I must get back to my packing. I hadn't realized how many things I had accumulated. I'm trying to organize it – to give Kitty some space.' Mair explained.

'Right ... yes ... well, thank you, dear ladies. It's time I was on my way,' Andrew said.

Mair sensed his reluctance to leave.

'Thank you, Dr Baxter. We shall look forward to seeing you the next time you call. Mair, perhaps you could show the doctor out,' Ada Turnbull suggested.

Mair heard Andrew's heavy sigh of relief. She wondered if the two women had heard it too.

'Of course,' Mair said, as she struggled to contain her excitement at having the chance to be alone with him, if only for a few minutes.

As Mair and Andrew left the room neither of them heard Ada Turnbull and the Sister's whispered comments.

'He obviously has something to say to Mair, that he doesn't want either of us to hear,' Ada said.

'Oh yes, and did you notice the excitement on her face when you asked her to show him out?'

Ada nodded. 'I do wonder if this attractive doctor hasn't turned her head too much. After all, we know so little about him.'

In the hallway with the door to the parlour safely closed behind them, Andrew Baxter took Mair's hand in his. 'Oh, Mair, I just had to see you. You do understand how difficult the next six weeks are going to be for us, don't you?'

Mair was flattered to think how much he was going to miss her.

'It won't be that bad. Apparently, I'm to have every Sunday off, and I'm sure there'll be occasions when we might bump into each other within the hospital itself,' she told him.

'That's what I've come to warn you about. At no time during

working hours must you acknowledge our … friendship. We need to be discreet. Matron has strict rules when it comes to us doctors fraternizing with the nursing staff, especially young trainee auxiliaries.'

'But surely Matron has already accepted you as "a friend of the family".'

'Even so, it's better to be safe than sorry,' he whispered as he leant over to kiss her cheek. 'Come on, don't look so gloomy. I promise it'll be as hard for me as it is for you. I really wouldn't like to be the one to upset matron. Trust me, it's for your own good. You do understand, don't you?'

She nodded. 'Yes, I understand.' Although in truth, she didn't understand at all.

The next morning Mair, along with fifteen other hopeful trainees, presented herself to the matron. The matron greeted them with a coolly efficient smile. 'Good morning and welcome to St Thomas's Hospital. If you would all care to follow me, I will take you to meet Staff Nurse Tomlinson, your head tutor.'

The matron led the way out of the hospital across the courtyard and into a large grey-stone building, where a stern-looking lady stood waiting to greet them. She was in her late thirties, dressed in a dark blue and white nurse's uniform and wearing a large white stiffly-starched headdress.

'Good morning, Matron,' she said.

'Good Morning, Staff. I trust we haven't kept you waiting long. These are your trainees.' The matron turned to the new recruits. 'Ladies, this is Staff Nurse Tomlinson and from now on she will be in charge of your training. You will address her as "Staff" and heed her every word. During your training, if Staff has cause to reprimand any of you, I will be informed. In the event of this happening you will be brought to my office. I will not tolerate bad or unladylike behaviour – if you do indeed abuse the privileges accorded to you on this course, there is a strong possibility you will be asked to leave the hospital immediately. My decision will be final. Do I make myself clear?'

'Yes, Matron,' the trainees meekly answered.

'Good. Well, Staff, they are all yours.'

'Thank you, Matron. Ladies, if you would like to follow me I will show you to your living quarters, housed on the second floor.'

Their living quarters turned out to be a long room with eight metal-framed beds either side – each with a small bedside cabinet and next to that a metal rail on which to hang their clothes. The stark furniture made the room feel cold and unwelcoming. The wood-block floor was polished to within an inch of its life. Everywhere was spotlessly clean. The bedding, the windows, the adjacent toilets and washroom, all looked and smelt so ... clinical.

'Ladies, this will be your home for the next six weeks. As you see it now is the order in which I expect it to be kept.' Staff's voice commanded attention, 'There will be regular inspections – so be prepared. Over the next three weeks you will spend six days a week within the walls of this building. On each bed you will find a comprehensive list of your daily schedule. You will all be expected to memorize it. There can be no excuse for lateness. Are there any questions?'

One of the girls alongside Mair put her hand up. 'I have one, Staff.'

'Yes. What is it?'

'When do we actually get to work on the wards?' the girl bravely asked.

'While I understand your eagerness to wear our uniform and start work on the wards, I assure you that you all have a long way to go before I let any of you loose on a single unsuspecting patient. You will need to have not only completed the course, but passed the final examination. Your first three weeks will be spent under my tuition, in the lecture hall. Only when I am sure that you have grasped the theory, will you be allowed onto the wards, to begin three weeks of practical training. I hope that answers your question?'

'Yes, Staff. Thank you, Staff,' the girl mumbled.

'Good. Now I shall leave you to get settled. Lunch is at 12.30. After lunch, you are free to explore the hospital grounds and find your bearings. Dinner is at 7.30. I suggest you all have an early night in readiness for tomorrow morning, the start of your six-week intensive course.'

*

Later that evening Mair lay on her allotted bed – the one nearest to the door – making her the first person Staff would see when she entered the dormitory. She knew she would be in the front firing line, but this was what she really wanted – to make Catherine proud of her.

Mair repeatedly read the training schedule, and worked hard at memorizing it.

Training Schedule: August/September 1912
Breakfast 7.30 a.m. Dining room Ground Floor.
1st Lesson 8.30 a.m. Lecture hall Ground Floor
Lunch 12.30 p.m. Dining Room
2nd Lesson 2.00–5.30 p.m.
Dinner 7.30 p.m.
The two hours between 5.30 and 7.30 will give trainees ample time to return to their dormitory and check their notes from each day's lesson.
On Saturday, the second lesson will be used for assessment – a small test to check on progress thus far.
Sunday – a day of rest.
9.30 a.m.: Every trainee will be expected to attend the Christian service held in the Hospital church, annexed to the main building. The rest of the morning should be spent on dormitory cleaning, laundry and personal hygiene. Trainees are at liberty to leave hospital grounds, but be advised that there is 6.30 p.m. curfew which every trainee is expected to observe – break this at your peril!

Mair made a mental note always to return on Sunday before 6.30. So far, everything about her day had been regimented and she wondered if it compared with what Frank had experienced when he first joined the army and had to report to Maendy Barracks in Cardiff. She gave a heavy sight. Since meeting Andrew, it was true that, while not a day went by when she didn't think of Catherine, she'd thought of Frank less and less. She wondered if he still thought of her. The truth was that whenever she thought of him, she always felt so guilty, knowing how hurt he would be if he were to find out how close she and Andrew had become, sure in her mind that he would see it as her two-timing him. Mair tried to justify her actions, reminding herself of how, when they had met in Southampton, she had tried to make him see that they had no future together.

On Sundays, the morning was allotted to attending church service, cleaning, doing the laundry, washing her hair and having a bath, so it was midday before she could head off to Grange House for lunch. In the afternoon, Andrew would call and take her for a stroll around Regents Park followed by high-tea. Mair often wondered why, with her being on such a tight timetable to ensure she arrived back at St Thomas's before curfew, Andrew always insisted on taking her north of the river. As she had so little time, surely it would have made more sense to stay on the Lambeth side of the river. On one occasion she had suggested they might visit Victoria Gardens situated not far from St Thomas's Hospital, after all there were plenty of suitable tea houses in and around Lambeth.

'I don't think that wise. There is a lot more chance of our being seen together south of the river,' he'd insisted.

One Sunday she had even mentioned how much she would like to visit the Florence Nightingale museum, annexed to St Thomas's.

'I really think that might be somewhere you visit on your own or maybe with one of the other trainees. You could even ask Kitty to go with you.'

'When we first met, you did say you might take me there one day,' she reminded him.

'That was then – long before you decided to become a trainee nurse. I'm afraid with the museum situated inside hospital grounds, we really can't risk it.'

This really hurt Mair. Although he'd previously explained the danger of them being seen together, she couldn't shake off the feeling that he was hiding something. Or was he simply ashamed to be seen with her?

At the end of the gruelling, six-week training period, Mair sat the comprehensive examination and passed with flying colours.

'Congratulations, Nurse Parsons. You did well. You are now a trainee auxiliary nurse. You can pack your things and return home to enjoy a well deserved rest,' the matron said.

'Thank you, Matron.'

'I shall expect you to present yourself to me, dressed in your newly issued uniform, on Monday 22 September – seven days' time, when you will be informed of your allotted ward.'

'Thank you again, Matron, I can't wait to start work.'

Mair left the grounds of St Thomas's and hailed a hansom. She couldn't wait to return to Grange House and get settled into her old room, the one she would now share with Kitty. This was no reflection on the girls she had trained with. They had all been friendly enough. It just wasn't the same as being with her friends at Grange House – a place she now fondly thought of as her home here in London.

Mair spent the next week catching up with everyone. Kitty was so excited to have her back and relished the thought of them sharing a room. She saw little of the remaining two Js, as they were on a full week of night duties. Sister Agnes was thrilled by her success, 'My dear Mair, I'm so very proud of the way you have completed your initial course and passed with commendation – well done.'

Ada Turnbull had actually hugged her and said how good it was to have her back in the fold.

Chapter Fifteen

THE WEEK BEFORE Mair was due to start work at St Thomas's Hospital had sped by. Although she was determined not to let anything dampen her spirits, she couldn't help feeling disappointed that Andrew Baxter had not called to see her. Instead, she had to be satisfied with the hastily scribbled note he sent her, explaining how busy he was at the hospital and unable to get away until Saturday afternoon.

On Saturday afternoon, as promised, Andrew Baxter called to take her out. At first, she'd thought him no different than all the other times he'd called for her – presenting himself to Mrs Turnbull as the perfect gentleman. It was only when they left Grange House that Mair suspected that something was not quite right.

The weather was warm, especially for the third week in September, the blue sky was sprinkled with only a few fluffy clouds and promised another fine and mild day. Mair had anticipated a stroll over Westminster Bridge to the other side of the Thames. Instead, Andrew immediately hailed a passing hansom cab, and as it came to a stop, practically bundled her inside before instructing the driver to move on.

'Andrew, is everything all right? You seem a little agitated,' she inquired.

His answer was to pull her to him and kiss her lips so passionately, it almost took her breath away.

'My dear Mair, this week has dragged by. You don't know how much I've been longing for this moment – to be alone with you, to kiss you, to hold you. My love, please say you feel the same way?' he asked.

Without waiting for her to reply, he once again pulled her to him, his mouth eagerly kissing hers, his hands exploring her body … her back … her neck … her breasts.

Mair felt light headed. All these weeks of polite hand holding and tender kisses, had now changed to this … unbridled passion. A passion that aroused her in a way she had never thought possible, making her eager to return his kisses with equal passion.

'My darling Mair, I'm so pleased you feel the same way.'

'Oh yes, Andrew, I do … I really do.'

Minutes later they came to a stop and having given her a few moments to compose herself, he helped her from the hansom. Andrew paid the cabbie. He drove away, leaving them standing in a street made up of small hotels.

'Andrew, where are we? I thought we were going for a stroll in St James's Park?'

He leaned over to whisper in her ear, 'I've planned a little surprise. I've booked us into a small hotel.'

Mair was taken aback. She looked into his eyes, to see if he might be testing or teasing her. His eyes stared back, almost pleading with her. She still wasn't sure. Had he meant what she thought he meant? There was only one way to find out. 'Do you mean for us actually to spend the night *together*?' she asked trying not to sound too shocked.

'Yes, that's exactly what I mean … but only if you want to. Look, why don't we just go inside? I'm sure we must look more than a little conspicuous, standing on the street like this. I've already picked up the key to our room. I also know of a private entrance, which means you won't even have to meet the proprietor or any other guests.'

Mair was dumbstruck. He seemed to have arranged everything. The thought crossed her mind that maybe he'd done this before, but these thoughts soon disappeared when his lips met hers. It felt so good that, when he took her hand in his, she let herself be led around the back of the hotel, up the stairs and into the bedroom.

As they entered the room, the first thing her eyes were drawn to was the large double bed – although she did also notice the room to be clean and well furnished.

Andrew began leading her towards the bed.

'Andrew, I'm really not sure about this. You do know that Mrs Turnbull will be expecting me in time for dinner, don't you?'

'I already thought of that. When I called for you this afternoon, I took the liberty of telling Mrs Turnbull that I had a little surprise in store for you.'

'You didn't tell her...?

'No, silly, I told her I'd booked us theatre tickets for tonight, to celebrate your success in becoming a Nightingale Nurse.'

'And what did she say?'

'She thought it a splendid idea, and said that on this occasion it was all right for you to stay out late.' His hands playfully tugged at Mair's leading her onto the bed.

'That's all very well, however, being late back and staying out all night are two entirely different things.' Mair pointed out.

'Look, the only person who'll know you stayed out all night is Kitty, and we both know she'd be the last person to give you away. Now, who's a clever fellow?' he flashed a mischievous smile.

His smile made her heart miss a beat. 'Clever? Devious more like. How long have you been planning this?' she asked, aware of his body siding up to hers.

'The truth is,' he whispered, his lips tenderly brushing the small of her neck, his hand expertly unbuttoning her blouse, 'the very first time I set eyes on you, I felt strangely attracted to you – since then my feelings for you have grown and grown. I've spent weeks longing to be alone with you ... to make love to you.'

As he held her close, Mair felt her heart beat faster, her whole being taking her to a place she thought she would never want to be....

As they lay entwined, the urgency of his kisses and the hardness of his manhood were matched by her new-found sexual yearning. As he kissed her his hand reached up to tenderly brush away the hair from her forehead and suddenly the memory of being in Frank's arms came flooding back. He had brushed her hair from her forehead that night in Southampton – the night she'd feigned sleep. Frank had always cared about her ... had loved her ... had wanted to *make love* to her. She had turned him away. She couldn't help but think how hurt Frank would be ... to think she could give herself to a man she barely knew.

'Andrew, I'm sorry. I can't do this,' Mair said, as she endeavoured to push him away.

'It's all right. I promise I'll be gentle,' he whispered.

'I can't. This is not what I want.' Moving away from him, she slid off the bed and stood to face him.

He sat up and stared at her, his face a picture of hurt, anger and disappointment.

'Andrew, I'm sorry, if I led you to believe—'

'Yes, you damn well did. Trust me. I know women and all the signs were there. Tell me what I've done wrong. What's changed your mind?' he asked, obviously bewildered.

'It's not you,' she whispered.

'So, if it's "not me", then who the hell is it?' he demanded.

Mair felt awful. It was then she decided to come clean and tell him about Frank, and suddenly she was blurting it all out … how she and Frank had planned to marry, how he'd always taken care of her, even meeting her in Southampton, how she'd left him and how, over the months, she'd come to realize how much he truly meant to her. 'Can't you see? To sleep with you would feel like the ultimate betrayal,' she argued. Mair said nothing about Catherine. It was far too private to tell anyone….

Andrew moved towards her taking her arm, 'Look I'm sorry if I tried to rush you. I know what it's like to be far from your home and loved ones. But we're together … here … now. You shouldn't let the guilt you feel for an old boyfriend stop us enjoying what *we* have.' He pulled her to him, 'Mair, I really want you. And I believe you want me too.'

Once again Mair pulled herself away, shaking her head. 'I'm sorry, Andrew. I can't. And if you don't mind, I think I'd like to go back to Grange House.'

Later that night, as she lay on the bed in the room she shared with Kitty, she cast her mind back to what had *almost* happened. Andrew had looked so hurt by her refusal – and who could blame him? He spoke the truth, when he'd said, 'all the signs were there'. She had let him kiss her, and yes, she'd kissed him back. And, if she was being honest with herself, she had also imagined what it would be like to be intimate with him – he had aroused her in a way she had never thought possible. So why had she pushed him away? And why had she felt the need to tell him about Frank? So what if Frank did find out about her and Andrew? Hadn't she already told Frank that she only wanted him as a friend? She was so confused. She decided to wait up for Kitty to confide in her.

Mair decided that first thing in the morning, she would seek out Andrew and apologize to him. Of course, there was always a chance that he might never want to speak to her again.

Mair was still awake, her thoughts in turmoil, when Kitty arrived back from the hospital. As soon as Kitty entered the room, Mair promptly sat up in bed.

'I'm sorry, Mair. Did I wake you?'

'N-no, it's just … I can't seem to get to sleep.'

'Shall I light the candle?'

'Yes, please. I need to talk to you … something has happened between Andrew and me, and I feel awful about it,' Mair blurted out.

In the darkness she heard Kitty fumble to light the candle on the bedside table.

'There … we have light. Now, tell me what's happened,' Kitty said, as she flopped herself onto the bed.

Mair took a deep breath. 'Well … when Andrew called for me this afternoon, I thought we were going for our usual stroll in St James's Park then, out of the blue, he hailed a cab and took me to this hotel and told me how much he wanted us to … well, you know?'

'Oh yes, I know. And I suppose he had pre-booked the hotel.'

Mair nodded.

'Oh Mair, please don't tell me you went along with it!' Kitty asked.

'The thing is … I almost did. And if I'm honest, I really wanted to. He made me feel like no other man ever has … but in the end … I just couldn't. And then I felt awful. He looked so hurt and disappointed.'

'I bet he did,' Kitty sniggered. 'He's probably not used to being refused.'

'What do you mean?'

'Look, Mair. I'm sorry. I probably should have spoken out before, but when I saw how happy you were … anyway, I'll not keep it from you any longer. The truth is that *your* Dr Andrew Baxter has a reputation for being something of a womanizer. It's a well known fact all around the hospital. He has already been taken to task by Matron, regarding his familiarity with nurses. While you may well have been one of the very few to turn him down, there has been many a young nurse who succumbed to his charms, only to find themselves having to leave the hospital in disgrace.'

'But I trusted him. I thought of him as ... a close friend,' Mair confided.

'Trust me. Your *friendship* is the last thing men like Dr Baxter want. For one thing, how would he explain you to his wife?'

'His wife, are you sure?' Mair put her hand over her mouth.

'Yes, I'm afraid it's a well-known fact,' Kitty assured her.

Mair felt betrayed. Andrew Baxter was a cheat and a liar! She couldn't believe how naive she'd been. He had taken her for a fool. She had come so close to giving herself to him – thankfully, the thought of Frank had stopped her. Once again Frank had been there looking out for her. To think she had even been prepared to apologize to Andrew. Well, not any more. Now she couldn't wait to confront him with the truth and have great pleasure in telling him that she wanted nothing more to do with him.

The next afternoon Mair knew Andrew was on duty, she went to the hospital to confront him.

'I've come to see Dr Andrew Baxter. I wonder, could you tell me what ward he's on?' Mair asked the hospital receptionist.

'I'm afraid Dr Baxter is no longer employed at this hospital – he left us on Friday.' The receptionist preened herself, obviously enjoying being in the know.

'Left ... to go where?' an incredulous Mair asked.

'Back to his wife and family in Scotland – he booked his travel arrangements early last week. His train was due to leave London at 10.30 this morning ... are you all right, my dear?

Mair rushed from the reception area to the nearest bathroom, her whole body shaking with anger, disbelief and contempt. How could he have just left without telling her? She was mortified to think how close she had come to sleeping with him and how he was prepared to seduce her and then high-tail it back to Scotland.... She couldn't believe how conceited he had been to think, that sleeping with her was an appropriate farewell gift.

Mair stood up straight, proud of the fact that, this time, she was not the wronged woman ... she had said no. It felt so good to at last be in control of her fate. Although it had been a close call, if she were being totally honest, part of her would always be grateful to Andrew Baxter for awakening in her feeling she thought lost forever.

On Monday 22 September, Mair, dressed in her smart nurse's uniform – a floor length dark-blue tunic, long white pinafore, white detachable collar and cuffs and a highly starched white hat – presented herself for duty on the men's surgical ward.

During her three-week practical training, like now, she had been amazed by the constant noise on the ward, There was a constant groaning of patients suffering pain and discomfort as they lay on metal-framed beds, as well as the noise of metal-wheeled trolleys pushed along the hardwood block floors and bedpans noisily flushed and washed in the porcelain sinks of the sluice – surely all this was not helpful to patient recovery.

With Andrew gone and no outside distractions, Mair threw herself into her work at the hospital and on her one day off, as a Red Cross volunteer.

When she was on a night shift, 8 p.m.–4 a.m., Mair would get up in time for lunch at Grange House, then head for the City of Westminster to explore the sights. Of late she had taken to purchasing postcards to send to Catherine. With her daughter almost three years old, Mair was sure that with Frank and Ethel's tuition, Catherine would be well on her way to reading and writing. She was determined to send Catherine a different postcard every week: the Houses of Parliament, the Tower of London, the Embankment, Nelson's Column, Trafalgar Square, the Thames and even one of St Thomas's Hospital. On each Mair would write, 'To Catherine, thinking of you, with much love and kisses, from your mother.'

For weeks now, Mair had been considering a trip back home to Wales. And she hoped these cards might spark in Catherine's mind a memory of her mother. If nothing else, they would at least act as a conversation piece – an icebreaker.

Chapter Sixteen

December 1912

THE NURSES ON the ward had drawn lots to decide who would have time off over Christmas and who would have New Year.

A week later the list was posted on the bulletin board in the hospital canteen. Mair approached it with anticipation – the outcome would determine whether she could travel home to Wales or not. She scanned the list for her name … and there it was: Nurse Mair Parsons on leave 20–27 December. Mair took a sharp intake of breath; surely this had to be fate and she was meant to return to Wales.

It was a cold December day when Mair, dressed in her new winter outfit of fur hat and muffler and a long midnight-blue woollen coat, and carrying her carpetbag, left her bedroom and headed down the stairs of Grange House, only to find Mrs Turnbull, Sister Agnes and Kitty waiting for her in the hallway.

'We couldn't let you go without saying goodbye and wishing you a safe and successful journey. Here, Cook has made you up a few sandwiches and a bottle of her homemade lemonade for the journey,' Mrs Turnbull gushed as she handed her the food parcel.

'That's so very kind of her. Please say thank you to her from me.'

'And may I say how very smart you look,' Sister Agnes offered. 'When I think of the young girl who made herself known to me at Waterloo Station – I cannot believe how much you have blossomed. You do your family proud.'

'And you three, I hope. Without your help and support over these past months, I don't know what I would have done. Kitty even helped me to choose this outfit.'

'Yes, and I'd like to see you in it again. So I want you to promise that you'll come back to us. I know how persuasive families can be.'

'Of course I'll come back. I'm due at work on 28 December and I've already booked my return train journey for the day before.'

'You promise?' Kitty pressed for an answer.

'Yes, I promise. Now come here and give me a hug.'

As the two girls hugged, they heard a hansom pull to a stop outside the front door.

'That will be my carriage. I'd better go. Goodbye, see you all in six days,' Mair said, as she headed for the front door.

'You take care of yourself. And don't you go talking to strangers and the like,' Mrs Turnbull called after her.

'And don't forget your promise!' Kitty yelled.

The hansom dropped her off at Waterloo Station. Mair went in search of a guard to find out the timetable for the next train to Paddington where she was to catch another train to Wales. On seeing a guard at the end of the platform she made her way over to him. She instantly recognized Albert, the friendly guard from before.

'Good morning, Albert, remember me?' she smiled.

'Of course I do, miss. I always remember a pretty face. You'll be that young girl who was looking for digs. I hope the Sally Army was of help to you.'

'Yes, thank you. Sister Agnes helped me find a really friendly establishment.'

'Glad to hear it. Now how can I help you?'

'I'm looking to find the time of the first train to Paddington. My next train leaves there in an hour.'

Taking a fob watch from his pocket, he checked the time. 'There's one due in five minutes. So you'll easily make your connection. Are you travelling far, miss?'

'I'm going home to Wales.'

'What? Have you found the big smoke too much for you?'

'Not at all, I'm training to be a nurse at St Thomas's Hospital. I'm going to spend Christmas with my family.

Just saying the words 'my family' gave Mair a warm feeling inside.

'That's grand, miss. Now, let me take your bag. I'll escort you to your platform.'

*

As Albert had said, Mair was in good time for her connection at Paddington Station – an unwelcoming, grimy-looking, intimidating place, full of dubious looking characters and barefooted street urchins, all intermingling with well dressed men and women. Mair did not like the crush of travellers and it was with relief that she boarded her train to Cardiff.

The journey from Paddington Station to Cardiff seemed to take forever. Mair felt restless, her mind filled with so many negative thoughts – all questioning the wisdom of the journey she was about to make. How many times over the past months had she thought about returning to Wales … only to change her mind at the last minute? The first time had been the night of her confrontation with Harry Stone – on reflection, with all ghosts put to rest, it would have been a perfect time to return to Ponty, to reunite with Catherine and make her peace with Frank and the family.

So why hadn't she gone? Why had she let herself be side-tracked by the charms of Andrew Baxter? Convincing herself that the prospect of becoming a Nightingale Nurse more than justified her living and working in London, when in truth, she was afraid to go home. Afraid of how everyone, especially Catherine, would react. What if her daughter didn't recognize her? She hadn't seen Mair for nine months – that's a long time when you're a young child. And if that were to happen – how would Mair feel?

She tried to focus her mind on the ever changing landscape as the train sped by. Mair had found she had a carriage to herself. At first she thought it a good thing but then, on reflection, she wondered if the journey may have been easier with the distraction of fellow travellers.

On arriving in Cardiff, Mair changed platforms. On platform twelve, through a haze of billowing steam, she found a locomotive waiting to take her to the small valley railway station in Llan and from there a charabanc to Ponty … and home.

The horse-drawn charabanc to Ponty was packed with passengers – some of whom stared at her with a hint of recognition, as if curious as to where they might have seen her before. Mair was only too aware of how much she'd changed. It was hard to believe that so much had happened since she had left Ponty – the fateful trip on the *Titanic*, her stay in hospital, her row with Rhiannon, her return to Britain, her quarrel with Frank, the death of her mother, Harry Stone ... Andrew Baxter. Each one a contributing factor in moulding her into the person she had now become. She had certainly grown up and was now able to see things as they really were – and not as she would have liked them to be.

The closer the charabanc was to Ponty, the more nervous she became. Part of her wanted to turn and run, but she knew that wasn't a possibility – the time had come to face the music. As the charabanc drove toward Ponty Square, passing John Jenkins' butcher shop, which was closed for trade and in complete darkness, in contrast, the family home next door was lit up with a warm amber glow from the oil lamp shining in the downstairs windows.

Then she was there. On the mountainside across from the square, she saw the winch wheel, looming high above the mine shaft of Ponty Colliery. Mair stepped onto the street. It was getting dark. A cold wind buffeted her face. She was glad of her warm coat, fur hat and muffler. It was always said that Wales was two overcoats colder than England. Well today certainly proved it to be true.

Mair slowly made her way toward the Jenkins house and within minutes had arrived at the front door. For a while she just stood there ... then, taking a deep breath, she raised her gloved hand, lifted the highly-polished brass knocker and knocked once ... twice ... three times. It seemed an age before anyone answered, when in truth it was only a minute. Mair felt her heart thump in her chest, causing her to once again question the wisdom of her decision to come back. And then the door opened.

Ethel Jenkins stood in the doorway. She stared open-mouthed, then blinked, as if not believing what she was seeing ... dumbstuck.

'Hello, Ethel. It's me, Mair. I've come—'

'Mair, my lovely, I can't believe it. Is it really you?' Ethel embraced her, hugging her so tightly Mair could hardly breathe. When she finally released her, she stood back, shaking her head in disbelief. 'To think the last time I saw you, was that dreadful moment aboard the

Titanic when I watched you disappear from view, to go in search of Rhiannon's locket.' Ethel gave a long sigh. 'I thought then that you were lost to us forever. You can't believe how good it is to see you ... alive and well.'

'Ethel, I'm sorry. I can understand what a shock it must be to have just turned up like this. I would have written but—' Mair was about to explain that she only recently heard that she could have the time off from her hospital duties, when Ethel interrupted.

'Don't you go giving it another thought. Shock or not, I'm just pleased to have you home. Your return has been such a long time coming ... my goodness, what am I doing, keeping you stood there in the cold?' Ethel took Mair's carpetbag. 'Come on in, *cariad*. Welcome home!' Closing the door Ethel led the way down the hall.

Mair felt tears well up in her eyes. Ethel seemed truly pleased to see her; no bitter reproach, no tirade of difficult questions ... just a 'welcome home'. This had not been what Mair had expected or, for that matter, what she deserved. She took a deep breath. She didn't want to cry. Not yet.

Ethel turned and caught Mair wiping her eyes. 'The cold wind always makes my eyes water, too,' Ethel said.

Mair nodded and smiled, she suspected Ethel had guessed how close to tears she was.

'That's better. Now, come on through. John and Catherine are in the kitchen. I know how pleased they'll be to see you ... especially Catherine.'

To hear her daughter's name and to know how close she was to at last seeing her again in person, suddenly filled Mair with joy – followed by anxiety ... there could be no turning back now.

'John ... Catherine! Look who's come home,' Ethel called out as she opened the kitchen door.

As Mair entered the kitchen, she felt a warm glow overtake her. She had almost forgotten how homely Ethel's kitchen was: its coal fire blazing in the large black-leaded fireplace that also housed the oven and cooking range; John and Ethel's well worn fireside chairs at either side; the wooden table with old chapel pews for seats and the Welsh dresser filled with crockery. It truly was a most welcoming place.

'Well now. There's a sight for sore eyes,' John said, as he rose up from his chair to embrace her, before standing back and giving her the once over. 'Why, look at you. You've turned into quite the young lady.'

'Hello, John. It's so good to see you. Although I'm not sure about the young lady bit. I'm still the same valley girl that I always was.'

'And still as mischievous I expect.' John chuckled to himself.

Mair smiled. John had always been so kind to her – she had always felt that he had a soft spot for her. As her eyes went around the room, she caught her first glimpse of Catherine, slowly emerging from behind Ethel's fireside chair. She looked as pretty as a picture. She was dressed in a white cotton tunic frilled at the yoke, white socks and black button-up shoes, her light-brown curly hair, bobbing up and down every time she moved and clutching a china doll dressed in blue satin. The sight of her daughter took Mair's breath away.

Catherine's piercing blue eyes stared curiously at Mair. Mair couldn't believe how much her daughter had grown – no more the tiny toddler she'd left in Ethel's arms aboard the *Titanic*, but a beautiful little girl – a daughter to be proud of. Mair was overcome with guilt for the way she had abandoned her.

Mair made to say her name, 'Ca—' For some reason the word stuck in her throat and wouldn't come out.

'Catherine, this is your mammy. Come say hello,' Ethel encouraged.

Ignoring her, the child ran back behind Ethel's chair.

Mair looked to Ethel for guidance as to what she should do.

Ethel smiled and gave her a knowing look, 'Don't worry. She'll come round. She reacted much the same when Rhiannon and Gus arrived here last week.'

'They've arrived then? Rhiannon wrote and told me that they hoped to be here in time for Christmas.'

'Yes, they arrived a few weeks ago. They're staying at the Angel Hotel in Cardiff, now there's posh for you.'

Mair smiled. 'How are they both?'

'They're fine. Anyway, you'll be able to see for yourself tomorrow. They're travelling up from Cardiff in the morning. They have an appointment at Bridgend Registry office to finalize their planned wedding. They intend to call up to see us sometime in the afternoon. Rhi will be so pleased to see you.'

'I can't wait to see her. A family wedding – how exciting is that?' Mair saw Catherine's inquisitive eyes peeping from behind the chair.

Ethel winked and shook her head, by way of telling Mair not to rush the child.

'Yes. You couldn't have arrived at a better time. They're to be married on 24 December. Rhiannon will be so happy to have you here with her for her special day.'

'She mentioned in her letter their plans to marry but I didn't expect it to be so soon,' Mair said, her eyes still seeking Catherine's. She edged closer to the chair.

'It appears they both wanted a Christmas wedding. Gus made a joke that he had to do it soon, in case Rhiannon changed her mind. Of course, there's no chance of that. At first Catherine didn't remember them. However, after a few hours in their company she warmed to them both – especially Gus. Mind you, that might have had something to do with that new doll he gave her.'

'Oh, I almost forgot.' Mair reached down into her bag and, taking out a small glass object, placed it on the kitchen table. 'This is for Catherine,' she said.

Ethel picked up the small glass dome and shook it to reveal a snow scene of Trafalgar Square. 'Look, Catherine. Look what your mammy's brought you.'

The child's eyes lit up. But she still didn't venture from behind the chair. Mair couldn't hide her disappointment.

'It's a lovely gift. Mind you, what better gift could there be than to have her mammy home?' Ethel said.

'I don't think she realizes who I am,' Mair whispered. 'I've been away such a long time, she has probably forgotten what I look like.'

'I doubt that very much. Frank made sure she wouldn't forget you. He put your picture – the one taken when John and I were married – above her cot in the bedroom. Your face is the first thing she sees of a morning and the last thing before she goes to sleep at night,' Ethel informed her.

'I didn't know.'

'No, how would you?'

'I'm sorry.'

An awkward silence followed the mention of Frank.

'Why don't you come and sit by the fire? You look frozen to the bone.' John beckoned for her to sit in Ethel's chair.

Mair looked to Ethel.

'Yes, *cariad*. You take my seat. I'll brew us a pot of tea.'

With Catherine still hiding behind Ethel's chair, Mair was eager to sit in it to be close to her daughter. Once in the chair, Mair felt Catherine's body press against it.

It felt so good to at last be this close to her daughter and yet, frustrating not to be able to talk to or touch her. She had to play a waiting game; Catherine had to want to come to her.

'We were just about to have something to eat. As you've travelled all day, you must be famished,' Ethel said.

'Just a little, although before leaving this morning, my landlady, Mrs Turnbull, handed me a packed lunch for the journey.'

'That was very kind of her. I can't wait to hear all your news. It seems you've been away from us for such a long time....' Ethel gave a long sigh. 'Still, you're home now and there'll be lots of time for us to talk.'

It was then Mair realized that Ethel had assumed she had come back for good. Mair wondered how, and more to the point when, she should tell her the truth. Certainly not here and now – that would be far too much of a shock.

'Here we are. It's nothing fancy, only cold meat and some bread and dripping. Mind you, I remember when you and Rhi first came to live with us, how I used to have to hide the bread and dripping from the two of you. It was always your favourite.'

'And it still is. Although I haven't had any since I left Ponty.'

'Good. Come sit by the table and help yourself. Funnily enough, bread and dripping happens to be Catherine's favourite too. I'm sure if you were to place a slice on that plate beside you, she'd come and sit next to you and eat it.'

Mair did as Ethel suggested and, sure enough, almost as soon as the bread and dripping was placed on the plate next to her, Catherine came out from behind the chair and sidled up onto the pew to sit next to Mair.

Ethel winked and nodded at Mair.

As the child, still holding tight to her doll, tucked in to the tasty snack, she gave Mair a shy look. Then, picking up the glass dome, she gave it a shake.

Mair smiled at her.

The child smiled back.

It was a start.

Over supper Ethel explained to her how Sadie and Martha, her stepdaughters, had gone to spend Christmas with John's relatives in Swansea. 'They pleaded to go. Apparently there's so much more to do in the city than here in the valley,' Ethel scoffed. 'Mind you, that was before we found out that Rhi and Gus planned to return to Wales to get married. And the last thing anyone expected was for you to come home too.'

'They'll probably kick themselves when they find out that they've missed a family wedding. And it'll serve them right for choosing to spend Christmas in Swansea, rather than stay here in Ponty with us,' John offered.

'And what about ... Frank,' Mair asked rather sheepishly.

'Rhi and Gus called to see him at his army barracks in Maendy only last week,' Ethel said. 'Sadly, he's unable to get leave from his regiment to come to the wedding or to spend Christmas with us. Although there's every chance he may get a few days off for New Year. So you'll see him then. I do hope you can set things right between you. He misses you so much.'

Mair felt a rush of guilt – she couldn't let Ethel believe she had come home to stay. Ethel would have to be told – but not in front of Catherine. She decided to tell her later, when Catherine was safely in bed and out of earshot.

'Can I hold your new dolly?' Mair asked Catherine.

The child nodded her head and handed Mair the doll.

'What a pretty dolly she is. Why, she's almost as pretty as you.'

Catherine smiled.

As Mair handed the doll back to her daughter, their hands touched. And much to Mair's joy, the child didn't pull her hand away. Instead, she took Mair's hand and, slipping down from the pew, proceeded to lead Mair out of the kitchen and up the stairs to her bedroom.

Mair followed. She had a lump in her throat – her daughter wanted her to follow ... to be with her ... how wonderful was that?

The bedroom – Frank's bedroom – was the same room that she and Rhiannon used to share, when they first returned to Ponty from Cardiff. Frank was so happy to have them both there, he had insisted on giving up his room to sleep in the parlour. Mair looked around the room and saw it hadn't changed much. The same wallpaper, the same iron-framed double bed that she and Rhi used to share. The only difference was the large wooden-framed cot at the bottom of the bed. Her eyes went to above the cot and, on the wall opposite, there it was; the family photograph of Ethel and John's wedding, with Mair stood at the front.

Catherine pointed at her picture, 'You're my mammy,' she said.

'Yes, that's right, *cariad*. I really am your mammy. And I'm so sorry that I stayed away from you for such a long time.'

Mair bent down and, taking her daughter in her arms, picked her up.

Catherine responded by throwing her arms around Mair's neck and hugging her. 'My mammy,' she repeated, pointing to the row of postcards that Mair had sent of the sights of London.

Mair soon realized that as Ethel had said, it was Frank that Mair had to thank for the strategically placed photograph and the postcards that adorned the wall. He had done a generous and so typically unselfish job of keeping Mair's memory alive in Catherine's heart and mind. How could she ever thank him?

'Yes, my love. I sent you all of them. Do you like them?'

The child nodded.

'Then I shall have to send you some more.'

Mair kissed her daughter and the child squealed with delight. Of course, she wouldn't have realized that for Mair to send her more postcards, it meant her having to return to London. One thing was certain, she vowed to somehow make amends to this dear, dear child. From now on she would keep in touch and visit her as often as she could. She couldn't bear to be away from her for so long again.

Later that night, with Catherine tucked up in bed and John at a chapel meeting of elders, Ethel and Mair sat down for a cup of tea and a heart to heart.

'I told you Catherine would come round, didn't I?'

'Yes, thank you. Although, part of me wasn't sure she would.

You've done such a great job with her. She's a delight and a real credit to you.' Mair spoke from the heart.

'A lot of the credit has to go to Frank. He simply adores her ... and she him. It's a wrench when he comes home on leave and then has to return to his regiment. I try to tell him it's his job. It's what he signed up for. But it doesn't seem to help him. At times I think he'd swap the regiment for a job back down the pit, if it meant he could be here with Catherine.'

'I know how much he hated working down the pit. Surely he doesn't mean to leave the army.'

'No. As much as he wants to be here for Catherine, he has to stay with his regiment.'

'He's obviously been a better father than I've been a mother. From the day she was born, he was a natural. Whereas I—'

'You were so very young. And the circumstances – what you went through with your mother and Harry Stone....'

'That's still no excuse for what I did. I abandoned her ... exactly like my mother abandoned me.'

'I was so sorry to hear about your mother's death. And as much as I questioned the wisdom of you running off to London in search of her, I think you were very brave to stick at it. You can be proud of yourself. You achieved what you set out to do. There aren't many who can say that.'

'I knew I couldn't go on with my life without finding out why my own mother had let such a terrible thing happen to me. In the end I had to come to terms with the fact that, while others saw him for the bully, abuser and pimp that he was, she truly loved Harry Stone. My friend, Sister Agnes of the Salvation Army, told me of the many women who fell for such men, only to end up abandoned on the streets of London. Thank goodness for the women's refuge, which helps so many.'

'Tell me, child, after you discovered your mother's sad demise, why didn't you just come home to us?'

'I suppose I was too ashamed to face you, Frank and Catherine. I felt I had failed you all. And when the chance came for me to train as a nurse ...' Mair shrugged her shoulders, 'it seemed the right thing to do, to learn to be useful to others. I know you probably thought of me as selfish, but I really believed that Catherine ... and Frank were better off without me.'

Ethel stood up and walked towards her and, putting an arm around her, gently kissed her cheek. 'I can't begin to think what a dark place your mind must have taken you to over the years. I hope now that you have come to terms with your mother's death, you can put the past behind you and look to the future. Frank helped you once before. Why not let him help you again? With a bit of luck he'll be home for New Years Eve and—'

'Ethel, I'm sorry if I led you to believe that I have come home for good. The truth is I'm due back on duty at the hospital on 28 December, this means I will have to leave Ponty the day before.'

'I see. I thought—'

'I know.'

'Do you realize what this will do to Catherine? I can't believe you could be so cruel, to walk back into her life, only to walk away again.' Ethel shook her head in angry disbelief.

'Ethel, please try to understand. The day I applied to train as a nurse, I knew that it would take four years to become fully qualified. When, after the initial training, I was accepted as a trainee Nightingale Nurse, I felt for the first time in my life that I'd really achieved something. It meant so much to me. But now that you have welcomed me with open arms, as well as John and my lovely Catherine, it would be so easy for me to turn my back on London and stay here. Part of me longs to do that. But if I do, then once again I'll be running away from doing something worthwhile with my life. Don't you see? I have to go back. I need to finish my training and make Catherine proud of me.'

'Oh, dear Mair, we are all proud of you already. But if it's what you really want, I'll do everything I can to help you. You know that Catherine will be safe with us. We love her very much, and I know you do too, but you must understand how confused and hurt she'll be when you leave again.'

Once more Mair felt overwhelmed by Ethel's continued support and understanding. 'Oh, Ethel, thank you. I will do everything I can to make things better this time. I'll have a long talk with Catherine. I know she's only young but, I will tell her that she will always hold a very special place in my heart and how I will think of her every day and write to her every week, sending colourful postcards and small gifts to keep in touch. And I promise to visit all the time.'

'Well, as sad as we'll be to see you go – I can at least rest easy, safe in the knowledge of the love you feel for your daughter.'

'Dearest Ethel. Without you—'

'I know. Hush now. Come on, let's finish our tea. It's almost time for bed. You've had a long and exhausting day. With Frank away, I thought you could sleep in his bedroom … to be close to Catherine.'

'Thank you Ethel, I'd like that. Thank you for everything.'

Mair slowly entered the bedroom. She didn't bother to light a candle. She didn't need to. Tonight there was a full moon shining brightly through the floral curtains that draped the window that lit up the room. Mair walked over to the cot where Catherine lay fast asleep. Overcome with such a deep feeling of love for this beautiful child, she lent over and gently brushed the child's cheek with a soft kiss. Mair's heart ached with longing for her daughter's love, a love she knew only too well she would have to earn. For a long while, Mair, stood watching Catherine sleep. Imprinting the image of her on her own heart, until tiredness overtook her, and she went to bed.

The next morning, with John Jenkins already at work in his butcher's shop, Ethel, Mair and Catherine were left to share breakfast together. Ethel fussed over them and acted as if all was well with her world. She made no mention of their talk the night before.

'I wonder what time Gus and Rhiannon will arrive. She will be so pleased to find you here,' Ethel said. 'Their wedding is going to be such a happy family time. I only wish Frank could be here too.'

At 2.30 that afternoon, Mair and Catherine watched every charabanc that rattled past the house in anticipation of their arrival, holding tight to each other's hand. They were finally rewarded when they saw Gus and Rhiannon waving frantically from inside the passing charabanc. As it came to a stop on Ponty Square, Mair lifted Catherine in her arms and ran to greet them.

'Rhiannon … Gus, it's so good to see you!' Mair cried out.

'Mair … you're here!' Rhiannon laughed with delight.

As the two girls met and were about to embrace, Gus reached out to take Catherine in his arms, 'Come to your Uncle Gus, I don't want you to be caught between these two. When they hug, you could get flattened,' he joked.

Catherine giggled and went to him with an ease which made Mair smile. She and Rhiannon hugged each other and cried with happiness, while Gus and Catherine looked on. After a while, when the two girls finally released each other, he beamed a smile and said, 'Can I take it that you two are best of friends again?'

'You can that. You can't believe how good it feels, for me to have my sister back and for Catherine to finally be reunited with her mother,' Rhiannon laughed.

'I think I can.' As Gus handed Catherine to Mair, he gently caught around her. 'We've missed you, Mair. Welcome back into the fold. Now, instead of us standing here in the cold, do you think we could move this happy reunion to the warmth and comfort of Ethel and John's house … please?'

Chapter Seventeen

GUS AND RHIANNON were married at Bridgend Registry Office on 24 December. It was a quiet family affair with John, Ethel, Mair and Catherine present and a few old friends. Sadly Frank was unable to get leave from his regiment, so couldn't be there. It surprised Mair how disappointed this made her feel. Her return to Ponty had gone much better than she could have expected. Catherine, after her initial reluctance, now seemed genuinely overjoyed and excited to have her there. And, with Ethel and the rest of the family so generous in their forgiveness – welcoming her with open arms – Mair really wanted … no … needed, to put things right between Frank and herself.

After the wedding, much to everyone's surprise, Gus didn't whisk Rhiannon away on honeymoon. Instead, he booked them into the Royal Hotel, in Ponty. 'So that we can spend our first Christmas as a married couple close to friends and family,' Gus announced.

This obviously pleased everyone, especially Rhiannon, who promptly showered Gus with kisses. 'If I had known you were going to make such a wonderful, understanding husband, I'd have married you sooner,' she teased.

'Now you tell me!' Gus joked.

Over the next few days they revelled in each other's company. Gus and John discussed the latest news and the daft business, as they saw it, of women getting the vote, or whether Mr Asquith, the prime minister, was right for the job. Mair, Ethel and Rhiannon simply enjoyed being together again. The three of them doted on Catherine by day, and spent their nights catching up with what had been happening in their lives since they'd been apart.

For Mair it was the best Christmas ever, and one she would treasure for a long while. The days passed so quickly and all too soon it was time for her to return to London. It was the night before she was due to leave Ponty that Mair finished reading Catherine a bedtime story and took the child's hand….

'Catherine, my love, I have something to tell you.'

The child's blue eyes looked up, the weight of her young body warm against Mair's shoulder. Mair had been so dreading this moment. She wrapped an arm tight around her daughter. 'The thing is, in the morning, I have to catch a train and go back to London.'

'Catherine come too?' The child's eyes pleaded with her.

'I'm afraid not, *cariad*. Do you remember the day when I told you about my work as a nurse?'

Catherine nodded.

'Good. You see, Mammy has to go back. But I want you to keep a look out for Jones-the-post. Every day I shall send you a pretty post-card with writing on. Mamgu Ethel will read them out, so you'll know how much I'll be missing you. I love you very much and will visit all the time.'

The child smiled, hugged her mother and, pointing at the postcards on the wall said, 'Pretty cards.'

'Yes, *cariad* … pretty cards.'

Mair reached down to place a tender kiss on her daughter's fore-head. Catherine snuggled beneath the bedcovers and closed her eyes, but she kept a tight hold on her mother's finger. She looked so peaceful and contented and, in a short while was fast asleep.

Mair entered the kitchen. She didn't need to speak. Ethel immediately knew.

'You've told her then?' Ethel said.

Mair nodded, 'Yes.'

'How did she take it?'

'It's hard to tell. I'm not sure she understands … oh, Ethel. I feel awful to be leaving her again.'

'My dear, girl, you are growing into a fine young woman and you have to do what you feel is right. Only time will tell if it has a lasting effect on the child. Children can be so resilient. In a couple of days Frank will be home on leave. I'm sure she'll buck up when she sees him, she always does. One things for certain, I know he'll be sorry to have missed your visit.'

'Perhaps it was for the best—'

'Mair, love,' Ethel interrupted, 'would it be all right if I gave him your London address, so that he may make contact?'

'After the way I've treated him, do you really think he'd want to?'

'It's not for me to say. At least having your address will give him the opportunity … should he choose to take it.'

Chapter Eighteen

MAIR RETURNED TO London. Everyone at Grange House was pleased to have her back. To celebrate her return Mrs Turnbull arranged a special dinner and invited Sister Agnes.

Her friends all wanted to hear about her trip to Wales. 'I bet your family was so pleased to see you,' Kitty gushed. 'Whenever I go home, they always want to feed me up.'

Mair felt slightly awkward. She had never talked much about those dear to her back in Ponty and while she regarded Ethel and John, Gus and Rhiannon, as family, in truth only Catherine was of her blood. A fact she had managed to keep a secret from everyone in London.

'Yes. I know what you mean,' she laughed, skating over the 'family' thing. 'One of the highlights of my visit was to see my sister and Gus tie the knot. They travelled all the way from America to be married in Wales.'

'How very exciting, it must have been quite a reunion,' Sister Agnes offered.

Mair so wanted to tell them all about Catherine, and how she had been the main highlight of her visit to Ponty. She wondered how they would react if they were to find out that, after all this time, the girl they thought to be an innocent, had a daughter out of wedlock. If the truth were to come out, Mair honestly believed that Mrs Turnbull, with her strict rules on how her guests should behave, would ask her to leave Grange House. Mair decided her secret was best kept to herself.

But she spent much of her time thinking about her daughter. Of course Catherine had always been in her heart, in her thoughts and dreams – even more so since her recent trip to Wales. How many nights did she dream she was *cutching* – cuddling Catherine – her lips brushing her daughter's hair, only to wake to find herself alone in her bed. Over the years she had trained herself to put the memory of the love she and Frank once shared to the back of her mind ... until now, that is. Now she so wanted to make amends ... to make things right between them. If only he would write to her.

Mair's life fell into a routine, which revolved around her duties at St Thomas's and her work as a Red Cross volunteer. The matron at the hospital had even passed comment on how well she was doing. 'I must say, the standard of your work is excellent. Keep this up and I'm sure you will achieve great things.'

Mair felt encouraged by this – a step closer to making Catherine proud of her. As promised, Mair sent her daughter daily postcards, and occasionally Ethel would write back to give her news from home. So far, there had been no news from Frank. Mair tried to tell herself it was for the best. What was the point of raking over old coals? He had probably moved on with his life – and perhaps it was time for her to do the same.

It was an early spring morning and Mair, having worked the night shift, proceeded to walk back to Grange House. Passers-by all seemed to have a spring in their step – no doubt pleased to have left the bleakness of an exceptionally hard winter behind them.

She entered Grange House and was greeted by Violet, the parlour maid, 'Good morning, miss,' she said. 'A letter arrived for you this morning. I pushed it under your bedroom door.'

'Thank you, Violet,' Mair said, and quickly crossed the hall. She ran up the stairs, her heart thumping in her chest.... could this be the letter she had been waiting for?

She opened the door of her bedroom to find the letter lying on the floor directly in front of her. She was almost too afraid to pick it up, not wanting to be disappointed. However, she need not have worried. As she bent down to pick it up, she immediately recognized Frank's neat handwriting. She hastily opened it and, sitting on the bed, proceeded to read it.

Dear Mair

I'm sorry for the delay in writing to you. This is the first opportunity I've had since my visit to Ponty for New Year. On my return, my regiment was sent on a six-week exercise up on Brecon Beacons. We were all billeted in tents – you can't imagine how cold it was. I never thought I'd be glad to get back to Maendy Barracks.

I was surprised to hear of your return to Ponty for Christmas and, as it turned out, for Gus and Rhi's wedding. I so wish I could have been there. It would have been wonderful to see you again. My mother couldn't wait to tell me how well you looked and how close you and Catherine became, in the short time you were there. I'm glad. She is so like you. Every time I look at her I feel my heart miss a beat, to think of what might have been.

I was sorry to hear of your mother's sad end. I feel so very proud of you. After all you have been through, I think training to become a nurse is such a worthwhile thing to do. I just hope that, when you qualify, you'll come back to Wales and find employment in a hospital close to the family.

I'm sure you'll be glad to hear that when I left Catherine, she was in good spirits and running rings around her Mamgu Ethel and John.

Mair, it would be so nice to hear from you sometime. However, if you don't write I will understand. It crossed my mind that my mother might have put pressure on you to let me have your address. I do hope not

Love, Frank

Mair read the letter over and over again. She felt deeply moved by the tone of his writing. Once again, just like Ethel and John, there had been no reproach. The letter was warm and generous and it proved to her something she had always known – what a loving and caring man he was. She shook her head. What a fool she had been. She had been so easily taken in by Andrew Baxter, desperate to find love … when all the while, true love had been hers for the taking. Was it too late? Had she wasted too much time? Well there was only one way to find out. She sat up in bed, took a writing pad and pen from the bedside table and began to write.

Dear Frank

It was so good to hear from you. And no, your mother didn't need to twist my arm. I wanted you to have my address. Although, after the way I've treated you, I wasn't sure you'd want to get in touch. I'm so glad you did.

I missed you at Christmas. When I returned to Ponty, I couldn't believe the welcome Ethel and John gave me – nothing like the bitter reproach I expected. It felt wonderful to be reunited with Catherine. She is such a joy and a credit to you and the family. When I think of the love you give her, it makes my heart ache. In the last twelve months I have missed so much of her growing up. I know I have no one to blame but myself. I want to try to make it up to her. Every day I send her a post-card, telling her how much I miss and love her and how I hope to see her soon.

The thing is, I only get one day off a week – a day I usually spend helping out as a volunteer for the Red Cross. The hospital matron does not like us taking time off. She's really nice, but very strict. In order to qualify for compassionate leave, I might have to resort to telling a little white lie ... maybe a family problem in Wales? We'll see.

Keep well,

Mair

Chapter Nineteen

April 1913

'GOOD MORNING, MRS Jenkins, My name's Selwyn Price – I'm a reporter with the *South Wales Echo*,' the lad in a raincoat announced.

'Well now, there's posh. A reporter you say? And what interest could I possibly be to the *South Wales Echo*?'

'Mrs Jenkins, I believe that you, along with your daughter-in-law and granddaughter, were survivors of the *Titanic* tragedy.'

'Yes, that's correct.'

'Are you aware that this coming weekend will be the first anniversary of that tragedy?'

Ethel pulled her shawl around her shoulders, 'N-no,' she lied, clarifying it with, 'It's not a date I care to remember.'

'My editor thought that, as your granddaughter was one of the youngest survivors, it would make a wonderful human interest story for our readers. I'm sure everyone would like to know how you have all fared during the past year. I promise I'll not keep you long.'

'Young man, you'll not be keeping me at all. You see, while there's not a day goes by when I don't thank God for saving me and mine, I have no wish to be reminded of that dreadful night. To me, anniversaries are usually a cause for celebration, and although we count ourselves lucky to be alive, we can never forget the many others that perished.'

'Can I at least quote you on that?' he urged.

'Yes, if you want.' Ethel fidgeted with her shawl. She didn't feel at all comfortable with this.

'A recent photograph of the three of you would be—'

'There will be no photograph!' Ethel snapped.

'Well, if *you* won't talk to me, what about your daughter-in-law?' the young lad persisted as he checked his note book. 'Her name is Mair … Mair Parsons, is that right?'

Ethel held her breath. If he knew Mair's real surname, then he had probably guessed that Mair and Frank were not married. Although he obviously wasn't aware that Mair was now living and working in London – or of her brief return to Ponty at Christmas. Ethel didn't want him raking over old coals or asking any awkward questions, especially when she didn't have the answers.

'You leave Mair be! She's been through enough…. I'll not have her being troubled, do … you … hear?' Ethel's voice quivered.

The reporter seemed taken aback.

'I'm sorry. I really didn't mean to upset you. Look, I'll make a note, for future reference, that Mair Parsons is strictly off limits. Is that all right?'

Ethel composed herself. 'Thank you. Now, if it's all the same to you. I'll bid you good day.' Ethel quickly closed the door.

A week later in London, 'THE ANNIVERSARY OF THE SINKING OF THE TITANIC' appeared in every newspaper. It seemed that everywhere Mair went people were talking about it. As much as she tried to avoid the subject, there was no hiding place. It brought to mind the dreadful images of the pain and suffering of those who drowned and of her own mother laughing at her and calling her names. All of which had haunted her dreams for such a long time. Thankfully, she was now free of them. She hoped and prayed they would never return.

Chapter Twenty

SPRING TURNED TO summer and at last Mair, who had to work extra shifts, had managed to secure a weekend off. She immediately booked her train ticket to Wales and in her regular postcard to Catherine, made sure to mention her planned visit.

It was late afternoon on 4 June. With only ten days to wait before her trip to Wales, Mair, with Kitty at her side, finished their shift at the hospital, and headed into London city centre to buy a new summer outfit and a present for Catherine. To save time they took a motorized hansom cab. The cab dropped them off at Regent Street. As soon as they stepped onto the pavement, they heard the loud cry of the newspaper seller.

'Read all about it! Suffragette activist trampled by King's horse at Epsom races! Read all about it!'

Mair and Kitty stopped to read the headlines. *Emily Wilding Davidson, a militant women's suffrage activist, threw herself under the King George V's horse at the Epsom Derby, earlier today. She suffered terrible injuries and was taken by ambulance to a local hospital.*

'Oh, Kitty, I wonder what possessed her to do such a thing. What did she think it would achieve?' Mair asked.

'I don't know. Perhaps she set out to show how far the suffragette movement will go to secure women's rights. I think to risk your life, for any cause, is taking things a step too far.'

Mair nodded her agreement. 'I wonder if Mrs Turnbull has heard the news. As a member of the movement she might even know her.'

'Do you think we should head back to Grange House and tell her?' Kitty asked.

'I must say, thinking of that poor woman being trampled by a race horse is terrible. I don't have the heart for shopping. I'll quickly find a gift for Catherine and then, if it's all right with you, we'll head back.'

In a toy shop called Noah's Ark, Mair purchased a brown teddy bear – small enough to carry in her carpetbag. She hoped Catherine would like it.

They arrived back at Grange House to find Mrs Turnbull seated in the living room with Sister Agnes. They had already heard the news and, as they expected, Mrs Turnbull was very upset.

'Do you know her well? Is she a close friend?' Mair asked.

'No. But I do know *of* her. She is well known as an extremist. While I might not agree with some of her methods, I greatly admire her and pray to God her injuries are not life-threatening.'

Mrs Turnbull's prayers went unanswered. Four days later the newspapers reported that Emily Davidson had died from her injuries.

Ten days later Mair, having abandoned her shopping trip to buy a new summer outfit, decided to wear her brown skirt, cream striped blouse with a brooch pinned at the neck and her straw hat trimmed with dried flowers. Across her carpetbag she carried her brown jacket. As she waited at Waterloo Station for her train to Paddington and then on to Cardiff, she heard a familiar voice.

'Well, hello again, Miss. I must say, you're becoming quite the regular traveller.' Albert Stubbs flashed a smile and doffed his cap.

'Hello, Albert. How nice to see you again. I hardly think I qualify as a regular. My last trip was just before Christmas. I wish I could get home more often. My work at St Thomas's Hospital makes it difficult for me to get time off.'

'With all that trouble in Europe at the moment, there's talk of Britain going to war. And if that happens, our boys will be off to fight for King and country. They'll need nurses to care for injured servicemen. That's when your training will prove its worth.'

Mair had read about the troubles abroad. 'Do you think it will come to that?'

'I hope not. But as a volunteer in the London division of the TF – Territorial Force – if there is a war, I'd want to go.'

'And leave your family behind?'

'The only family I've got is my ageing mother. Mind you, there is a girl I'm rather sweet on – nothing serious you understand.' He gave a cheeky grin, 'She loves a man in uniform. She likes me dressed as a station guard. Just think how impressed she'll be to see me dressed as a soldier! No doubt I'd have women falling at my feet.' He laughed.

Mair chuckled. 'I don't think that qualifies as a reason to enlist.'

'I'm sure you're right. But you must admit it's an added benefit.... Here's your train, Miss.'

Mair boarded the train. Albert had certainly given her something to think about. On such a beautiful summer day, as she watched the ever-changing landscape flash by, war was such an unthinkable prospect. She decided to put such depressing thoughts from her mind. She did not want anything to spoil her reunion with Catherine.

It was late afternoon when Mair arrived in Ponty. The sky was blue and the sun was shining high above Carn Mountain. Even the coal-tips of slack – sub-standard coal, normally a blot on the landscape – glistened in the sunshine. The valley looked so welcoming and for once all seemed well with her world. As Mair stepped from the chara-banc, it felt so good to be home. This time she had no feeling of dread as to how she would be received, she knew she would be welcomed with open arms. As she walked toward the Jenkins' house she had a definite spring in her step.

When she lifted the knocker, the door suddenly opened … and, much to her surprise, there stood Frank Lewis. He hadn't changed much, a little more muscular perhaps, the rough material of his khaki uniform sitting well on his broad shoulders. She thought how hand-some he looked.

She dropped her carpetbag to the floor. 'Frank! What on earth are you doing here?' she cried, her voice unable to hide her delight.

'Well now, there's a welcome I didn't expect.'

'I-I didn't mean it's not a nice surprise. It's just, well, you were the last person I expected to see.'

He beamed a smile and took her hand. His hand felt rough yet at the same time … gentle.

'As soon as Mam wrote and told me of your planned visit, I did everything I could to wangle a twenty-four-hour pass. It's not long. But I just had to see you.' Frank gave her a long look, then, pulling her to him, he place a kiss full on her lips.

Mair didn't pull away. It felt too good.

Frank kissed her harder and more passionately and she responded with all the emotion she had been holding back for so long. The kiss seamed to go on forever, only stopping when they both ran out of breath.

Their eyes met and Frank flashed a smile. 'Now, that was well worth a twelve month wait,' he said.

'Yes, I suppose it has been over a year since ... Southampton.'

'Far too long, if you ask me. But that was then. This is now.' He caught around her. 'It's so good to have you back,' he whispered. 'Come on, John, Ethel and Catherine are in the kitchen. John and Ethel are expecting you. We thought it best not to tell Catherine. We didn't want her to be disappointed, if something happened and you couldn't make it.'

'Wild horses couldn't have stopped me,' Mair said.

Taking her hand he led her down the hall and into the kitchen to find John sitting in his chair and Ethel and Catherine at the table. They looked up.

On seeing Mair, Catherine squealed with delight. 'Mammy, Mammy!' She ran to Mair's side.

Mair blinked back the tears of happiness that threatened to spill over. She was home. Frank appeared to hold no grudge against her, and her daughter was obviously pleased to see her. She felt the luckiest woman on earth. Mair reached down and, taking the teddy bear from her carpetbag, handed it to Catherine. The child instantly clutched it to her. 'My lovely teddy,' she almost purred with delight. Mair's arms went around her daughter and, picking her up, she hugged her tightly. Frank responded by throwing his arms around the two of them.

'What a great family photograph that would make,' John said.

'You won't believe the times I've prayed to see the three of you together again. At last my prayers have been answered,' Ethel sobbed, and taking a handkerchief from her apron pocket, loudly blew her nose. 'Now look what you've made me do. The last thing I wanted was to cry.'

Ethel had prepared a welcome home meal of meat and potato pie, fresh vegetables and gravy, followed by a creamy rice pudding with blueberry jam. It was delicious. After the meal they stayed at the table reminiscing about old times. There was no talk of London, the threat of war or any long-term plans. It reminded Mair of how they used to spend their evenings ... before she and Ethel had left Ponty and headed for New York.

When it was time for Catherine to go to bed, she insisted that Mair took her – the child eager to show her mother all of the postcards sent from London, now filling one wall. Mair was overcome with so much love for the child, and so warmed by her daughter's genuine pleasure at having her there. Catherine handed her a book.

'Mammy, read me?' Catherine asked, her blue eyes staring hopefully into Mair's.

'Yes, my love. Of course I will.'

Catherine settled down in her cot, her new brown teddy bear was placed next to her on her pillow. Mair read and, long before she finished the story, she looked down to see the child was fast asleep, her face flushed with happiness. Mair leaned over and kissed her daughter, inhaling the sweet scent of her.

She entered the kitchen to rejoin Ethel, John and Frank and made to sit with Frank at the kitchen table.

'There's no need for you to sit there. While you were upstairs with Catherine, John went to light the fire in the parlour. As we seldom use the room, we thought it might need an airing. So why not take yourselves off in there and spend some time alone. I promise you'll not be disturbed.'

'Thanks, Mam,' Frank said, already taking Mair's hand and heading for the door. 'I've told Mair that she can sleep in the bedroom with Catherine. I'm happy to sleep on the couch in the parlour.'

'That's what I was thinking too,' Ethel agreed. 'You'll find a blanket and pillow in the cupboard next to the fireplace.'

'It gladdens my heart to see you two back together,' John said, followed by, 'God bless you both.'

'Amen to that,' Ethel said.

In the parlour they settled themselves on the sofa in front of the fireplace. Frank put his arm around Mair's shoulder. 'So, was John right, are we back together again?'

'Is that what you truly want? I really wouldn't blame you if you told me you'd found someone else ... someone more worthy....'

'Don't be daft. Ever since that day when you left me in

Southampton, I seem to have been wandering in a wilderness of unhappiness and, as I thought, false hope. Mair, the truth is, I still love you with all my heart and that's never going to change.' He stared lovingly into her eyes.

'Oh, Frank, I've been such a fool. If only … you won't believe how many times over the past year I've thought about coming back.'

'What? Back to me, or Catherine, or just to Ponty?'

'I can't answer that.'

'Can't or won't?'

'Frank. I walked away from you and Catherine. How can you ever forgive me?' Mair argued.

'As far as I'm concerned, there's nothing to forgive. You had your reasons. And as misguided as I felt they were at the time, you had to do what you truly believed right at the time. And just think, if you hadn't gone to London, you might never have found out what happened to your mother…. Mair, love, I've been meaning to ask you, did you ever catch up with Harry Stone?'

'Oh yes, I did get to see him. And what a sorry excuse for a man he turned out to be – when I think of the years I wasted—'

'You've been through a lot. And I truly believe that in surviving the *Titanic* tragedy, it affected your way of thinking.'

'I'm not sure I can blame the *Titanic* for all of my actions. Yes, it made me realize how precious life is … and the recurring nightmares did prompt me to seek out my mother … but that done, I should have returned to Ponty. Instead I … you don't know how close I came to—' Mair felt warm tears run down her cheeks.

Frank handed her a handkerchief. 'Why are you crying? I don't understand … you came close to what? Please tell me. Mair, love, if we're to have a chance of a future together you need to trust me. Whatever it is, I'm sure we can work it out.'

As she wiped away the tears, she nodded her agreement. 'I know. I so want you … *need* you to know the truth….'

For the next hour Mair poured her heart out to Frank. She told him everything that had happened to her since the morning she crept from the hotel room, leaving him in Southampton, and Catherine in Ponty. She hid nothing telling him all about Andrew Baxter and of the way she believed they truly felt for one another.

'So you see, Frank. I came so close to giving myself to him—'

'But you didn't,' Frank interrupted. 'The thought of betraying *me* stopped you. And, while it hurts like crazy to think of you in another man's arms … if the end result was you thinking of me … then I can live with it. What you have experienced since you've been away has helped mould you into the woman you now are. The woman I so love … please say you feel the same way.'

Mair flung her arms around him. 'Yes. Yes, I do. I love you so much it hurts,' she cried, as she showered his face with kisses.

Frank pulled her close and kissed her passionately. They spent the night wrapped in each other's arms, both wanting so much more, yet both knowing this was neither the time nor the place.

Chapter Twenty-One

STORM CLOUDS GATHERED over Europe. It all began with the assassination on 28 June 1914 of the Archduke Franz Ferdinand, heir to the Austro-Hungary throne. On 28 July the conflict opened with the Austro-Hungarian invasion of Serbia, followed by the German invasion of Belgium and France and a Russian attack against Germany.

Prime Minister Asquith and those of His Majesty's Government assured the country that they were keeping a close eye on events as they unfolded. An ultimatum for Germany to withdraw from Belgium was being considered. The British people, surrounded by gloom and fear, held their breath.

Until now, no British troops were involved. Frank, along with a platoon of some sixty men from his regiment, drilled up and down the Maendy Barracks parade ground. He guessed something was on the cards. As used to parade-bashing as he was, today the intensity of the training had increased tenfold; the men were ordered to wear their khaki battle dress and to carry a full kitbag. They were made to march for longer and harder than they had ever done before.

Over the last few weeks the newspapers had been full of the inevitability of Britain being at war with Germany. While the majority of men in his regiment relished the chance to put their training into practice, Frank felt differently. Although he was more than willing to fight for King and country the thought of being sent to fight overseas and again separated from Mair for God knows how long, filled him with dread. Against all odds they were together again. He so wanted to be close to her ... to woo her ... to always share his life with her. A declaration of war with Germany would make this impossible. If his regiment was, in fact, sent overseas, he wondered if her love would sustain yet another separation. Having just found her, he couldn't bare the thought of losing her again.

On the evening of Tuesday 4 August 1914, Mair felt herself being pushed along, almost lifted off her feet, by the crowds running down the Mall, headed for Buckingham Palace.

'Kitty, try to stay close. It wouldn't do for us to become separated,' Mair urged.

The girls had read in the newspapers how Prime Minister Asquith had given Germany an ultimatum, 'to respect Belgium's neutrality'. They had until eight o'clock that night to comply. Should they choose not to, then Britain would have no other option than to declare war on Germany.

Mair and Kitty had ventured into the city, despite knowing that Mrs Turnbull would think it too dangerous. They followed the crowds heading for Buckingham Palace

'Come on, Mair. This is history in the making, and we don't want to miss it,' Kitty enthused.

At around eight o'clock, when they, along with the crowds, eventually came to a stop outside Buckingham Palace, Mair looked up and saw the King and Queen, as well as the Prince of Wales and Princess Mary, came out onto the balcony, closely followed by Mr Herbert Asquith, Mr Lloyd George and Mr Winston Churchill, all waving to the noisy crowds of loyal subjects below.

There was a large police presence but, on seeing the orderliness of the crowd, they made no attempt to force people back. However, they did pass word among the crowd that the King was holding a very important meeting in the palace and their silence would be appreciated. And apart from a few spasmodic renditions of the national anthem, *God Save the King* , there was a respectful silence.

At 11 p.m. the King and Queen and the Prince of Wales made a further appearance on the balcony and the crowds once more sang the national anthem, following this with hearty clapping and cheering and caps thrown in the air. There was a real party atmosphere. And only after the departure of the royal party, did the crowds begin to disperse, many still shouting and waving flags.

Mair and Kitty were exhausted but exhilarated by the events of the day and headed for Westminster Bridge and across the Thames to Grange House. Later that night, as she lay in her bed, Mair reflected on what Britain going to war would mean to those whom she held dear.

In anticipation of that day's announcement *The Times* and many other newspapers had appealed for able-bodied men over the age of eighteen to join the army.

Her thoughts went to Frank. She remembered how, after the 1909 accident down the pit in Ponty – the one that took her dear father's life and fifteen other men as well – Frank was one of the lucky few to survive and made the decision to join the army to escape ever having to work below ground again. Now, the thought of his regiment being sent to the front, to fight for King and country, filled her with horror. She tried not to imagine him wounded ... or dead, yet in her heart she knew this would be the fate of some, never to see their homeland again.

Since their reunion in Wales, when they had both declared their love for each other, she had been thinking long and hard about her future ... a future spent with Frank and Catherine as a family. She had been given a second chance and was determined to grab it with both hands. To achieve this, Mair had made up her mind to approach the matron and make inquiries as to the possibility of completing her nurses training in a hospital in Wales. Now, with war imminent, she knew this was out of the question. Her duties lay at St Thomas's. And Frank's with his regiment. No doubt at sometime in the near future, along with many other regiments around the country, he would be sent overseas to fight. She prayed that Frank's wouldn't be one of the first to go. Either way it seemed as if they were destined to spend their lives apart. She prayed with all her heart that their love could sustain the separation and asked God to keep him safe.

The next morning Mair read the announcement in the *Daily Mirror*:

4 August, 12.13 a.m.: Reuters Agency is informed that following the expiration of the ultimatum at 11.00 p.m. London time (12.00 a.m. Berlin time) His Majesty's Government of Great Britain has declared to the German Government that a state of war exists between Great Britain and Germany as from 11 p.m. on 4 August.

It was now official.

Chapter Twenty-Two

October 1914

SIX WEEKS AFTER the declaration of war with Germany, the orders came for Frank's regiment to leave for Ypres, a small Flemish market town just over the border from France. Each soldier was given the option of a twenty-four-hour pass to say goodbye to his loved ones. Frank instantly wrote a letter to his mother and the family to tell them of his imminent departure to the front. He thanked Ethel for the way she looked after everyone, especially Catherine. He sent his love and hoped they would all understand his decision to use his precious pass to seek out Mair in London.

At 12.15 the very next day, Frank's train arrived at Paddington Station. To save time, he decided to take a motor cab.

'Where to, mate?' the cabbie asked.

'St Thomas's Hospital, please,' Frank answered, crossing his fingers that Mair would be on duty. Although armed with the address of Grange House, he was loath to go directly there. Mair had told him how strict her landlady was about gentlemen callers, and as a complete stranger, there would be no way he could be alone with her.

It was a dreary day, made worse by the surrounding thick black fog. As the taxicab wove its way through the streets of London, he thought of Mair venturing across this vast city in search of Nellie and Harry Stone. He hoped Mair could now put all of her bad memories behind her. It was time for her to be happy and enjoy the rest of her life … hopefully with him and Catherine.

The taxicab came to a stop. 'Here we are, mate.'

'Thank you,' Frank said. He exited the cab and paid the driver.

Frank straightened his uniform before heading up the steps to the entrance of the imposing building that was St Thomas's Hospital. He entered the reception area and headed straight for the inquiry desk.

'Good afternoon. I wonder can you help me,' he said politely.

'I can try,' a surly looking woman replied.

Frank thought she looked to be in her late forties, and not at all happy in her work.

'I'm looking for a nurse—'

'This place is full of nurses – a name might help,' the woman quipped.

'Her name is Nurse Mair Parsons, and she's a trainee auxiliary,' Frank offered.

'Any idea of the name of the ward she works on?'

'No. But I do know it's a men's surgical ward.'

The receptionist proceeded to check a long list. After a while she looked up and said, 'Well, you're in luck. There's a Nurse Mair Parsons working on Nightingale Ward.'

'Thank you. Directions would help,' Frank said, a note of sarcasm in his voice.

The woman gave a heavy sigh. 'Straight down the hall, first left, then first right. Mind you, if Nurse Parsons is on duty, I doubt if you'll get to speak to her.'

'You let me worry about that,' Frank said, as he turned and walked away, his stomach doing somersaults. He couldn't believe how nervous he felt … he hoped she would be there.

As he approached the entrance doors to Nightingale Ward, the doors opened to reveal two orderlies pushing a patient on a stretcher. Behind them holding the door open was … Mair. As the stretcher cleared the doors, Mair followed it out closing the doors gently behind her. Then she saw him.

'Frank! What are you doing here? Is there something wrong? Is it Catherine?'

'No. The last I heard Catherine and the family are fine. I'm here because … I just needed to see you,' he gushed.

'I can't believe that you're really here. Look, you stay where you are. I have to go back onto the ward to ask my friend Kitty to cover for me.' With that she turned and left him standing alone.

It felt an age before she returned but before long she rushed towards him and took his hands in hers. 'Oh Frank, it's so good to see you.'

'My love. I had to come in person to tell you that our orders have come through. My regiment has been called to the front and I just couldn't leave without seeing you.'

'Oh, Frank, no! I hoped the fighting would all be over before your regiment was called upon. How soon do you go?'

'We sail from Cardiff at 6 p.m. tomorrow.'

'That soon?'

'Yes, I'm afraid so.' But he changed the subject quickly and smiled at her. 'If I'd realized how great you look in your nurse's uniform, I'd have come sooner. I bet you have to fight off all your male patients.'

She laughed. 'I have to admit that a few do try it on. Thankfully Matron has strict rules about us nurses fraternizing with the patients.'

'I'm glad to hear it,' Frank smiled.

'Anyway you don't look too bad yourself in uniform. I bet you have ladies falling at your feet,' Mair teased.

'All the time,' Frank joked.

For a while they stood in silence gazing longingly at each other, unable to touch.

'Christ. This is unbearable, standing here making idle chit chat, when all I want to do is take you in my arms,' Frank said, leaning towards her and whispering in her ear.

'I feel exactly the same … but I should be getting back. I don't want to get Kitty into trouble.'

'Your Kitty sounds like a really good friend.'

'She is. She's one of the best. We lodge together at Grange House.'

'I hope to meet her one day, only not today. Today I only want to be with you. What time do you finish?'

'My shift finishes at four o'clock.'

'Great. So I've got plenty of time to find myself overnight accommodation, and whatever happens, I'll be back here waiting for you dead on four. Perhaps we can go for tea.'

Mair's heart missed a beat. 'I can't wait,' she said. Every part of her so wanted to be in his arms – the wait would be unbearable.

She was about to make her way back to the ward when she saw her friend, walking through the swing doors toward her.

'Kitty, is everything all right?' Mair asked.

'I'm not sure. Matron has asked to see us both in her office.'

'Do you think we might be in trouble?' Mair asked.

'We'll soon find out. She wants to see us straight away. Anyway, who's the good-looking soldier boy?' Kitty asked, as they walked towards the matron's office.

'He's an old friend from Wales.' Mair blushed.

'Well, you've certainly kept him a secret, you dark horse, you. I thought you promised there'd be no secrets between us.'

'You've heard me mention Frank Lewis, a friend of the family? Anyway, he's coming back to meet me at four to take me for tea.'

'You lucky thing, and come to mention it, his name does ring a bell. But you never said how good-looking he was.'

'Kitty, I was wondering … if I happen to be a little late back this evening, would you cover for me with Mrs Turnbull?'

'Of course I will. In fact, if you were of a mind to stay out all night, I'll just tell her that you've been asked to work an extra shift.'

Mair blushed. 'I'm sure that won't be necessary.'

'You don't know. The way your "old friend" was looking at you, I'd say he had a lot more than tea on his mind!'

Mair's heart gave a flutter. Could it be true? And if so, how would she react?

The girls knocked on the door of Matron's office.

'Come in,' she called.

Mair and Kitty entered. Matron was sitting upright at her neatly organized desk. It was from this office that she controlled the running of the hospital. She did it with what appeared to be such ease but no one was ever in doubt as to who was in charge.

'Good afternoon, ladies. Please take a seat.' The matron indicated to the two seats immediately in front of her desk.

The girls did as she asked.

'Ladies, no doubt you have heard the speculation among the hospital staff, concerning the new wing being added here at St Thomas's. Well the time has come for me to put the record straight. With the impending war against Germany, the purpose of the new wing is to accommodate any injured servicemen. It is imperative we prepare for the worst and hope for the best,' the matron announced. She stood up from her chair and, walking to the window, picked up a small watering can and proceeded to water the plant box on the window ledge, before making her way back to her seat.

Mair and Kitty looked at each other, both still puzzled as to why the matron had asked to see them. It was true that everyone in the hospital was talking about the new wing. While some were sure it was to be a new children's ward, others felt the timing meant it had to be linked to the war. The latter would now be proved right.

'You are probably asking yourselves what this has to do with you,' the matron said, as she settled herself back in her chair. 'To staff this new wing I have put together a highly trained team of nurses, all with considerable experience in dealing with serious injuries. I am pleased to tell you that you have both been chosen to assist this elite team.'

Mair and Kitty gasped in unison.

'Over the past months I have watched you both – you work well together. And while you, Nurse Slater, are more than qualified to take the position, I do believe that, as a second-year trainee, you, Nurse Parsons, will be up to the job in hand. I feel assured that your previous work on men's surgical will stand you in good stead.' She stood up and gave a firm smile. 'While I fully understand what a huge undertaking this is for you both, I have every confidence in you. You may go now.'

'Thank you, Matron. I promise, we'll not let you down,' Mair said, getting up from her chair.

Kitty followed her. 'Yes, thank you, Matron,' she said, her eyes bright with excitement.

For the remainder of the day Mair went about her duties in a daze. She still couldn't believe she, Mair Parsons, had been chosen as part of an 'elite' nursing team. This day was certainly turning into one to be remembered. Against all odds, her dear Frank was here in London. She hated to think of him leaving for France tomorrow evening, as today might be the last time they meet for a long time … maybe even— She stopped herself abruptly. She couldn't bear to think the unthinkable. At least they had today. She vowed to make the most of the precious time they had together. It was then she made her decision.

*

At precisely four o'clock, Mair finished her duties and picked up her navy-blue cape from the cloakroom, prepared to leave.

As promised Frank was waiting in the lobby outside the ward. He smiled and his smile warmed her heart. He took her hand. 'Let's go. I don't want to waste another minute of the short time we have together.'

Outside, Frank hailed a passing motor cab, and asked the driver to take them to the Kardomah Café on the Strand. During the journey Frank held her close. It felt so good to be in his arms. The busy streets in the City of London bustled with traffic, horse-drawn hansom cabs vying for position with motorized vehicles and cyclists. It was a frenzy made worse by the low lying fog and she was glad when they had reached their destination.

The café was packed. They just managed to get a table for two at the back of the room. As Mair looked around she couldn't help but notice the number of servicemen, army, air force and navy personnel, each in the company of a woman. Mair wondered if they too had arranged to meet with their mothers, sisters, wives or lovers, in order to say … farewell – 'goodbye' sounded much too final a word. The strange thing was that no one appeared sad – quite the opposite. Everyone seemed in good spirits. All smiling and laughing as if, like Frank had said earlier, they were determined to enjoy every last minute together.

Frank ordered a pot of tea for two and a cake stand full of assorted fancy cakes.

Mair made to lift the teapot. 'Shall I be mother?' she asked.

'I'd rather you didn't. I'd much prefer you be you. I'm pleased to say, the feelings I have for you …' he nodded his head and gave a wicked grin, 'are definitely not the ones a son should feel for his mother.'

'Behave yourself, Frank Lewis. Remember where we are.' Mair struggled to suppress a giggle.

'I'll try. It's just that I'm finding it hard to be this close to you, and yet not able to touch you – it's driving me mad.'

They gazed at each other across the table, both understanding each other's needs. Mair tried to eat one of the cakes but found she couldn't swallow, she was too nervous … too excited … all the while his eyes stared longingly into hers.

'Frank,' she whispered, 'please, take me away from here. Take me somewhere where we can be alone.'

'Are you sure?' Frank asked, wrapping his hand around hers.

'Yes. I'm sure,' she whispered.

Frank instantly called the waitress and paid the bill. Mair noticed how his hands shook and wondered if he was as nervous as she was. She had more or less made the decision to give herself to him back at the hospital, because their time together was so precious. They loved each other and he was going to war. If the unthinkable happened ... at least she would have the memory of his lovemaking to cling to.

They took a cab to Sussex Gardens, a terraced quadrangle of small Victorian hotels close to Paddington Station.

'I decided to book a hotel here because of its proximity to the railway station. It means I won't have far to go for my train in the morning,' Frank said as he took her hand and led her through the foyer and past the reception area to the lift. Mair noticed a middle-aged man standing behind the counter at reception. Was it her imagination or had he raised an eyebrow at the sight of a regular soldier and a nurse heading for the bedrooms. She gave him a shy smile. He smiled back giving her a knowing wink.

Although her knees felt like jelly and her pulse was racing, she let herself be led by Frank to the lift, eager to be alone with him. Once in the bedroom Frank hastily removed his cap and khaki jacket. Mair followed suit, unbuttoning her cape and placing it on a small chair close to the door. She raised her hand to remove her starched head-dress, only her hands were shaking so much she struggled to remove the hairpins holding it in place.

'Here, let me help you,' Frank said, moving closer to her, and raising his hands to her head to gently remove her hairpins. He was standing so close she could smell his musk-perfumed shaving soap and hair oil, his muscular body almost touching hers.

When he had successfully removed her headdress, Frank looked down on her. 'Are you all right?'

She nodded her head. Afraid to speak, afraid she might spoil the moment. Frank kissed her lips. She kissed him back. He kissed her again this time more passionately. As his hands went to her blouse, nervously he unbuttoned her tunic to reveal her young breasts. As he bent down to kiss them she attempted to unbutton his shirt. The next thing she knew she was being lifted off the floor and carried over to the bed.

Somehow they managed to undress one another, as if there was no time for such practicality, both eager to fulfil their longing for each other.

When at last she was lying beneath him, Frank looked down at her. She was aware that this was the first time he had seen her naked. She wondered what he thought of her.

'God, you are so beautiful,' he said.

Frank looked into her eyes and Mair felt swamped by a rush of emotion. For a moment she was sure her heart stood still.

'My darling Mair, as eager as I am to make love to you, I have to know if it's what *you* really want.'

Mair remembered all the times in the past when, plagued by the memory of being raped, the resulting pregnancy and the birth of Catherine, she had pushed Frank away. He had been so patient with her then. Now with the past well and truly behind her, the time had come to give herself to this man, whom she loved with all her heart.

'Oh yes-yes. Frank, it truly is what I want ... I love you so much.'

'*Cariad*, my love, I've waited so long to hear those words. To have you here in my arms makes me the luckiest man alive.' He kissed her eyelids, her nose, her cheeks, his mouth lightly brushing her lips before moving to her neck, her breasts, her stomach....

Mair felt the warmth of his body ... his manliness ... and felt no fear, just overwhelming pleasure. She closed her eyes and joy swept over her as her body yearned for his touch. She gave herself willingly to him.

They had waited so long for this moment. Their lovemaking was made all the sweeter for it.

They spent the night with their arms and legs closely entwined, as if clinging together might delay the moment they had to part. But the next morning, Mair awoke to find Frank gone. He had left a note on the bedside table; in it he had written just three words:

I LOVE YOU.

When the day arrived for his regiment to leave for France, it was with much trepidation that Frank climbed aboard one of the six army trucks loaded with soldiers and equipment, waiting to drive them to Cardiff docks where they were to board one of the troop-ships, passenger steamers seconded for the war effort.

At the docks the soldiers, rifles slung over their shoulders and fully loaded kitbags on their backs, left the truck and proudly marched towards the troop ship all singing *Men of Harlech*. Frank spent the crossing sharing a billet with one of the seconded territorial, part-time volunteer soldiers. This one had been sent from the London Brigade. His name was Albert Stubbs, a man in his early twenties. The first time they met, his new room-mate was having trouble unhitching his rifle from across his shoulder.

'How long have you been in the TF?' Frank asked. 'If you don't mind me saying, judging by the trouble you're having with that rifle, I'd say not long.'

'I joined as a young lad,' Albert proudly announced. 'The truth is we seldom trained with real rifles, only fake ones. Mind you since the day Britain declared war on Germany, we've been given training in Aldershot and issued with full kitbags and rifles.'

Frank shook his head in disbelief. 'That was only a month ago. How much training have you had?'

'In London all of those in the TF, able bodied and willing to fight for King and country, were sent to Aldershot for four weeks' intense training, before being seconded to different regiments. Our sergeant major advised us, if and when we saw action, to stick close to a regular soldier and to follow his lead.'

'So us regulars are meant to babysit you lot. Is that it? What sort of an army is that?'

'It's a proud one. And I can assure you you'll not need to "babysit" me. You may want to consider that while you regulars are not here from choice, but simply following orders issued by your CO, we in the TF signed up to be here, we couldn't wait to join you "professionals". And I'm sure that together we shall scupper the Germans in quick time.' He stood tall and made a salute. 'Sapper Stubbs at your service, sir.'

Frank had to smile. There could be no doubting the man's commitment. Although Frank did wonder, when all talk was of this war 'not lasting until Christmas', why those in power felt it necessary to send the TF at all. Albert had given him food for thought. If he hadn't already been in the regular army, would he have been as keen to put his hand up to fight? He really wasn't sure. Especially with Mair waiting for him.

Frank and Albert hit it off straight away and by the time they reached France they were the best of friends.

Chapter Twenty-Three

IT WAS A Sunday morning and the new wing at St Thomas's was completed. There were two new wards, Florence Ward for amputees and Asquith Ward for all other injuries. Now that everything was ready, Matron was giving Mair and Kitty their orders.

'I want you to get yourselves off to Charing Cross Station to meet the hospital trains bringing the injured soldiers from the front. Once there, you will join other nurses from various hospitals, all co-ordinated by the Red Cross volunteers. Aware of the connection you two already have with this charity, I thought you might welcome working alongside them.'

'Yes, Matron. Thank you, Matron,' Mair said.

'While at the railway station, the injured will be assessed by doctors and sent to a hospital, some as far afield as Scotland. Your job is to escort by ambulance those allocated to St Thomas's. The time has come to put the new wards to work.'

'What, if any, treatment should we administer?' Kitty asked.

'No treatment will be necessary at this stage. Your job is to assist the Red Cross volunteers as much as you can, and to do your best to make the journey from the station to St Thomas's as comfortable for these brave men as you possibly can. Once safely delivered to the new wing, our highly trained team of doctors and nursing staff will take over and do the rest.'

Mair and Kitty arrived at Charing Cross and immediately went to seek out Sister Agnes, whom they just knew would be there.

'Kitty ... Mair, I'm so glad you came. I'm working with the Red Cross today – they need all the help they can get,' Sister Agnes said.

'Matron sent us to escort those assigned to St Thomas's for treatment, back to the hospital. In the meantime, what would you like us to do?' Mair asked.

'Well, if you could be there to greet and talk to these poor injured servicemen, maybe offer them a cup of tea, I know they'd be so grateful,' the Sister informed them. Then, shaking her head, 'I have to warn you to be prepared, most are in a pretty bad way. I couldn't even begin to describe the injuries – and not always physical. The carnage these boys have witnessed has certainly taken its toll. Many will need your help with even the simplest of tasks.'

Mair felt confident that the work she had done on Nightingale Ward had more than prepared her to minister to the injured soldiers, no matter how horrific their injuries might be. But in truth, nothing could have prepared her for rows of badly injured men, some dreadfully disfigured, many missing arms and legs. Stretcher upon stretcher of men, all spread out before her, almost too many to count, covering the length of the platform.

Taking a deep breath, Mair led Kitty among the wounded, slowly making her way along each row. The first to meet Mair's gaze was a young soldier, who in her mind didn't even look old enough to *be* in uniform. He lay in a sorry state. His face and uniform caked in mud and both arms swathed in bloody bandages.

Mair knelt down beside the stretcher and gently touching his shoulder said, 'Hello. Would you like a cup of tea?'

The young man's eyes stared into hers. 'Thank you, Miss, that would be good. Only I don't think I could manage to hold it right now.' His eyes looked down at what was left of his arms.

Mair swallowed hard and reaching up took one of the baby feeding beakers from an adjacent tea trolley. 'That's what I'm here for. Look, take a sip from this.'

As she placed the beaker between his lips, the lad took a big sip. The sweet strong tea made him cough, but it also brought a smile to his face, 'That feels so good. I can't remember the last time I had a cup of tea – we couldn't get any in France, see.' The lad coughed again, this time harder and louder.

Mair called for a medic, but with so many to attend to, no one came. With blood trickling from the side his mouth, the lad's frightened eyes stared into hers. Mair's free hand grabbed her handkerchief and softly dabbed his mouth to remove the blood.

She gave him a gentle smile, 'Is there anything you'd like me to do?' she asked, her arm supporting his head.

'Another drop of that tea would be nice ...' and with that his eyes closed and his body went limp.

Mair shuddered and stroked his young cheek. This was the first dead person she had seen, although she knew it wouldn't be the last. She wiped away her sudden tears and looked around the busy station, along the platform and past the rows of stretchers filled with military personnel. There was a British army officer, a French officer and a woman and other civilians waiting to board the passenger train newly arrived in the station. In the centre of the platform stood a man with a luggage cart, and directly behind him, a young woman carrying a wicker basket full of items for sale. Everyone was going about their business – all oblivious to the death and suffering not ten feet away from them.

Mair and Kitty spent the next hour doing what little they could to make the injured comfortable while awaiting transportation to their allotted hospitals. To Mair it seemed a logistical nightmare. However, against all odds, they were soon informed that sixteen of the injured were destined for St Thomas's, and two ambulances were seconded to take them. With four to an ambulance and one nurse in each, two journeys were necessary. It was decided that Kitty should take the first ambulance and Mair the second. But before they left, Sister Agnes came over to see them.

'You two did well today,' the Sister said. 'I wanted you to know what a difference you made. I'm sure, after what these men have been through, seeing such a pair of pretty young nurses tending to them went a long way to lifting their hearts and minds.'

She hugged both girls. 'I'm so very proud of you.'

The transportation of the sixteen injured servicemen seemed to take forever. As the comfort of the patients was a priority, each of the ambulance drivers endeavoured to make every journey to the hospital as smooth a ride as possible. Finally, with the injured safely in the care of the nursing team, Mair and Kitty could go off duty. It had been a harrowing day, a day they expected would be one of many. And although physically and mentally drained, they felt satisfied at having done a good day's work.

Later that night, as Mair lay exhausted on her bed, her thoughts went to the numerous young men she had tended that day – some wounded beyond repair, some with horrific burns, their faces distorted in pain, many others missing a limb, all desperately in need of help and comfort. However, for all that, the one face that she couldn't shake from her mind was of the first young soldier who had died, with her arm under his head.

From then on, every time the hospital train arrived at Charing Cross Station, Mair and Kitty were sent to assist. Nearly every day more and more injured returned from the front; doctors, nurses, ambulance men and women and volunteers were pushed to the limit.

Chapter Twenty-Four

May 1915

IT WAS EARLY morning at Grange House. With no hospital train due in until 2.30, Mair and Kitty looked forward to a leisurely breakfast and then a trip into the city, before heading over to Charing Cross Station.

'Good morning, Mrs Turnbull,' they said in unison as they entered the dining room for breakfast.

'Good morning, girls. I trust you both slept well. You've both been working such long hours of late. Mind you, I'm glad to see that you, Mair, haven't been asked to work any extra shifts. I think it's asking too much of anyone to work two shifts back to back like you did before.'

Mair almost choked on a piece of toast.

'It doesn't happen often ... only when there's an emergency, isn't that right, Mair?' Kitty quickly interjected.

Mrs Turbull's eyes stared directly at Mair. Mair felt her colour rise. It had been months since Frank's visit to London. With Kitty making the excuse of her working an extra shift – and no awkward questions from Mrs Turnbull, she thought she had got away with staying out all night.

'Isn't that right, Mair?' Kitty prompted.

'Yes. That's right,' she said, taking a large swig of hot tea. 'It's only when there's an emergency.'

'I should think so too,' Mrs Turnbull said.

For a while there was an awkward silence. Then, by way of a timely intervention, the dining room door opened and Violet entered.

'The morning newspaper, Mrs Turnbull,' she said handing it to her.

'Thank you, Violet,' Mrs Turnbull said. With newspaper in hand, she proceeded to read the headlines.

Mair and Kitty breathed a sigh of relief.

'My God, such terrible news,' Mrs Turnbull cried.

'What is it?' Kitty asked.

'The *Lusitania*, a Cunard passenger liner, has been sunk, torpedoed by a German U-boat off the coast of Ireland. It says almost 1,200 passengers are thought to have perished.'

'That's terrible. I can't bear to think of German U-boats so close to us … on patrol in Irish waters. I know we're at war, but why sink a passenger liner?' Kitty asked.

'I'll read it to you,' Mrs Turnbull said, her hands visibly shaking with shock. '"*The German Embassy recently printed a warning in the* New York Times *saying that any ship that strayed into the European War Zone would be a legitimate target for their submarines; these vessels are capable of breaking certain codes of practice i.e. carrying arms and armaments.*"' Mrs Turnbull looked up from the newspaper.

'Whatever way they try to justify it, it is never right to knowingly kill innocent civilians.' Kitty shook her head in disbelief. She looked to Mair for support, and on seeing her friend's ashen face, she got up from the table and went to her. 'Mair, are you all right?'

Mair shook her head. 'When I think of those poor lost souls … hundreds of them … some of whom may have been stranded in the water for hours before … too weak to tread water any longer … perished.'

'Oh, my dear girl, whatever was I thinking? Hearing this news has no doubt reminded you of your own experience in the *Titanic* tragedy.'

Mair nodded her head. 'Yes. The difference is – what happened to the *Titanic* was the result of human error. To me this is a blatant act of murder!'

'I'm afraid this is the reality of war,' Mrs Turnbull said.

Chapter Twenty-Five

FRANK LEWIS SAT propped against the cold, damp, shaft wall of the stinking muddy pit, his allotted space among other soldiers from his regiment, in the trenches at the Somme region of France. While they waited for the order to go over the top to face German machine guns, his new mate, Albert Stubbs was grabbing, what he called, 'a bit of shut-eye'. He certainly had nerves of steel.

It was early October, and although most days were still fine and warm, the nights were growing increasingly cold. Somewhere out there a long line of German soldiers lay in wait, high upon a hill, armed with machine guns.

It was getting dark and after a day spent waiting for the order that never came, everyone was feeling cold, tired and hungry. Frank tried not to dwell on the terrifying fact of how close to death he might be. He had seen so many killed. He longed to be back in the arms of his darling Mair. He wondered how she was faring in London. There was talk among the lads that, if this war continued, the Germans would aim to take France and cross the channel to Dover ... then on to London. His darling Mair was there. He thanked God that Catherine and the family would be, at least for the time being, reasonably safe in Ponty. Although he was petrified by the thought that he might never see Mair, Catherine or his family again, he desperately clung to the hope that this dreadful war would end soon. After all, hadn't everyone said the war would be over by Christmas 1914? That was almost a year ago.

'Are you all right, butty?' Frank whispered to the big, rough-looking ginger-haired man not two feet away from him.

'What's it to you?' the man demanded.

'Nothing at all ... I just thought you looked—'

'What ... scared shitless? Well, I am. And I don't mind admitting it.'

'You're not on your own. I bet there's not a man here who doesn't feel the same. And I'm sure that goes for the enemy too.'

'That's as maybe, but as an ex-professional boxer, I intend to treat this fight like any other. A fight is only as good as its contestants. And usually it's the better man who wins.'

'Except this fight is not a fair one.' Frank scoffed.

The men sized each other up.

'Look, I'm sorry if I was a bit sharp. Jake Brewer's the name ... I'm from Cardiff.'

'I thought I recognized the Welsh accent. I'm a valley lad from Ponty myself ... Frank Lewis.' Frank stretched over and offered Jake a cold muddy hand.

Jake accepted the handshake. 'It's good to meet a fellow Welshman. I arrived last night with fifty other new recruits. Talk about being thrown in at the deep end.'

'I thought I hadn't seen you before. New recruit you say?' Frank offered him a roll-up from his tobacco tin.

'Thanks,' the man said, his hand visibly shaking as he removed a misshapen cigarette that had been rolled in haste from Frank's well-used metal tin. 'And I know what you're thinking ... a bit old in the tooth for a new recruit, eh?'

'Sorry, but most of the previous new recruits were so much younger and still wet behind the ears. I'm just a bit surprised, that's all. No offence intended.'

'All right, none taken. Look, I might be knocking fifty, but, as I still do a fair bit of training to keep my hand in at the boxing ring, fitness is not an issue. All I had to do was shave off my beard and lie about my age. The truth is I needed to get out of Cardiff a bit rapid.' Raising his index finger, Jake tapped the side of his nose. 'A bit of bother, if you know what I mean.'

'That's none of my business.' Frank said, not really taking to the man.

'I'm classed as one of "Kitchener's Volunteer Army", supposedly spurred on by the posters hung on almost every lamp post. You know the one – showing Lord Kitchener's face, his finger pointing and in bold letters printed, "Your Country Needs You!".' Jake mimicked Lord

Kitchener's pose on the poster. 'Mind you, the recruitment centre didn't seem too choosy. I felt that as long as I could stand and looked fit enough to hold a rifle, I would be accepted,' Jake scoffed.

'I'm not surprised. With the death toll as high as it is – it stands to reason that a constant flow of replacements is needed.'

'Bad is it?'

'They call us the PBIs – the Poor Bloody Infantry, all waiting for the dreaded sound of a whistle, the order to climb that ladder, go over the top and march across no-man's-land. It's bloody madness! We lost forty men in this section alone yesterday, mowed down by German rifles. I tell you it's just suicide, man. And no one seems to give a fuck!'

'So why not just up and leave? I've only been here a day, and I'm seriously thinking of doing a runner.'

'No, when you're caught and brought back as a deserter, you'll be put up against a wall and shot by a firing squad, made up of the very men you've previously been fighting alongside.'

'So we're well and truly fucked?' With the back of his hand Jake angrily wiped loose bits of tobacco from the side of his mouth.

Frank shrugged his shoulders. 'Yes, I'm afraid so,' he said.

A loud whistle echoed along the trenches. It was time for them to go over the top. A heavy shell exploded. It came very close – far too close for comfort. The noise was deafening ... Frank watched Jake fly into the air. Then everything went black.

Chapter Twenty-Six

January 1917

IT WAS FOUR days after New Year. Ethel, John and Catherine were warming themselves by the fire in the parlour. A small fir tree stood in the corner of the room adorned with home-made lanterns and painted fir cones, the walls and ceiling draped with paper chains – all put up to make the most of Christmas, war or no war.

'Shall I start to take the decorations down?' John asked.

'No!' Ethel snapped. 'We can't take them down until tomorrow – the twelfth night after Christmas.'

'Why?' Catherine asked.

'Because it's bad luck, that's why,' Ethel explained.

'I really don't think you should go filling the child's head with such stuff and nonsense,' John admonished.

'Well, with our Frank out fighting the Hun, I'm taking no chances. It's always been twelfth night, and that's how it'll stay, so there,' Ethel stated firmly.

John walked across the room. He put his arm around his wife, 'I'm sorry, *cariad*. I didn't mean to upset you.'

'No, it's all right. It's only me being a bit touchy. With Frank so far away and another Christmas without him … it's just … I miss him so much. We haven't heard from him for ages. It's the not knowing if he be dead or alive—'

'You mustn't think like that. I've told you before. If it was bad news we would hear soon enough.'

Ethel shuddered, 'It doesn't bear thinking about.'

*

The very next day a letter arrived, postmarked France.

'Oh John, it's from Frank. He's coming home ... Frank's actually coming home ... he's due to arrive the day after tomorrow,' Ethel cried.

'What else does the lad have to say?' John asked.

Ethel scanned the letter, 'He says he's in the thick of it but we're not to worry. He hopes we're all right and can't wait to see us. The food there is so nasty he's looking forward to some of my home cooking. He wants to know if we've heard from Mair. He says he hopes to see her in London before coming home to us. The lad loves her so much.' Ethel sniffled into her handkerchief before turning to Catherine. 'Your daddy sends you lots of hugs and kisses.'

Catherine chuckled, 'Daddy?'

'Yes, child. Your daddy's coming home.'

It was Tuesday, 4 January. New Year had been and gone, and there was still no sign of the war with Germany coming to an end. Mair was at the station, moving along from stretcher to stretcher giving what aid and comfort she could to the wounded soldiers, when she heard some-one call her name.

'Mair!' a man's voice called out.

Mair looked across the busy platform. A soldier had just stepped off the hospital train. He raised his hand and waved to her.

'Mair!' he called.

She stared at him, not believing her own eyes ... could it be ... was it him? He was walking towards her ... 'Frank!' she cried, running into his arms.

He caught around her, squeezing her so tightly she could hardly breathe. 'Mair, love, you don't know how long I've dreamt of seeing you again. There was a time back there when I thought I never would,' he whispered.

His voice sounded weary. She stood back to look at him. He was thin and gaunt looking, his eyes, once so bright, now dull and ... almost lifeless.

'Frank, why were you on the hospital train, are you injured?'

'Not so you'd notice. I suppose I'm what they call, "one of the walking wounded". A heavy shell exploded close to our dugout. For a while, it rendered me deaf. It's left me with shell shock – there are occasions when I shake so bad I can't control my limbs – it's shameful. My CO decided that I was no use to my regiment like this.' Frank's eyes glazed over, he shook his head, as if the memory were too painful. 'I once saw a fellow who had it so bad he couldn't go up the ladder from the dug-out and over the top. The poor bastard was shot as a coward.'

'What, by his own regiment?'

'I tell you, Mair. Some of the things I've seen—' He turned his head away again, his hand brushing a tear from his eyes. When he had composed himself, he turned to face her. 'Anyway, I'm one of the lucky ones. I've been sent home to be medically assessed. Next Monday I'm to report to the 3rd Western TF General Hospital in Cardiff, where a panel of doctors will decide my fate – and hopefully tell me if I'm fit for duty or not.'

'Oh, my poor Frank.' She took his pale face in her hands and studied his stunned eyes. 'In the meantime, I suppose you have to head home to Ponty.'

'Yes, but I couldn't bear to go without seeing you. My plan was to turn up at St Thomas's and surprise you like I did before.' He tried to smile but failed. 'The truth is, I'm not sure I have the strength to make it across London. When I spotted you here on the station, I couldn't believe my luck.'

'I'm so glad you did. Did you get my letter, the one with the photograph you asked for?'

'Yes.' He tapped the inside pocket of his mud-stained khaki jacket. 'I keep it close to my heart. I read the letter and look at your picture at every opportunity – to remind me of what I have to come back to.'

Mair reached up and gently kissed his cheek. 'I can't believe that you're actually safe here in London. It's been such a long time … but I never gave up believing you would return, Frank.'

He gave a long sigh. 'The weeks turn to months, the months into a year … and still no end to this damn war.' He seemed close to tears again.

This broken man was not the Frank she remembered. Her heart went out to him. She didn't want to think of the scenes he must have witnessed, to have affected him this way. 'I had a card from your mother today.' Mair smiled, in an attempt to lift his spirits. 'Apparently our little Catherine played Mary in the chapel's Christmas nativity play – perhaps she's taking after her Aunt Rhiannon.'

'I wish I could have been there to see her. It's hard to believe we've missed so many Christmases with her.'

'I know. I feel the same way. Surely this war has to end soon.'

'I can't see it. If anything, the fighting is more intense than ever…. Mair, love, are you able to get away? I'm sorry I'm not the best of company right now, but tomorrow morning I'll be on a train heading for Wales. I'm longing to spend some time alone with you – away from the noise and the crowds.'

'Oh Frank. I would love to, but I can't leave here yet. Why don't you get yourself off to the hotel in Sussex Gardens and book us a room for the night. I need to stay here for a while longer. My job is to escort some of the injured to St Thomas's. As soon as I'm done, I promise I'll rush over and join you. You just rest up and wait for me. Get some sleep, Frank.'

Taking his arm she walked him from the station and into one of the waiting hansom cabs that were queuing for fares.

'Sussex Gardens, please,' she instructed the driver, as Frank stepped aboard and slumped in the seat.

'Come as quick as you can,' Frank said, his eyes almost pleading with her.

'You get some rest.' She leaned forward and kissed his lips, tasting the sadness on them. 'I'll be with you soon. I promise.'

As she watched the hansom drive off her heart ached for her poor Frank. She vowed that whatever it took, she'd be there to nurse him back to health.

Back inside the station Mair went to seek out Kitty and found her outside, in the ambulance bay.

'Thank goodness. Where have you been? Our injured patients, eight in all, are already loaded in two ambulances. I was about to send out a search party,' Kitty admonished.

'Kitty, you'll never believe it. Frank was here. He was on the hospital train. He's suffering shell shock. He looks awful.'

'Where is he now?' Kitty asked.

'I sent him on to the hotel in Sussex Gardens. I'm going over there, just as soon as I finish my shift.'

Kitty flashed a knowing smile. 'And I suppose you'd like me to cover for you with Mrs Turnbull.'

'Thanks, but I don't want you to lie for me again. The thing is, he's in a bad way ... this is not like the other time. This time he really needs me to be there ... to hold him ... to love him. And if that means facing the wrath of Mrs Turnbull, then that's what I shall do.'

'Good for you. I so wish I had a man to spend the night with, any man ... able-bodied or not.'

When the injured were safely delivered to the hospital, Mair went to see the matron.

An hour later Mair entered the hotel foyer. At reception she asked the middle-aged man behind the counter, what room Frank Lewis was in.

'May I have your name?' he asked.

'Nurse Parsons,' she answered, not sure where his question was heading.

'Miss Parsons, Mr Lewis asked me to give you this spare key to his room,' he said, handing it to her. 'It's not something we encourage, you understand. Only, under the circumstances ... with him looking so poorly and all—'

'Thank you,' Mair said.

He nodded, then shaking his head muttered, 'This bloody war has a lot to answer for.'

Out of politeness, Mair gave a light tap on the door before letting herself into the bedroom. 'Frank, love, I'm here. I told you I wouldn't be long.'

The room was in darkness. She walked over and pulled open the drapes to find Frank sitting in an armchair in the far corner of the room, staring into space. His eyes focused on nothing.

Her heart was banging in her chest as she walked over and knelt beside him. 'Frank, love. It's me, Mair,' she whispered, tenderly taking his hand in hers.

At the touch of her hand, he turned his head to face her. His eyes filled with tears, a few spilled over onto his cheek.

'Frank. Please tell me what I can do to help.'

He shook his head. And for a while, he didn't say a word, then breathing heavily he said, 'The truth is I don't know. At times I feel beyond help. I hate being like this. I feel so weak … so damn useless.'

'My love, you're not well.'

Again he shook his head. 'You don't understand. There are many doctors who don't even recognize shell shock as an illness. There's every chance that the ones I'm going to see will be of that mind. They have it in their power to send me back to the front … without treatment. If that happened then I'd be labelled a coward, a Jessie – a weak man … and for all I know, they could be right. The truth is, I'm not sure about anything any more. Last week, I witnessed a man called Jake Brewer – a new recruit, who had only arrived that very day – blown to pieces by a shell that exploded right next to him. And while Albert, my best butty, is still out there fighting in the thick of it, here I am, with no visible injuries, crying like a baby. It makes me feel a disgrace to my regiment.'

'Frank, love, don't be so hard on yourself.' She lifted his hand to her cheek. 'You need to rest up and be taken care of. For what it's worth, since this war began I've seen many physically injured soldiers who also suffered shell shock, on the wards at St Thomas's.' She was about to say how, in many cases, their wounds healed quicker than their minds, but thought better of it. Instead she added, 'The doctors at St Thomas's recognize shell shock as an injury to the nervous system. And like every other injury, it needs time to heal.'

Frank shook his head. 'Mair, the truth is … I'm a different man to the one who left you at the beginning of the war. I spend my days in fear, unable to cope with the smallest of tasks. I jump at the slightest noise. I burst into tears at the drop of a hat and … my nights? My nights are haunted by such vivid memories, I'm afraid to go to sleep. This is what war has done to me.'

'Believe me, my dearest Frank, that I really do know how you feel. When I woke up in the hospital in New York, I felt exactly the same. Even now, when I hear anyone mention the *Titanic*, I struggle with having to remember the events of that night.'

Frank nodded. 'Before this damn war, I couldn't understand why my mother never wanted to talk about the *Titanic*. I do now.'

'I was the same,' Mair said. 'Somehow the experience, like your senses, becoming numbed; the dreadful memories haunt your dreams by night and your consciousness by day. The last thing you want to do is to discuss it – no amount of discussion could ever succeed in making sense of it.'

'My darling Mair, you're right. You do understand.'

Taking him by the hand she walked him into the bathroom. There she ran him a warm bath, gently undressed him and helped him into it, her skills and expertise as a nurse standing her in good stead. She gently bathed him, shocked by the thinness of his body and the state of his blistered feet, and afterwards towelled him dry. Then, leading him to the bed, he lay between the bedclothes. Mair quickly undressed herself and slid in beside him. For a while, they lay close together in silence, their naked bodies touching yet still.

'I feel I want to pinch myself,' he whispered in her ear. 'If you only knew the number of nights I spent wishing for this moment – to have you lying next to me ... to make love to you. And now that you're here, I feel so useless – impotent even. I want you, but I want sleep more. It's so peaceful to hear no noise of artillery or machine guns firing at will. No sounds of men screaming in pain. No—'

'Frank, my love, you're safe now. Go to sleep. I'll still be here when you wake up, I promise.'

Brushing a strand of hair away from his forehead, she placed a gentle kiss on his lips.

'Thank you,' he whispered. 'I love you so much.'

'I know, Frank. And I love you, to.'

Frank slept for eight hours – a restless sleep; all the while tossing and turning, at times calling out ... crying. For a long time Mair didn't sleep. She spent most of the night holding and comforting him, eventually giving way to sleep at 4 a.m.

She awoke at 7.30, daylight lighting the room, to find Frank, his arm bent under his head, raising him from the pillow, staring across at her.

'Good morning,' he said.

'Good morning. How do you feel?' she asked.

He leaned across and kissed her.

She kissed him back.

'At this moment, I feel the luckiest man alive.' He moved to lie on top of her. His arms went around her waist pulling her naked body closer to his. The touch of his manhood aroused her. She knew he wanted her ... and she so wanted him. They made love, their love-making far less intense than the last time they stayed at that hotel, yet nonetheless satisfying.

Afterwards they bathed together and slowly towelled each other dry – savouring every minute of this shared experience.

Later when they went down for breakfast, the dining room was practically empty; only two elderly ladies sat at the table in the window. After nodding a 'Good morning', Frank and Mair sat as far away from them as they could, not wanting to risk having to make idle conversation with strangers. They wanted to be alone.

'I'm famished,' Mair said.

'Me too, I don't think I've eaten for days – if I have, I can't remember it.'

'You take a seat. I'll order us breakfast,' Mair instructed.

'Yes, ma'am,' he joked.

As pleased as she was to see him in such good spirits, something told her to be prepared for his mood swings.

They ate a hearty breakfast of scrambled egg on toast, followed by a warm bread roll and preserves. On a large notice above the kitchen door was written, 'The Hotel Manager apologizes for the lack of bacon, tomatoes and mushrooms – availability of such products is scarce in the marketplace due to the war effort.'

They had almost finished eating when Frank reached across the table and took her hand. 'I don't want our time together to end. I've loved being with you and ...' he stopped then whispered, 'sleeping with you.' He smiled.

Mair, seeing a hint of the 'old' Frank, smiled back.

'This feels a bit like the last supper.' He looked pensive.

'But we know it's not. In fact, I've got something to tell you.' She held his hand to her lips and kissed it. 'Frank, love, I'm coming with you.'

Frank looked puzzled. 'What do you mean? Coming where – to the station to see me off? I'd rather you didn't, I hate saying goodbye.'

'No, silly. I meant, I'm coming back to Wales with you!'

The shocked look on his face said it all – he was rendered speech-less.

'My darling Frank, it's the truth. Yesterday, as soon as I finished my shift, I went to see Matron. I told her I had a sick relative in Wales who needed me. I pointed out that, if I stayed in London, my mind wouldn't be on the job. She agreed to let me take compassionate leave.'

'How long has she given you?'

'Three weeks. Now if I'm to make the train at eleven, I have to get myself over to Grange House as soon as I can. I need to pack my carpetbag and tell Mrs Turnbull of my plans. If Kitty's not there, I'll leave her a note and our address in Ponty. With a bit of luck, I should be at Paddington at around 10.45.'

'I still can't believe that you're actually coming home with me.'

At Grange House, Mair, having given Mrs Turnbull the same speech as Matron, braced herself for her landlady's reaction.

'This is all a bit sudden. When exactly did you hear about this sick relative?' Mrs Turnbull asked, looking mightily suspicious.

Mair knew she couldn't continue the lie – this lady had been so kind to her. She deserved the truth.

'I only heard today.'

'Today … I don't understand. How did you hear? Was it by letter or did someone call to see you?'

Taking a deep breath, Mair decided to come clean. 'His name is Frank Lewis. We've been friends for as long as I can remember. His mother gave me and my sister a home. I've known the family all my life,' she said.

'And tell me, did this young man have anything to do with you staying out all night?'

'Yes, I can't lie. I stayed with him at a hotel in Sussex Gardens.' She quickly added, 'Frank's not well. He arrived off one of the hospital trains yesterday morning. He's suffering shell shock … he needed me.'

'I see,' Mrs Turnbull said.

Mair tried to read the woman's expression, and couldn't decide if it was one of sympathy or disappointment. She settled on the latter.

'Mrs Turnbull. I understand how disappointed you must be with me. Unfortunately there is so much about my life before the *Titanic*, New York and arriving here in London that you don't know about me.'

'Everyone has a past. And for the most part, I believe that it's of no one's business but your own,' Mrs Turnbull offered.

'And that's what I originally believed too. However, I was wrong. After all you did for me, I should have confided in you and Sister Agnes. I should have told you a lot more. And one day … if you let me, I will. Although as I broke the house rules last night, I'll understand if you want me to leave the house permanently.'

'Now why would I want you to do that? My dear, you get yourself off to Wales and look after your young man. Your room will be waiting for you when you return. I'll explain everything to Sister Agnes. I'm sure she, like me, will understand.'

'Thank you so much. It was never my intention to lie to you. I really didn't set out to be a disappointment to you.'

'And you're not.' Mrs Turnbull caught around her and gave her a peck on the cheek. 'Now be off with you. You don't want to miss your train.'

Mair reached into her carpetbag, 'One last thing. Could you give this letter to Kitty? I've left a forwarding address … so if any of you want to get in touch….'

Mrs Turnbull nodded. 'Kitty's going to miss you, you know?'

'And I her,' Mair said.

Mair arrived at Paddington Station with only five minutes to spare. She found Frank pacing the platform, but when he spotted her his eyes lit up. He rushed towards her and embraced her.

'I thought you'd changed your mind.'

'I'm sorry I'm late. I just couldn't rush off. I felt Mrs Turnbull deserved a truthful explanation – she trusted me and took me in when I needed a roof over my head. I didn't mean to worry you.'

'You're here now. That's all that matters and, by the look of it, not a moment too soon – here's our train.'

It felt strange, yet so right, to be travelling back to Wales with Frank. After all this time, they were returning as a couple. Frank might be unwell, but she hoped that with her love, care and support, he'd make a full recovery. They shared a compartment with a young family, a man, woman and a boy who looked to be about nine or ten years old. They kept themselves to themselves and for most of the time the young lad had his nose in a comic book.

Mair, having had only a few hours' sleep the night before, cuddled up to Frank and slept for most of the journey. Frank held her close, occasionally kissing her forehead. When they arrived in Cardiff, they found they had an hour to wait before the next train to Llan, and from there, a charabanc to Ponty.

'What say we take ourselves over to the station café for a pot of tea and a sandwich?' Frank asked.

'A cup of tea would be nice. I'm not sure about the sandwich. I'm still full of the breakfast we had this morning.'

'Me too,' he said. Then, with his kitbag sitting firmly on his back, he reached down and picked up her luggage. She didn't argue. She knew how futile it would be. He was a proud man.

In the café they sat at a table and a young waitress served them a pot of tea. When she had left them alone, Frank took Mair's hand.

'Mair, love, I've got something I want to ask you. And while I know this is probably not the time or the place ... if I don't do it now, I may never will.'

'Frank. What is it?'

'Well, I was thinking ... with your twenty-first birthday only two weeks away ... look. I know that, with me suffering shell shock and all, I might not be the best catch in the world ... but I will get better.'

'I know you will. It may take a bit of time but—'

'I promise you that whatever it takes, I'm determined to beat this. What I can't wait another minute for, is to ask you to be my ... wife!'

Mair stared in silence. This was the last thing she expected to hear.

'Mair, I know it's a bit sudden. I just so want us to return to Ponty with some good news for a change. What do you say?' Frank asked, his eyes pleading for an answer.

She squeezed his hand, 'Yes, yes, yes! I can't think of anything I'd like better than to be your wife, to finally be Mrs Frank Lewis. Just the thought of it warms my heart.'

'I'm so happy you feel like that. Now you leave everything to me. Tomorrow when I'm in Cardiff, I'll pay a visit to the registry office and book it for 20 January, the day after your birthday. Then no one can claim it's not legal.'

'Frank, love, as much as I want to marry you, there's no real rush, is there? Why not wait until you're fully recovered?'

'You're not regretting saying yes, are you? I couldn't bear it if you rejected me … I lost you once. I'll not lose you again.' Frank appeared agitated.

Mair couldn't fail to notice how quickly his mood had changed.

'Don't be daft. I promise I'll never reject you.' She was about to add 'again' but no doubt he'd remember the time in Southampton when she'd left him to go to London. She had to somehow make him believe this was not the case. 'How could I? I love you too much for that! I'm just so worried about the assessment tomorrow.'

'Don't you see, that with the assessment hanging over my head, the thought of us being wed gives me hope … whatever the army may decide. I know I have a future with you and Catherine.'

'Then that's settled.' She kissed his hand. 'Cardiff Registry Office it is. Mind you, the registry office in Bridgend is closer to Ponty.'

'I thought if we got wed in Cardiff, it would make it easier for Rhiannon and Gus to attend. You know how difficult it is for them to get time off from the theatre.'

'Frank Lewis, sometimes you're a real wonder to me. You really have thought of everything, haven't you?'

'Not everything. I hadn't prepared a contingency plan, in the event of your refusal.'

'I'm glad. Surely, deep down, you must have known that it was what I wanted too?'

'I hoped so.'

At that moment the announcement over the loudspeaker told them that their train for Ponty was about to arrive. Frank led the way from the café and onto the platform. Mair followed on as if in a dream – a dream in which her prayers had been answered. In two weeks' time she would become Mrs Frank Lewis, and she, Frank and Catherine, would be together as a family at last.

Arriving in Ponty, Frank and Mair proudly walked arm in arm across the square and towards the Jenkins' house – they were home, and they wanted to show the world that they were a couple.

They reached the family butcher shop. On seeing them, John immediately stopped what he was doing and rushed from behind the counter and out of the shop to greet them – much to the surprise of the customers in the shop, causing the three women to turn to see what had caused such unusual behaviour.

'Frank … Mair. What a lovely surprise.' Then, seeing Frank's arm resting on Mair's waist, 'Does this mean what I think it means?' he whispered, not wanting to give fuel to the valley gossips.

Frank nodded. Mair beamed a smile.

John caught around the two of them. 'Welcome home! Your mam and Catherine will be so pleased to see you. Frank … your mother has been so worried about you. She'll probably want to fuss over you. Be patient with her.'

'I will, John, I promise.'

'Are you all right, Frank? I must say you don't look too grand.'

'I'm a little tired, that's all. I'll explain later.'

'I hope so. Now you get yourself next door. You're home now. I'll catch up with you later – when I close up.'

Frank shook his hand. Mair placed a kiss on John's cheek.

'We didn't expect a welcoming committee.' Frank nodded towards the women staring at them from inside the shop.

'Yes, I'd better go serve them. No doubt I'll be bombarded with questions – although they'll not get much out of me. Ethel's trained me too well.' He gave a loud laugh before heading back into the shop.

Frank took a key from his jacket pocket and let himself into the house, closely followed by Mair. 'Mam, I'm home,' he called out.

Mair recognized the tiredness in his voice. The trip home had obviously taken more out of him than she had first thought.

'Frank, son, is it really you?' Ethel cried out as she rushed down the hall to greet him. On seeing Mair and Frank standing arm in arm, she stopped in her tracks and took a sharp intake of breath. 'I can't believe it … the two of you home together. It's such a lovely surprise.' She stared into Frank's eyes. She knew him too well not to notice his look of fatigue. 'You look tired, son, and … so very thin. Doesn't that army of yours feed you?' she asked.

'We're at war, Mam. We eat and sleep when we can. But it's nothing a good night's sleep and a bowl of your *cawl* won't put right.'

'Well, come on, get yourselves into the kitchen. I've a big pan of *cawl* waiting for you on the hob – my lamb stew was always your favourite.'

As they entered the kitchen they caught sight of Catherine playing on the floor with her wooden building blocks. She looked up.

'There she is, our little girl – although not so little now, eh? I can't believe how much you've grown.' Frank smiled with pride.

In a rush the child got up from the floor.

Mair knelt down and held her arms out to her daughter. 'I've missed you so much,' she said and, fighting back tears, she gave a wide smile.

Catherine leapt into her arms. 'Mammy … Daddy,' she squealed, hugging her mother, then she pulled at her father's trouser leg, urging him to pick her up.

Frank tried, but with his kitbag on his back, and feeling as tired as he was, he found it difficult.

'Catherine, you've grown so much, you need to let your daddy get his kitbag off before he can pick you up.'

The child stood up straight almost standing on tiptoe. 'I am a big girl,' she said proudly.

'Catherine, why don't you go up to your bedroom and get your brown teddy? I bet your mammy and daddy would love to see him.'

'Yes. I haven't seen him for ages,' Mair agreed.

'I get teddy for you,' the child said, as she turned and ran towards the stairs.

'Thanks, Mam,' Frank said, as he removed his kitbag and flopped into his mother's fireside chair. 'It's been a long trip. I hadn't realized how tired I was.'

'You sit there,' Ethel said. 'I'll get you both a bowl of *cawl* and a slice of Tom *bara*'s freshly baked bread. Mair, you sit at the table. I'll put Frank's on a tray.'

As Frank tucked in to the soup, Ethel's eyes never left her son, and her concern was obvious. She walked over to him. 'You look done in, son. What's wrong?' she asked, removing his tray.

Frank looked to Mair for help.

'The thing is, Ethel. Frank's been given sick leave.'

'Oh my God, I knew it! I felt it in my bones. I just knew something wasn't right. Where are you injured? Is it serious?'

Frank shook his head. 'Mam, I've got no visible injuries. I've got shell shock,' he announced.

'Shell shock, what does that mean exactly?'

Again his eyes looked to Mair to explain.

'It means he's suffered a trauma to the head.' Mair went on to explain about the exploding shell and its effect on Frank.

'Will he get better?' Ethel demanded.

'Yes … in time. What he needs right now is to rest – to recuperate and be nursed back to health.'

'I see. Is that why you came back home … to nurse him?'

'Yes … and no. He's due in Cardiff tomorrow to have his injuries assessed. We'll know more then.'

'What, another long trip? Are you sure you're up to it, son?' Ethel asked.

'Don't worry, Ethel. I'm going to Cardiff with him,' Mair announced.

'Mair, love, I really don't think that's necessary,' Frank argued.

'Necessary or not, I'm coming with you. No argument.'

'Have you noticed how bossy she can be, Mam? And that's before we're married.' He gave a weary laugh.

'Married? What's this?' Ethel flopped onto John's armchair. 'I need to sit down.'

Leaning across, Frank took his mother's hand. 'Mam, Mair's agreed to marry me. Our plan is to get wed in Cardiff on the twentieth of this month.'

'Frank, Mair. That's the best news I've had for ages.'

Mair caught around her future mother-in-law and gave her a hug. 'We knew you'd be pleased for us.'

'I can't wait to tell John. This calls for a celebration. We'll drink a toast to the two of you as soon as he gets home.'

'That'll be nice, Mam. Now, if you don't mind, I'd like to go for a lie down.'

'Of course you would, lad. You take yourself up to bed. Mair, go up with him and see what's keeping Catherine. She's probably gathering up all her toys to show you. Just bring her down to the kitchen.'

Two hours later, when John arrived home, Ethel sent Mair and Catherine upstairs to check on Frank. 'I think it best not to let him sleep for too long or he might have trouble sleeping through the night,' Ethel advised.

'I think you're right. Come on Catherine, *cariad*, let's go and see your dad,' Mair said, taking her daughter's hand.

When they were out of earshot, Ethel turned to her husband. 'John, love, I know it's great to have them home, but Frank's not at all well.' She proceeded to tell him about the shell shock and his forthcoming assessment. 'I don't need the result of an assessment. It's plain to see that he's in no fit state to go back to the trenches. And yet, if he's asked to leave the army, I fear for his state of mind.'

'Let's cross that bridge when we come to it. They're home … and are obviously a couple, surely that counts for a lot.'

'Oh yes, it does. And there's something else. They're soon to be married.'

At that moment Mair entered the room, followed closely by Frank, looking much better for his rest and with Catherine in his arms. He smiled across at John, 'I see Mam couldn't wait to give you the news?'

'No. In fact I'm surprised she waited until I came home. My congratulations to both of you and … although it's been a long time coming, I always believed you were meant for each other.'

'Thank you. I know I'm a very lucky man. Mind you, the way I am at the moment, I'm not sure if Mair is getting such a good deal.'

'Don't be daft. If the two women in your life have anything to do with it, you'll be back to full health in no time. Ethel, love, bring out the sherry. It's time for a toast,' John said.

With their glasses filled, John said, 'Here's to a happy and long future together.'

They all raised their glasses.

After tea, the four adults spent a relaxed family evening sitting in the parlour, with Catherine happily playing on the carpet with an assortment of toys.

Mair inquired about Ethel's daughters. 'How are Sadie and Martha? I haven't seen them for that long, I probably wouldn't recognize them.'

'The girls, well not really girls any more – they're young women now. They work at the ammunition factory in Bridgend.'

'I think it shows strength of character to want to do their bit for the war effort,' John boasted.

'Isn't it dangerous?' Mair asked.

'We're told it's as safe as the powers that be can make it. And we have to believe them. Of course, as it's too far to travel every day, they lodge in digs in Bridgend. They used to come home every weekend, but they said it was too much of a rush to get back for Monday morning.'

'Well, I think what they're doing is very admirable. When you next see them, be sure and say how proud we are of them,' Frank said.

'I will. Now, Mair, love, as you probably noticed when you went upstairs earlier, Catherine has outgrown her cot, so I moved her in to Martha and Sadie's room. With the two of them working and living in Bridgend, it seemed the most sensible thing to do. Mind you, she insisted I moved the family photograph and all the postcards as well. I didn't mind, as long as it made her happy.'

'But won't Martha and Sadie be upset?' Mair asked.

'No. The bed in their room is that big, if they do come home, the three of them can bunk up together. I felt it was only right that, as the eldest, Frank should have a bedroom to himself when he came home. As it's turned out – with him needing his rest and you two planning to get married – it's as if I knew.'

'And in the meantime, where will Mair sleep?' Frank asked.

'In with Catherine, of course…. You weren't thinking of—?' Ethel looked shocked.

Mair felt her colour rise; she knew exactly what Frank was suggesting.

'Well, we *are* soon to be married,' Frank pointed out.

'Yes, in two weeks' time. Until then, I'll not have you … the valley gossips would have a field day.'

'Frank, I've already had words with your mother,' John intervened. 'I've told her that from now on your bedroom is off limits. You're a grown man, for God's sake. So if you want to entertain company in your *private* quarters, then it's no business of ours,' John winked, 'if you know what I mean.'

Ethel gave a loud, 'Tut-tut, John Jenkins. How could you? I fully understand that, in a perfect world these two would already be married. All this time they wasted – unable to marry until Mair was twenty-one. If only either of her parents had been around to sign their consent, they might have been married years ago. How much heartache might that have saved?'

'Ethel, John, Frank was only teasing,' Mair said quickly. 'The last thing we want is for the two of you to fall out over us. We would never do anything to upset you. I'm more than happy to sleep in with Catherine until we're married. That way there'll be no cause for anyone to talk about us.'

'I'm probably being a silly old fool. The thing is most of the valley folk think the two of you are already married. I never thought it my place to set them straight.'

'She's a cunning one, that mother of yours,' John scoffed.

'If that's the case, then our plan to get married in Cardiff is a good one.'

'I feel so lucky to have you both home with us. I intend to go to chapel this Sunday and thank God for answering my prayers.'

Frank, knowing how his mother hadn't stepped foot inside a chapel since the *Titanic* tragedy, put his arm around her. 'And we'll all be there to give thanks too, Mam.'

When it came to eight o'clock and Catherine's bedtime, Mair walked over to her, 'Come on, *cariad*,' she said. And, remembering what her stepfather, Dai Hughes, used to always say when he took her and Rhiannon up to bed, 'It's time to go up the wooden hill.'

The child giggled.

'Now there's a saying that takes me back a while,' Ethel said.

Mair smiled and nodded. 'Me too…. Frank, love, if you don't mind, I think I'll take myself off to bed with Catherine. We've an early start in the morning, and I don't want to sleep late.'

'I think that's a good idea,' he said. He rose and placed a kiss first on Mair's cheek and then on Catherine's. 'I'll not be long for *my* bed either,' he said, looking directly at his mother.

'Tut-tut,' Ethel admonished, as Catherine skipped over to give her and John a kiss goodnight.

'Good night, *cariad*. Sleep tight,' they said.

It was 4 a.m. when Frank, unable to sleep, tiptoed down the stairs and headed for the kitchen where he made himself a hot drink. He was still there at 5.30 when John got up for work.

'Whatever are you doing sat here in the darkness, son?' John asked.

'I couldn't sleep. The nightmares … sometimes I like to sit alone in the darkness – a quiet place to hide.' Frank began to shake. 'I can't stand noise. Even in silence, I get these really bad headaches.... Where's Mam?' Frank asked, starting to rise from his chair. He didn't want her to see him like this.

'I told your mother to have a lie in. She plans to get up just before seven to make you and Mair breakfast before you leave for Cardiff. You sit back down and I'll make us a fresh pot of tea.'

'Thank you. I don't want to make you late for work.'

'Don't you worry, son. The shop will still be there whatever time I get in. You're far more important.'

Over a cup of tea, Frank and John had a heart to heart. It felt good for Frank to have another man to talk to.'

'Does it help to talk about it?' John asked.

Frank nodded. 'Yes ... and no. I have this theory that if I don't talk about it, I'll never get better. Keeping everything bottled up is driving me mad.'

'I can understand that. Sometimes the mind can play strange tricks on you. I suppose you saw some pretty serious fighting?'

'All of the time, especially during October and November at the Somme. Sixty of our lads were killed going over the top. They chopped us all to pieces with their machine guns. My mate Albert and I saw one of our mates blown up by a heavy shell. We saw him fly up in the air; I was knocked unconscious. When I came round later, Albert told me that when the smoke cleared, he saw him hanging from a barbed-wire fence shot to ribbons. We were lucky to survive.'

'That's enough to shake anyone up. Such a waste of life ... and try to justify it by saying, "It's the price we have to pay for freedom". Yet none of those politicians are ever the ones to pay the price.'

Frank and Mair breakfasted early that morning. Ethel made sure they were well fed and watered, and Frank made no mention of his sleep-less night or of his early morning chat with John.

'So what are your plans for today?' Ethel asked.

'After the assessment we intend to go book the registry office and after that we'll go and see Rhiannon and Gus, to tell them our plans. Mam, I don't think we'll make it back much before late evening,' Frank said.

'Whatever time you get back, I'll have a meal waiting for you. I'll be thinking of you all day.'

His appointment at the TF Hospital was booked for 11.30, so Frank and Mair left the house to catch the 8.00 charabanc, on the start of their long journey to Cardiff. It was still dark and the ground was covered in frost. Mair hoped the weather wouldn't take a turn for the worse – at least not until they safely returned home. They arrived at the hospital with only minutes to spare. Frank looked nervous and Mair sensed that the last thing he needed was small-talk, so she just sat holding his hand. There were three other servicemen in the waiting area, all dressed in khaki and all looking equally as nervous as Frank.

A door opened. 'Private Frank Lewis,' the large sergeant major called out.

Frank stood to attention. 'Yes, sir.'

'Follow me,' the sergeant ordered.

Frank, following his lead, marched into the room. Not long after, one by one the other soldiers were called into different rooms to await their fate – a fate that was no longer in their hands.

The wait seemed to last forever for Mair but after an hour an ashen-faced Frank emerged from the room. He walked over to Mair. 'Let's get out of here,' he said urgently, taking her hand and leading her quickly out of the hospital and into the open air.

Once outside he led her to a wooden bench situated within the hospital grounds. Although it was a frosty January day with the air filled with the promise of snowfall, Frank seemed oblivious to the cold wind buffeting them. Mair pulled her coat collar up around her neck and tucked her hands into her muffler for some protection.

'Frank, my love, tell me. What did they say?' Mair asked, unable to contain herself any longer.

'It was as I expected. The panel was made up of three doctors, two of whom were split on the whole shell shock debate. One even accused me of "merely looking for an excuse not to fight". How I controlled my temper, I'll never know.'

For a moment he dropped his head in his hands and Mair felt the tremors run through him, but he raised his head again and continued. 'Thankfully, the second doctor was very sympathetic. He spoke about recent writings in *The Lancet* – a newspaper for surgeons and practitioners – referring to shell shock as an accepted nervous and mental shock injury. He believed it to now be a recognized condition, and one affecting servicemen from all backgrounds and not always connected to an explosion. But it was the third doctor who asked me the most questions … how I was dealing with everyday life … the sleepless nights … the fighting. I answered as honestly as I could.'

'And?' Mair prompted gently.

'In the end, the vote went 2–1 in favour of my suffering shell-shock. The thing is, they want to admit me to a hospital in Whitchurch, a small village on the outskirts of Cardiff. For "complete rest", they said. The hospital specializes in treating mental illness. I'm to spend a month there. In two weeks' time I'm to be reassessed.'

'That's good, isn't it?'

'I'm not sure. What if it turns out to be an asylum for mad people and they don't let me out?'

'You mustn't think like that. Remember your promise to me? "Whatever it takes", you said. Well, this could be what it takes.'

'I hope you're right. I'm to report back to them within the hour when transport will be waiting to take me to Whitchurch.'

'You mean you're to be admitted today?' Mair hadn't expected this.

'Yes. I'm afraid this scuppers our wedding plans. I suppose I could always refuse to go?'

'I'll not hear of it. The sooner you begin treatment the better.'

Frank looked despondent. 'I so want us to be man and wife.'

'Frank, love. The fact that we're back together again is good enough for me. I can wait for as long as it takes. Will I be able to visit you in Whitchurch?'

Frank shook his head. 'I'm afraid not. The doctors seem to think complete rest and isolation are what I need for recovery.'

'Then I shall write every day. I'll stay in Ponty until it's time for me to return to London.'

'I'm glad. It will be good for you to spend time with Catherine. And just knowing you're in Wales will make you feel closer to me.' His eyes welled up, and he began to shiver.

Mair caught around him and smiled up at him. 'As much as I hate to leave you here, I'm sure it's for the best.'

'Mair Parsons, as soon as I'm fit we're going to be wed, do you hear?'

'Yes, Mr Lewis. I hear.' She laughed to lighten his mood and kissed his mouth warmly. 'Now let's get you back inside before we both catch our death.'

Mair left the TF Hospital feeling extremely low. She hated leaving Frank. That morning when they'd left Ponty, they'd had such definite plans. All now sadly dashed. She hoped this wasn't a bad omen. With a visit to the registry office on hold, she felt at a loss, but she could at least still visit Rhiannon and Gus, so headed for the Angel Hotel.

As she made her way across the busy streets of Cardiff, she was reminded of the time she and Rhiannon first arrived in the city, and how the Angel Hotel and the Empire Theatre had both played such a huge part in both their lives. They had come a long way since then.

On the train journey back to Llan, Mair reflected on her reunion with Rhiannon and Gus. They had both been so pleased to see her, though obviously saddened to hear of Frank's confinement to Whitchurch Hospital.

'I'm sure it's for the best. None of us actually know what the lad had to endure. We hear such horrific stories … I can't imagine what it must be like, having to live through the hell of this war. When you write to him, please send him our best wishes,' Gus had said.

Mair thought Rhiannon looked as radiant as ever, despite having increased her workload from seven to twelve shows a week. She had even taken a cut in her fee so that ticket prices could be reduced and make a trip to the theatre more affordable for the man in the street.

'In the hope of boosting morale – my bit for the war effort,' Rhiannon said.

Mair hugged her warm and generous stepsister with affection.

'During this time of trouble, I can only marvel at the way you British all pull together,' Gus said.

As Mair neared Llan, she reflected on this, and felt, although she was Welsh through and through, she was indeed proud to be British.

It was late when the charabanc stopped on Ponty Square. It had been a long day and Mair felt exhausted. She didn't relish having to explain to Ethel and John why Frank hadn't returned home with her. The wedding was off … at least for the time being. She vowed to make the rest of her stay as helpful and as happy as she could for Catherine, Ethel and John.

Chapter Twenty-Seven

FRANK LEWIS WAS admitted to the Whitchurch Hospital, and it was as he thought, a mental hospital. He found himself surrounded by mental health patients – some in a really bad way. This truly worried him. He began to question why he was there. Surely he wasn't mad. He was merely fatigued.

If Frank believed the sum total of his treatment would be rest and recuperation, he found he was sadly mistaken. On his second day he was subjected to electric shock treatment – sending shock waves to the brain – which left him both physically and mentally drained and for a few days afterwards unable to do the simplest of tasks – not knowing who or where he was … almost in limbo … virtually knocked out … his brain given complete rest.

As the days passed, he was astonished and bemused to find that he began to feel better – the nightmares, shaking and cold sweats had stopped. He began to feel less suspicious of his surroundings. It was only later that he found out that the electric shock treatment, while proven to be effective, was also deemed successful at identifying malingerers from the genuinely ill and once identified, malingerers were immediately sent back to the front in disgrace. During Frank's stay, Mair, as promised, had sent him a letter every day – each one confirming her love for him, how much she longed for them to be together and keeping him up to date with news about Catherine and the family.

The last letter told him of her planned return to London, and what a wrench it would be to leave everyone. And he was shocked to read that she had seriously considered not returning to London at all, so that she could stay close to him. In the end, it was his mother who had insisted she returned to her duties at the hospital, 'to do what she could to help those injured in this terrible war'.

Also enclosed was a letter sent to his home in Ponty and post-marked London. Frank opened it. Much to his surprise he found that it was from Albert Stubbs. Apparently, he'd been injured – shrapnel in the buttocks, 'Trust me to be shot in the arse,' Albert had written. This made Frank smile. Albert had been admitted to St Thomas's Hospital in London and Frank made a mental note to write to Mair and ask her to seek him out.

As soon as Mair returned to London and Grange House, she reported for duty at St Thomas's, only to find the new wing full to capacity, with extra beds set up in the corridors to accommodate the injured servicemen recently shipped in from the front – so many young men … some with such horrific injuries. On 1 July 1916, it was reported that in one day of battle at the Somme, 20,000 British soldiers were dead and 40,000 injured – the heaviest day of casualties in British history. Mair couldn't help feeling that the price of this war was far too high.

Frank's recent letter had made mention of Albert Stubbs, who'd been admitted to St Thomas's, so Mair eagerly went onto the ward to seek him out before reporting for duty. Surely it would be too much of a coincidence if it turned out to be Albert Stubbs, the station guard. She found him among the twenty or so patients on Asquith ward. He was lying face down on the bed, his behind heavily swathed in bandages.

'Albert … Albert Stubbs. Is that you?'

'Yes. And if you've come to stick another needle in my ar—' he stopped in mid-sentence. 'Nurse Parsons! Well, I must say you were the last person I expected to see – I'd forgotten you worked here at St Thomas's.'

'As soon as I heard you'd been admitted, I came to look for you. What are your injuries? Not serious, I hope.'

'No, Miss. Just some shrapnel wounds, it's obvious where they are.'

'Very painful, I'm sure.' Mair fought to suppress a smile.

'To be honest, I thought I'd fallen lucky when I saw myself surrounded by young nurses. But having them change your dressing and stick needles into … well, such a tender and … private area, is very embarrassing. Mind you, there is one nurse who's a bit special. Her name's Kitty Slater. She not one of the ones caring for me. She just comes to have a chat occasionally.'

'I know Kitty – we share a room. She's my best friend.'

'In that case, maybe you could put in a good word for me....' He laughed. 'Anyway, who told you I was here?'

'Frank, Frank Lewis … my fiancé. He wrote from his hospital in Cardiff and asked me to seek you out. I suppose you know about him having shell shock? Thankfully, he's well on the road to recovery.'

'Thank God for that. He had us all worried. I still can't believe you're his fiancée – what do you think the chances were of me making friends with your bloke? Mind you, he talked about his girlfriend all the time – constantly looking at her … your photograph. I never took much notice. I was more than a bit jealous. You see, I didn't have anyone "special" to write to or take my mind off…. Anyway, suffice to say that your Frank is a good man – one of the best.'

'Albert, Frank mentioned another man who fought along side you. His name was … Jake Brewer.' This name was like acid on her mouth. 'Do you remember him?'

'Yes, I do. The poor bugger … sorry, Miss, I didn't mean to swear. I've been too long in the company of men. Jake Brewer caught it on his first day in the trenches. How unlucky was that? I do believe he was originally from Cardiff. Now don't say you knew him too?'

'No,' she lied. 'I just wanted to make sure Frank had his facts right. When he first arrived back, he was so confused.'

It was the day of Frank's re-assessment. He was confident he would pass it with flying colours. He felt so much better – almost back to normal. Although he was also under no illusion, he knew his recovery had a lot to do with being in Wales and away from the conflict. His only fear now was if … *when* he was declared fit enough to return to duty and returned to the front, what were the chances of him suffering a relapse? He knew that only time would tell.

'Well, Private Lewis, I'm pleased to see you so much improved. Our treatment has obviously worked.'

'Does that mean I can be discharged?'

'I'm afraid not. I want you to stay with us for a little longer, because at the moment you're on quite a lot of medication. Over the next ten days, we will look to gradually reduce it. We will of course monitor the effects.'

A week later Frank received a letter from Mair, postmarked London. She told him that Albert had been discharged and had returned to the front. She went on to tell him of the coincidence of her having met him before and how he, a station guard on Waterloo Station, had befriended her on her first day in London. It warmed Frank's heart to know that the man he called his friend, was also Mair's too. And, with Frank's own discharge from hospital imminent, he could at least look forward to meeting up with his old butty again.

Mair said she needed them to promise that the next time they found themselves together in the middle of this war, that they look out for each other ... or else.

Chapter Twenty-Eight

1918

THE WAR WITH Germany dragged on. Then finally, at the 11th hour of the 11th day of the 11th month in the French town of Redonthes, Germany signed an armistice with the Allies – the official date of the end of the Great War.

Frank and Albert returned to London together. They met up with Mair and Kitty and the four of them booked into the hotel in Sussex Gardens. The celebrations on the streets of London went on for days, a joyful outpouring of relief, and during that time Frank took it upon himself to arrange a special licence for him and Mair to marry. The night before the wedding, Mair made the decision to spend it back at Grange House and Kitty agreed to go with her. 'It's bad luck to see the groom, the night before the wedding,' Kitty informed her.

Although Mair wanted to avoid bad luck, this was not the reason she wanted to return to Grange House. As soon as she and Kitty arrived back she asked Mrs Turnbull if Violet, the maid, might go and fetch Sister Agnes.

'I have something to tell you – something I should have told you a long time ago,' Mair announced.

Twenty minutes later, Violet arrived back closely followed by Sister Agnes. With Mrs Turnbull, Sister Agnes and Kitty all gathered in the parlour, each of them looking curious, Mair took a deep breath and began....

'Let me start by saying how fortunate I am to have you as my friends – a fact I hope won't change when I tell you my secret.'

'You don't have to—' Mrs Turnbull began.

Mair interrupted her, 'Oh but I do. Tomorrow I'm to be wed and, in a few days' time, I'll be moving back to Wales. It just wouldn't feel right to leave without telling you the truth.'

'What truth?' Kitty asked.

'The truth about … Catherine.'

'The little girl who travelled with you and your friend aboard the *Titanic*?' Mrs Turnbull asked.

'I'm afraid that, when I told you I was travelling with a friend and her daughter, I lied. The truth is … the little girl was my daughter … and my friend was actually Frank's mother.'

'And is Frank Lewis the child's father,' Sister Agnes asked, her voice full of concern.

'No … yes … I need to explain.' Mair began at the beginning, telling them about Dai Hughes, and what a good man he'd been to take her and her mother in, his subsequent death and all the events that followed. She hid nothing. She even told them of the rape when she was only thirteen, and how Frank had always looked after her since … and Catherine.

'So you see, although Catherine is not of his blood, I truly believe that Frank has more than earned the right to be called her dad.'

When Mair finished, the room fell silent. Her heart was filled with dismay. What if they didn't want to ever see or hear from her again…? What if they—

But the three walked over to Mair and threw their arms around her.

'My dear, dear, girl, it's hard to believe how cruel some people can be … you were just a child,' Mrs Turnbull said.

'To think of what you have endured in your short life, makes me feel humble,' the Sister offered.

'You should have told us sooner,' Kitty admonished.

'I couldn't. I was too ashamed … not of Catherine, you understand. I love her more than life itself.'

'Then maybe it's time you told us all about her,' Mrs Turnbull suggested.

Mair smiled. 'I'd love to.'

The next day Mair and Frank were married. Albert and Kitty were witnesses – and Catherine, Ethel and John arrived in time for the ceremony. Afterwards they all went back to Grange House for the wedding party. Frank and Mair spent their wedding night at the hotel in Sussex Gardens.

The next day they all returned to Wales to find a huge street party in progress on Ponty Square, attended by everyone in the valley to celebrate the end of the war. The following day John handed them a wedding present – the lease of a property in Bridgend – shop premises with a three bedroom living accommodation above and an inside bathroom and toilet facilities. John's proposition was to open the shop as a butcher's. He would, of course, train and oversee Frank in the initial period.

A place to call home – Mair, Frank and Catherine were at last a family.

Chapter Twenty-Nine

April 1922

'GOOD MORNING, MRS Jenkins. It's that time of the year again,' Gareth Brewer, a reporter with the *South Wales Echo*, cheerily greeted Ethel Jenkins.

'And it's a good morning to you, too. Tell me, Gareth, when is Selwyn Price, that editor of yours, going to stop sending you on this wild goose chase? He visited me for years when he was a reporter, so he knows I have nothing to say to you.'

'Mrs Jenkins, it is ten years to the day since the *Titanic* tragically sank....'

'Yes, ten years of your newspaper asking me for my story and ten years of my saying no.'

Ethel certainly admired their persistence, returning year after year and getting more or less the same response. She wondered what he'd have made of it if he knew the rest – of Mair's dramatic return, her marriage to Frank and the fact that above all odds, Mair, Frank and Catherine were together as a family at last.... Now there was a story worth telling.

Chapter Thirty

1926

MAIR LEWIS SAT in her kitchen, giving thanks to God, as she often did, for how her life had turned out. She was truly happy. The butcher's shop was now going from strength to strength – Frank had worked so hard to prove to John and his mother that the faith they had in him was justified, and that he had it in him to make the business work. It had been a hard struggle, especially during the post-war years when produce was scarce.

There had been a time when Frank had even considered going back down the mine but Mair wouldn't hear of it. Instead she had gone back as a part-time nurse on the children's ward at Bridgend Hospital – only working while Catherine was at school. Having missed her daughter's early years, she was determined to now be there for her every need. Mair loved her so much. And as for Frank, Catherine was and always would be his pride and joy.

Every day, Mair thanked God for the love of her family. And her dear friends Albert and Kitty Stubbs, who visited whenever they could and Mrs Turnbull and Sister Agnes, companions for each other now that they were older and both living at Grange House. On the rare occasion Mair and Frank went up to London, Grange House was always their first stopover.

Frank Lewis was about to close the shop, eager to sit down with his wife and Catherine, when a young man entered.

'Good afternoon, Mr Lewis. I hope you don't mind me calling to see you at your place of work.' The young man held out his hand. 'My name's Gareth Brewer. I work as a reporter for the *South Wales*

Echo, and I wondered if you could spare me a few minutes of your time.'

'Well, a good afternoon to you,' Frank said, shaking the young lad's hand. 'You were lucky to catch me. I was just about to close up. I close early every Wednesday. If you'd like to take a seat over in the corner, I'll lock the door, and you can tell me what I can do for you.'

A few minutes later Frank returned to talk to the lad.

'I'm all done. Now you say your name's Gareth Brewer.'

'That's right, sir.'

Frank rubbed his chin. 'I knew a Jake Brewer during the war, an ex-boxer who came from over Cardiff way ... I don't suppose he's any relation?'

'Yes. As a matter of fact Jake Brewer was my father. He was killed in the war. I always thought a life of excess would do for him.'

Frank heard the bitterness in the lad's voice.

'I'm sorry about that, lad. I can't say I really knew him. We met in the trenches at the Somme. What I will say is that he was truly up for the fight against the Hun, you can be proud of him,' Frank lied – in the hope of giving the lad and his family some comfort.

'It's strange to hear someone actually praise him. I'm afraid he lived something of a chequered life. He wasn't the best father or husband in the world.... I'm sorry, you don't want to hear my sob story, enough to say his death was no sad loss.'

'Don't be sorry. We can only speak as we find. All I saw was a fellow soldier, trying to do his bit for King and country.'

The lad nodded and smiled.

'Now, Gareth. What brings you to my shop?'

The lad cleared his throat and, taking a notebook and pen from his jacket pocket, looked every bit the reporter.

'I believe your wife and daughter were aboard the *Titanic* on that tragic night of 14 April, 1912.'

'Yes, that's correct. But that was a long time ago.'

'If our records are correct, your daughter was only two years old at the time, which makes her one of the youngest survivors. The youngest was a Miss Millvina Dean, only nine weeks old and a babe in arms. I believe she now lives in Hampshire.'

'Where are you going with this?'

'Am I right in thinking that your daughter will be celebrating her sixteenth birthday soon and no doubt you have a party planned?'

Frank nodded. 'Yes, on Saturday 20 March.'

'The thing is … my editor has asked me to do a piece, an article on her reaching such a landmark in her life – her leaving school … her plans for the future. I can promise a sensitive account. I'll not intrude on you or your wife. Apparently, your mother warned my editor off approaching your wife regarding the *Titanic* years ago.'

'I wasn't aware of that. Mind you, I can well believe it. My mother has always been very protective of those close to her.'

'Mr Lewis, if you and your wife could see your way clear to letting me cover your daughter's birthday party, I promise a sensitive coverage.'

Frank looked at the lad. A good-looking upstanding young man and one that any father would … should have been proud of.

'May I ask how old you are?' Frank asked.

'I'm nearly twenty, sir.'

'And would I be right in thinking that, if allowed to do this article, it would be a feather in your cap?'

'Well, let's just say it wouldn't do me any harm.' The lad flashed Frank a wide smile.

'Look, I can't promise anything. All I can do is mention it to my wife and Catherine. It has to be their decision.'

When Frank broached the subject, as expected, Mair wasn't sure it was such a good idea. 'What if the reporter asks awkward questions about us … how long we've been married and—'

'The lad has assured me that he's not interested in us,' Frank told her. Apparently, my mam warned him that you were off limits years ago. All he wants is an article on Catherine … one of the youngest survivors of the *Titanic*, her hopes and aspirations for the future … nothing too solemn.'

'And you think we should let him do it?' Mair asked.

'I think we should at least put it to Catherine and see how she feels about it. The thing is … I really like the lad. I actually met his dad during the war. Do you remember me telling you about Jake Brewer, and how he was killed on his first day in the trenches?'

Mair's blood ran cold. For years she had put all thoughts of her attacker to the back of her mind ... as dead and buried as the hateful man himself. And now Frank was about to invite his son into their home and there was nothing she could do about it. She had never told Frank that the rapist was Jake Brewer – she believed, with him now dead, he was no threat to them. Had she been wrong and could his son be a threat to their happiness? She made the decision to remain watchful and wary.

When Frank put it to Catherine, she was all in favour of it.

It was just after her tenth birthday that Catherine first found out about the *Titanic* ... and her involvement. She had been visiting Ponty when she overheard a reporter who called at the house asking *Mamgu* Ethel about the tragedy. When he had left, she asked why the man had come asking questions. *Mamgu* had sat her down and told her the full story. Up to then Catherine had never been aware that she, along with her mother and Ethel, were survivors of this famous tragedy.

Mamgu had explained how, when her mother was given the gift of 'a trip of a lifetime' by Catherine's Aunt Rhiannon and Uncle Gus, and as her father was unable to get time off from his regiment, the three of them had set off.

When the iceberg struck, *Mamgu* Ethel truly believed, 'If it hadn't been for your mother's quick action – in getting us up onto the Boat Deck, I'm sure we would have all perished. While we were on the Boat Deck, your mother noticed she'd lost her locket – a present from Rhiannon – something of a family heirloom. Your mother went in search of it, leaving you in my care. That's when we became separated.' She went on tell her of the ordeal ... being rescued ... repatriated. Then came the news that her mother had been found safe and well, and of her own repatriation to Southampton.

Now a reporter wanted to interview her. How exciting was that? The story of the *Titanic* seemed to be embedded in their lives.

On the night of her party Catherine was introduced to Gareth Brewer – a fair-haired handsome young man, who looked to be a few years older than she was. He was full of confidence ... a bit of a show-off and – to her fury – he made her blush every time he looked at her.

They were instantly attracted to each other, and Gareth Brewer, true to his word, wrote a sensitive and moving piece for his paper. As a result, he soon became a regular visitor to the Lewis's home.

Catherine was obviously taken with him and he with her. She was pleased that her father seemed to like him and happily welcomed him into their home, but she was baffled that her mother, always so protective of her, seemed strangely against him. Stating her objections, in no uncertain terms, 'He's far too old for you,' her mother had said, and 'I find him too full of confidence – beware of a man oozing confidence.' In the end her mother forbade her to see him.

Unfortunately, her father, who she had expected to take her side, sided with her mother. 'I'm sure your mother has her reasons. And you are still very young. Maybe if you wait for a year or two she'll come round to the idea,' he'd suggested.

But Catherine couldn't wait. Going against her parents' wishes she continued to secretly meet with Gareth at every opportunity but when their need for each other became intense it was showed control. 'We mustn't. As much as I want to make love to you, knowing how your parents feel about me, it just wouldn't feel right. Cathy, I love you and want to marry you. Please say you feel the same.'

'Yes – yes, I do.'

Gareth took her in his arms and kissed her passionately.

'Then we must tell your parents how we feel about each other. No more going behind their backs. I'm sure when they know how much we truly love each other and when I ask your father for your hand in marriage, they'll come round to our way of thinking.'

'I do hope so. I've hated having to lie to them.'

'It's 6.30. Your parents will be expecting you home for tea. This time, I'm coming with you. I want this sorted out once and for all.'

Frank and Mair were just about to sit down to their meal, when the front door opened. 'Is that you, Catherine?' Frank called out. 'You're just in time for tea.'

'Yes, Dad, it's me. And I've brought someone to see you.'

As the kitchen door opened, Mair looked up to see Catherine and Gareth Brewer standing in the doorway hand in hand. Her knees felt weak. She made a grab for the back of the chair. 'Tell me this doesn't mean what I think it means,' Mair said, unable to control the shake in her voice.

'Mair, love, are you all right? You look as if you've seen a ghost. Sit yourself down. I'll deal with this,' Frank said. 'Catherine, answer your mother. What does this mean?'

'It means we're a couple – and that we love each other—'

'I've come to ask for your daughter's hand in marriage,' Gareth interjected.

Mair let out a cry.

'Mam, what's so terrible about that?' Catherine demanded. 'I don't understand.'

'Frank, love … could we have a private word in the parlour?' Mair's eyes pleaded with him. She felt sick to her stomach and knew the time had come to tell him the truth.

'Of course, my love,' he said, then turned to his daughter and Gareth, 'You two sit yourselves down. I'll speak with you shortly.'

Once in the parlour, Frank caught around Mair and hugged her she sobbed into his chest.

'There, there. I know it's a bit of a shock but Gareth Brewer is a good lad. I, like you, feel cross that they've obviously gone behind our backs. The thing is, I really believe he loves her … and she him. Why should we stand in their way?'

'Frank. Please listen to me. Gareth Brewer is Jake Brewer's son.'

'I know that, wasn't I in the army with him?'

'So you said, but what you don't know is—' she took a deep breath 'Jake Brewer is the man who raped me. He's Catherine's real father. Do you know what that means?'

Mair watched the blood drain from Frank's face. 'Oh God, please don't let this be true. Why have you never told me? No wonder you were so against them seeing each other. This will break Catherine's heart. She loves the boy. I can't believe you never told me! When did you realize it was the same man?'

'I recognized his name when you first mentioned seeing him killed. At first I thought, I hoped, it was another man with the same name. Then, when you were in the hospital in Whitchurch and I met up with Albert in St Thomas's, I questioned him about it. He confirmed the man was an ex-boxer who lived in Cardiff. It was too much of a coincidence not to be the same man. I thought, with Jake Brewer dead and buried, that would be the end of it … and now this.'

Frank fell into the easy chair, his head in his hands. 'For years I've been dreading the day she found out that I am not her real father. Now the poor girl not only has to deal with the reality of that, but she has to find out that the man she has given her heart to is her half-brother … it's all so cruel.'

They entered the kitchen, the sorrow of what was about to unfold written on their faces.

Catherine stared at them, instantly realizing something was wrong. 'Mam? Dad? What is it?'

Mair and Frank slowly walked over to the kitchen table and sat next to Catherine and Gareth.

Mair took Catherine's hand in hers. 'Catherine, my darling sweet girl, what I have to say to you will come as a great shock. I hoped you would never have to know. The thing is … young Gareth here is your brother!'

'That can't possibly be true, Dad? What's Mam saying?'

'I'm sorry Catherine. I'm afraid it is the truth.'

As Mair looked at Catherine, she saw the anguish in her daughter's eyes as she tried desperately to understand the nightmare that was going on around her.

'But how do you know it's the truth?' Gareth asked. His young face was set rigid.

'Jake Brewer … your father, was the first man I ever slept with.' She was about to add 'he raped me' but stopped herself – Gareth and Catherine didn't need to know the sordid details.

Her daughter, white-faced, turned to Frank. 'It's all lies. It can't be true. Dad? Tell her to stop now. How could Gareth's father be my father?'

'I'm afraid your mother is telling the truth,' Frank suddenly spoke, making his way from the other end of the table. 'I'm sorry, *cariad*. I wish with all my heart that it wasn't … you must know how much I genuinely love you. To me, you've always been *my* daughter, and it's how I will always think of you but—'

'I'm *not* really your daughter … is that what your saying? Well, I don't believe it! This is all some sort of plan to stop me seeing Gareth … I thought you both liked him—'

'We do. He's a good lad. And under normal circumstances.... Catherine, love, I promise you that when we agreed for him to come to the house to interview you on your sixteenth birthday, I didn't know. Your mother never told me. Damn it, I fought beside Jake Brewer during the war – when I think how I befriended the man who had done such an injustice to your mother ... makes me feel sick to my stomach.'

'What injustice? I don't understand. My mother got herself pregnant with the first man she met ... the only injustice I can see is the way you've both lied to me.'

Frank shook his head. 'I think it best if we leave you and Gareth together. No doubt you need to talk.' And, taking Mair's hand, he led her from the room.

When they had gone, Catherine sat staring at the roaring fire in the grate. She felt Gareth's arm reach out to her. She instantly pulled away.

'Cathy love, whatever happened was a long time ago. That was then. This is now!' Gareth pleaded.

On hearing the desperation in his voice, Catherine closed her eyes. Never mind how much they wanted it to be otherwise, the terrible truth was that Gareth Brewer was her half-brother ... they could never marry. Their lives had suddenly been torn apart.

Catherine swallowed hard, fighting the urge to be angry with her mother.

Gareth moved closer, 'Cathy, love ...' his eyes pleaded with her. 'This doesn't change anything.'

'Have you gone completely mad?' she hissed, 'Didn't you hear what they said? I'm your half-sister. Of course, it changes everything!'

'I love you, Cathy. Nothing will ever change that.'

'Don't even dare to say that. You can't ... we can't love each other. Not any more. Not like *that*.... When I think—'

'We haven't done anything wrong,' he argued.

'We both know we might have, though. We both wanted to. When I think of the feelings your kisses aroused in me, I feel dirty and ashamed. Don't you understand?

He shook his head miserably. 'No, Cathy, I don't. How can you let something that happened all those years ago affect the way we feel about each other?'

'I don't know.' She gave a shudder. 'But one thing is for sure, whatever we might or might not feel for each other, it has to stop now. I never want to see you again ... do you hear!'

The weeks that followed were unbearable ... for Mair, for Frank and especially for Catherine, who seldom came out of her room and had even threatened to leave home. Mair tried to comfort her but she was beyond comfort.

In desperation Frank decided to visit Gareth. He needed to talk to the lad and see how he was taking it. He went to seek him out at his newspaper depot, only to find he was on sick leave. Thankfully, the friendly receptionist gave Frank his home address and when he sought out the house, Gareth's mother answered the door – a frail, timid looking woman, who invited him in. Frank, eager to state his friendship for Gareth, explained how he came to know him and how he had also known her late husband during the war.

She told him how angry Gareth had been, and how much he hated his pig of a father. 'The truth is, Mr Lewis, we all have secrets.' She shrugged her thin shoulders and looked around the drab room as if she expected to see them hiding there. 'My secret, which I hoped to carry to the grave, is that Gareth is neither Jake's nor my son. He was my sister's child. My sister died giving birth to him. His dad was a young dock-worker, who left Wales as soon as he knew she was pregnant. I persuaded Jake to let me adopt him, but he never accepted the poor child. Later, when I gave him a son of his own, it was as if Gareth didn't exist. Over the years I tried to compensate. The truth is, Mr Lewis ... Jake Brewer was not a nice man. He was a drunkard, a womanizer and a blaggard. The only good thing he ever did in his life was to let me adopt Gareth. And with all that's now happened ... with your Catherine and all ... I'm not so sure.'

'Mrs Brewer, surely you must see that for the sake of his and Catherine's future, you have to tell him.'

Frank left Cardiff feeling a weight lift from his heart. Gareth Brewer was not Jake's son. A fact he couldn't wait to tell his wife ... and daughter.

*

Catherine was busy packing her bags. She was going to leave ... to go where? Mair wasn't sure, and she didn't think Catherine knew either.

Mair stood outside the bedroom and made a last ditch attempt to stop her. 'Catherine, love, I can't make you stay. However, before you go, I think it's time you knew the truth. One thing you have to believe is that it was never our intention to hurt or deceive you. At least give me a chance to explain.'

The bedroom door opened and a bleary-eyed Catherine stepped out. 'All right, Mam. I'll listen. I need to know everything ... I still can't believe that my dad ... Frank, isn't—'

'Now you listen to me, girl. While he may not be of your blood, your dad ... and yes, I will keep calling him your dad, he has more than earned the right. Unlike myself, *he* has always been there for you ... sit yourself down, child. It's time I explained.'

Mair talked for what seemed like hours. It was growing dark outside when she finished. Through the glow of the fire, she saw tears flow down her daughter's face.

'I'm sorry, Mam. I didn't understand.' Catherine said catching around her mother. 'All I could think of when I heard was how knowing the truth had spoilt my chance of happiness with Gareth.... I didn't mean to be so cruel to ... dad. Do you think he can ever forgive me?'

At that moment, the door opened and Frank entered the kitchen.

Epilogue

1986 Excavating the Titanic

Dr Robert Ballard Returns to the Titanic

In July 1986, some eleven months after Dr Robert Ballard discovered the wreck of the RMS Titanic, *he returned aboard the* Atlantis II, *equipped with the submersible* Alvin *and the ROV Jason.*

The exact location of the wreck of the Titanic *where she lay on the seabed was a closely guarded secret.* Titanic – *no longer lost, no longer out of reach, no longer beyond approach.* Titanic *is once again, after seventy-four dark and silent years, receiving visitors. With each dive a new discovery, a piece of history, another piece added to the never ending puzzle which is the* Titanic!

RMS Titanic, Inc. Recovery Expedition

Under the leadership of Company President Arnie Geller, RMS Titanic, Inc. conducted its seventh research and recovery mission to Titanic's wreck site. Expedition 2004 left Halifax, Nova Scotia on 25 August, 2004 onboard the vessel Mariner Sea.

The goals of this expedition were to recover artifacts for exhibition, identify objects for future recovery, inspect the wreck site for alleged harm caused by previous visitors and, if necessary, to establish guidelines for future visitations.

IN THE AUTUMN of 1994, Catherine Brewer stood among the specially invited guests at the National Maritime Museum in Greenwich, at a viewing of the exhibition of artefacts recovered from the seabed around the wreck of the *Titanic*. Among the 200 items on display were numerous pieces of jewellery, a shaving brush, watches, a purse and travellers' cheques, and much, much more, all well preserved by the cold, dark conditions at the bottom of the North Atlantic, 500 miles off Newfoundland.

Also invited to this historic event was 82-year-old Miss Millvina Dean – she was only nine weeks old the night the tragedy struck. Catherine had been two years old and was now a sprightly 84-year-old.

As Catherine grew up, she was never consciously aware of the *Titanic* tragedy. In the early years she had been mainly brought up by *Mamgu* Ethel and John Jenkins, and although she missed her parents when they weren't there, Ethel and John never failed to make her feel always loved. The first she heard about the *Titanic* was just after her tenth birthday, when her *Mamgu* had sat her down and told her how she, Catherine and her mother were all survivors from that terrible night in 1912.

This had been such exciting news for Catherine, although, even then, something told her ... there were still unanswered questions. Why had her mother taken a job as a nurse in London? Why hadn't she come back to live in Ponty? All Ethel would say at the time was, 'I'm in no doubt that when you are older, your mother and father will tell you everything.'

And of course her mother had. The same day that Gareth proposed. And the same day that her father had returned home from Cardiff with the news about Gareth Brewer ... that changed her life forever. As Catherine Brewer viewed each artefact with interest, her eyes were suddenly drawn to a metal flask and alongside it, on a red satin pouch, lay ... a small gold locket....